NEW YORK TIMES BESTSELLING AUTHOR

KAYLEE RYAN

The following story contains sexual situations and strong language. It is intended for adult readers.

Cover Design: Lori Jackson Designs
Cover Photography: Wander Aguiar
Special Edition Cover: Emily Wittig Designs
Editing: Hot Tree Editing
Proofreading: Deaton Author Services, Jo Thompson, and Jess Hodge
Paperback Formatting: Integrity Formatting

KAYLEE RYAN

CAN WE
TRY?

LACHLAN
PROLOGUE

T WO BY TWO, MY BEST friends and their wives head up to bed. The fire is still roaring in the fireplace, giving off not only warmth but a comforting glow. Maggie and I remain on the loveseat with her feet in my lap, and I'm too damn comfortable to move.

"Are you going to bed on me too?" Maggie asks. Her voice slurs just slightly from the alcohol we've all consumed tonight.

"Nah, not yet." Not only am I relaxed, but I'm enjoying her company. "This has been a good trip, getting away and just hanging out with everyone."

"It has been. Who knew the men of Everlasting Ink were really just big, old snuggly bears."

"Hey, we're not all snugly bears," I counter.

"Are you trying to tell me that you don't like to snuggle?"

I shrug. "I don't usually stick around long enough to find out."

"Lachlan!" Maggie scolds me playfully.

"Would you rather I lie to you?" I ask, holding in my laughter. "I've never had someone in my life who I wanted to spend time with. The women who come on to me in bars want the bad boy.

They don't care about anything but hooking up with the guy covered in ink, who puts it down on people's skin for a living."

"That's sad," Maggie says softly.

"It is what it is." You can't miss what you've never had, right?

"Don't you want more?" she asks.

I give myself some time to mull over her question before answering. "Maybe. Watching the guys with their wives, yeah, I can see the appeal, but I don't know. It might happen for me and it might not."

"You have to manifest it." She grins. "And maybe get some practice."

"Practice?" I huff out a laugh. "Trust me, Mags. I'm good." I wink at her, and I like the slight blush that coats her cheeks.

"Not that." She rolls her big blue eyes that remind me of a cloudless sky. "Snuggling."

"I get plenty of snuggle time with the kids." I know that's not what she's referring to, but that's the extent of my snuggle sessions these days. Hell, ever.

"It's different," Maggie insists.

"So what you're telling me is that you're clingy after sex?" I watch as the slight blush turns to a bright red coasting across her cheeks.

"No. I mean, yes, I like the intimacy of it. I think cuddling can sometimes feel more intimate than sex. That's precisely why my ex hated it. He was a closed off, narcissistic asshole."

"Fuck him," I say, feeling the words as they wrap around my being. "You deserve better." A protective feeling washes over me.

"Yeah," she agrees softly. "It took me some time to believe that, after all the shit he put into my head. Sometimes, I still struggle with believing it."

"What did he do?" There is a demand to my voice that even I don't recognize. I try to mask it by picking up her foot that's resting on my lap, and start to massage.

"Oh, that's... heavenly."

I chuckle. "Good. I'll keep going and you tell me what the fuck off of an ex said to you."

"You know, I'm a nurse, right? And that I spend hours on my feet. If talking is all it takes for you to keep up with that, then you better settle in."

I grin. I love her sass. "Good to know. But if you don't say the words I want to hear, this stops," I say, digging into the arch of her foot. She moans, a deep throaty sound that has my cock twitching in my sweatpants. I only hope she tones it down, because I can't hide what that sound does to me in these. I'm a man, after all, and Maggie, well, she's beautiful. It's a natural reaction.

"Eric was sweet at first. He said and did all the right things. Until he didn't. It started slow. He'd ask me if the outfit I was wearing was really what I wanted to wear. Then we'd be at dinner and I'd order a steak and he'd ask me if a salad might be better. Little by little he tore me down, and I know you don't have to tell me that I'm the fool that let him."

"Did you love him?" I don't know why I ask, but I can't take the words back now.

"I thought I did at the time, but once I was away from him, and I could see the abuse for what it was, I knew it wasn't love. I think maybe I was in love with the idea of him."

"What do you mean?"

"I wanted to be wanted. I wanted that one person who was all mine. I wanted someone to look at me the way those guys upstairs look at my friends."

"You deserve that," I tell her, leaning a little closer than before.

She rests her hand on my arm. "Thanks, Lachlan. It would also help for him to want me... like, *really* want me," she says.

"You said you wanted to be wanted," I remind her.

"I did, and I do. But I just want someone who wants to spend their time with me. It would also be nice if they wanted to be inside me just as badly." She slaps her hands over her face. "Forget I said that. Why am I spilling all of this to you?"

Abandoning her foot massage, I move in even closer and pull her hands from her face. "You have nothing to be embarrassed about," I assure her.

"Having your boyfriend tell you that he no longer finds you desirable and that's why he had to get his rocks off somewhere else, that destroys a girl's ego, you know?"

"He's a moron," I spit out. "Maggie, look at me." She lifts her head from where she's been staring down at her lap. "He lied. You're beautiful, and any man would be damn lucky to have you in his bed."

She stares at me as if she's trying to decide if my words are sincere. They are. She's not going to find any deceit. Maggie is a fucking knockout with blonde hair, clear blue eyes, and a body I'd like to wrap myself around. She's also an amazing person. She's been there for Emerson, Monroe, Briar, and Brogan. She's great with the kids, she's a hard worker, and I've seen her in her scrubs.

Sexy as fuck.

"Would you?" she asks, her voice soft.

It takes me a minute to understand what she's asking. "Yes." I swallow hard. My cock thinks that her question is an invitation, and I'm hard as stone. I shift to try to hide the evidence of my arousal, but her eyes drop to my crotch, and when she licks her lips, I can't stop the moan that falls from my lips.

"Mags, you can't look at me like that," I warn her.

"Like what?" she asks innocently.

"Like you want to find out what it's like to be in my bed."

Her eyes find mine. "What if I do?"

"Aren't you worried that's going to complicate things?"

"We're both adults, right? I know the score, Lachlan. This is a one-time thing."

"So, when we wake up in the morning, you're going to pretend like this never happened? That you didn't spend the night riding my cock? Because I promise you, it's going to be all night. If we're doing this, I'm getting my fill of you."

"Is that supposed to scare me away?" she asks with a small laugh. "Lachlan, it's been years since I've felt a man's hands on me. His body hovering over mine. Hell, I haven't kissed a guy since breaking things off with Eric."

"How long?" My voice is gruff as desire courses through me.

"Years." I stare at her, and she gives me what I want. "Since I graduated from college three years ago. He missed my graduation, and I went to his place worried about him, only to find him on the couch, with some random woman, both of them naked as the day they were born, exploring each other's bodies. Something he hadn't done with me in months. So, yeah, three years, probably more like four. I can't remember exactly. I just know it's been a long damn time."

I take a minute to process what she's said. "No dates since then?"

"Yeah, but none that I wanted more from. Part of that is my issue. I just... don't want to go through that again, so my trust of men is tainted."

"But you trust me?"

"Yeah, I mean, I know you. I know you're a good man, and I know you won't expect anything else from me other than a hot night between the sheets. That's your thing, and for once, just this once, I want it to be my thing too. Maybe it's because I've been surrounded by loved-up couples all weekend, and maybe it's the gentle massage you were giving me, but whatever the reason, I want to do this with you."

I stare at her big blue eyes, trying to find a chink in her armor, that she doesn't really mean what she's saying, but all I find is desire and absolute honesty, which appears laced with the pain of what that asshole did to her and how he made her feel.

"Lachlan?"

I don't say a word as I stand and offer her my hand. She grins widely, placing her palm in mine before she leads me to my room. I chose the sole basement bedroom because I didn't want to have to hear my buddies making babies or practicing with their wives all night long. It turns out that was a smart move on my part, because I meant what I said. If I get to have it, it's going to be all night long.

I try not to notice how perfect her delicate hand feels in mine as I turn off all the lights and turn off the gas fireplace as we head toward my room in the basement. With each step that carries us closer, my heart rate kicks up. The anticipation is as thick as the chemistry that's flowing between us.

I didn't see this night turning out with me buried between Maggie's thighs, but I'm also not one to kick a gift horse in the mouth. Maggie knows what this is; hell, she basically laid out the terms, and as she said, I don't know if it's because I had my hands on her or the fact that our friends are upstairs doing this very thing. Hell, maybe it's the forbidden aspect. Our lives are tangled together; so much so, that I should tell her that I've changed my mind, but that's not going to happen. I've always been one to trust my gut, and my gut is telling me that this night with Maggie will be one I'll forever remember, and when she tells me it won't be weird, I believe her.

Pushing through my bedroom door, I flip on the light—a lamp that gives off a soft glow—and lead her into the room. I close the door softly and engage the lock. Dropping her hand, I grip her hips and turn her so that her back is against the door. I push her up against it and stare down into her bright blue eyes.

"You sure about this, Maggie?" I don't want to give her an out, but what kind of asshole would I be if I didn't?

"Shut up and kiss me."

I grin. "Yes, ma'am." Sliding my hand behind her neck and beneath her long blonde hair, I guide her lips to mine. I mean for the kiss to be slow, to ease us both into this, but when Maggie buries her hands in my hair and tugs, all bets are off. I kiss her harder, nipping at her bottom lip, and she opens for me, allowing my tongue to explore her mouth, to get a thorough first taste of her.

She tugs again, and my cock throbs in response. "Hold on." My words are the only warning she gets before I bend, grip the backs of her thighs, and lift her into my arms. My lips mold with hers as I blindly carry her to the bed. As soon as my knees hit the mattress, I toss her gently on the bed. Her laughter rings out in the quiet room, and it sounds like music to my ears.

I pause, just staring at the beauty laid out before me. Have I ever said a woman's laugh sounded like music? Damn, the guys and their mushy shit they have for their wives are in my head. There's been far too much coupled-up love since we've been here. That has to be what that thought was about. Shaking out of my head, I focus back on Maggie.

"I'm going to need you naked, Mags."

"Race you?" she says, scrambling to her knees.

I stand back and watch as she rips her sweatshirt over her head and tosses it behind her before reaching around her back and unclasping her bra. That too gets tossed, and my eyes zero in on her tits. Damn, they look like the perfect handful, and those dark pink nipples of hers have my mouth watering for a taste. I lean in to do just that, but her hand to my chest and more laughter stops me.

"I'm going to need you naked, Lach." She smirks, tossing my words back at me.

"That's right; this was supposed to be a race," I muse as I pull my sweatshirt over my head and drop it to the floor. My hands slip beneath the waistband of my sweats, and I tug them over my thighs.

"No underwear?" she asks.

I shrug. "We were in for the night." I nod to her bottom half. "Looks like I won." I wag my eyebrows.

Maggie just grins and moves to sit on her butt, leaning back on her elbows. She lifts her hips. "I think I need your help."

I shake my head, because I'm once again grinning. Have I ever had this much fun during sex? I try to think back to a time, and the answer is a resounding no. Maybe it's because we know each other so well or because we know we're both on the same page. I'm not worried about Maggie trying to convince me she's the one for me. This is pleasure between two consenting adults.

Leaning over her, I press a kiss to her lips, ignoring her tits that are begging for my mouth. Grabbing on to the waistband of her leggings, I tug those, as well as her panties, down at the same time. She lifts her hips, allowing me to pull them over her ass and down her thighs. I yank until they're off and on the floor with the rest of our clothing.

Maggie turns and crawls up the bed, giving me the perfect view of her round ass and her pussy that's already glistening for me. My hand goes to my cock, and I squeeze before stroking myself a few times while her eyes track my movements.

"Want some help with that?" she asks, licking her lips.

"Not yet," I tell her. "If you touch me now, this is going to end before it starts."

"What? The great Lachlan Noble is a two-minute man?" she teases. There's a happy glint in her eyes.

"It's been a while for me too, and you're a fucking knockout, Maggie. A man can only resist so much."

"How long?" She tilts her head to the side, her blonde hair splaying over my pillow. She looks like a goddess.

"Over a year."

"What?" She rises, resting her weight on her elbows. "Really?"

I nod. "I'm picky."

"So, we both really did need this."

"Yeah," I agree.

"What are you waiting for?" She eases back on the pillow. She looks perfect, and I can't help but imagine her in my bed at home.

"Just admiring the view."

"You about done admiring? I'm lonely here."

Again, I chuckle, knowing my grin matches the one she's wearing. "Spread those thighs, Mags."

"Oh." Her mouth falls open. "You don't have to... do that," she says. "I know guys don't really like that. Well, some don't."

"I want his full name and last known address because I want to kick the shit out of him. Real men eat pussy, Maggie." I slap my hand over my chest. "That's me. I'm going to devour you, and I'm going to love every single taste, and every moan that falls from those plump pink lips while I do it."

She swallows hard, and I imagine my lips pressed to her neck, feeling the action against my lips and tongue. Climbing on the bed, I nod toward her thighs. "Open for me, Mags." A shy look crosses her face, but slowly, she parts her legs. I keep my eyes on hers when I say, "Pull my hair, ride my face, take what you need, because I'm not coming up for air until you've soaked my face. Understood?"

Her face is a beautiful shade of pink, but she nods. Good enough for me. I settle on my belly, slide my arms beneath her legs, and place my hands on her ass, pulling her pussy to my mouth. I don't start slow, and I don't take my time. I do exactly as I told her I would and devour her. Her taste explodes on my tongue, and my hunger for her intensifies. I suck on her clit, while exploring her with my tongue.

"Lach—" she starts, and then her hands are buried in my hair.

I lift my head just slightly. "Good girl," I praise, and go back to my meal. Her hips lift off the bed as if she's seeking more, and who am I not to give her exactly what she needs? Moving my arms from under her legs, I press one hand flat on her belly to hold her still. With the other, I slide one finger inside her, and the moan that I'm gifted with lights a fire inside my soul. I thrust toward the mattress, needing friction. I need to get her there, because my cock is weeping.

As I add another finger, I keep working her clit with my tongue, and it doesn't take long for her to call out my name.

Best. Fucking. Sound.

I don't let up until her body slumps to the bed. Only then do I remove my fingers and lift my head to smile at her. I wipe my face with the back of my hand and slowly kiss my way up to her. I stop on my travels to taste those perfectly pert nipples, giving both of them equal amounts of my attention until I finally reach her lips.

"Hey," I say, kissing her lightly.

"Hi."

"You still with me?" I smirk.

"Definitely."

"Good." I kiss her again, because her lips are soft and inviting, and I like kissing her. Not that I need an excuse. Not right now. Quickly, I climb off the bed and dig through my suitcase for a condom, only to come up empty. "Fuck," I mutter.

"What? What's wrong?"

I stand to face her, my cock pointing at her like a beacon. The ache of not being inside her has already started to set in. I dig around in my suitcase again. I thought I had a couple in here from my last trip. Not that I thought I'd be getting any action on that trip or during this one. It was more out of habit. And better safe than sorry. I'm starting to feel like this night is going to end in disappointment. I reach to the very bottom of the front zippered compartment and smile when I feel the small, foiled strip. Pulling it out, I smile at the three condoms.

That will have to do.

Ripping one off, I bring it to my lips and tear it open with my teeth. It takes mere seconds to be sheathed and back on the bed, nestled between her thighs. "I need to hear you say it."

She rolls her big blue eyes. "Again?"

"Humor me, beautiful."

"Yes, Lachlan, I want your massive cock inside me."

My body shakes with silent laughter. "That'll do," I say as I push inside her. She gasps, and once she's taken all of me, I still, giving her time to get used to my size.

"Eggplant is more like it," she mumbles.

"What's that?" I smirk. I heard every word, and we both know it.

"Do you know how to use that bat between your legs?" she taunts.

"You're about to find out." Pulling out, I thrust back in and repeat the process over and over. Maggie's hands dig into my back as she tilts her head back and bites down on her bottom lip. With every thrust of my hips into hers, my orgasm builds. Her pussy squeezes me like a vise, and it's been too long. She's too hot, too wet, and way too fucking tight for me to be able to last. I open my mouth to tell her to touch herself, that no way do I come before she does, but she cries out my name, and her nails I'm pretty sure draw blood—her grip on my back is so intense.

However, it's not until she opens her eyes, when they lock on mine, and I see desire, and longing in her eyes, I lose it. I grunt out my release, and when we're both finally spent, I rest my forehead against hers.

"You still alive there, big guy?" Maggie asks.

"I'm not sure," I tell her. I lift my head, then drop my lips to hers and kiss her slowly. It's not until we eventually come up for air that I allow myself to leave her body. I rush to the en suite bathroom to take care of the condom. Grabbing a rag, I wet it with warm water, and help her clean up, much to her dismay.

"I just need about fifteen, and we can go again."

"I think we should nap." She pulls the covers up over us and snuggles into my side.

This is new for me. I don't snuggle. I'm not a complete asshole, but I don't have women in my bed, which makes it easy to leave theirs or the hotel or wherever we end up. I never wanted to stick around and snuggle, but this is Maggie, and there is no denying her. At least not for me.

Instead, I wrap my arm around her and take a quick nap before I ravish her twice more before she sneaks out of my bed and back to hers. My room feels empty without her, and this bed is far too big for just me, but I ignore those feelings and close my eyes, hoping to get a few more hours of sleep before we head home later today.

MAGGIE 1

S ITTING ON THE BLANKET, I close my eyes and tilt my head back. Today was a hot one, but now that the sun has gone down, it's not so bad. I brought a few blankets down to spread them out for everyone to sit on to watch the show and decided to go ahead and take a seat myself. This has become our tradition, at least according to Maddox and Forrest. Two years in a row is enough to call it a tradition, right? Fourth of July will forever be celebrated at Maddox and Brogan's place.

It really is the best spot to watch the fireworks, not that any of us will tell them that. We like to tease them, but if I'm being honest, it's sweet that these men want to make traditions for their kids and wives. I'm just lucky enough to be included as a friend of their wives, and I'd like to think I'm their friend as well.

"How are you feeling?" Brogan asks, taking a seat next to me on the blanket. I'm all spread out and ready for the fireworks show to start.

"Better." I smile at her. "It must have been something I ate. I made a bacon, egg, and cheese sandwich for breakfast. I guess it didn't agree with me."

"Well, I'm glad you're feeling better."

"Me too. Being sick is the worst."

"Agreed," she says, laughing as Maddox and Lachlan head our way. My belly does a flip as Lachlan's vibrant blue eyes lock on mine. I always thought my eyes were a rare blue, but Lachlan, his are like blue glass or marbles. They're stunning, just like the man they belong to.

"I see how it is," Maddox says, smiling. "You ladies wanted to score the best spot."

"Is there really a bad spot?" Brogan asks him.

"I guess not." Lachlan chuckles as he takes a seat next to me on my blanket. He leans his shoulder into mine. "Hey, Mags."

My body heats just from being near him. It's as if it can't forget the night we shared. I know I can't forget. In fact, it keeps me company at night, along with my battery-operated friend, but that's information that will remain locked inside the Maggie vault, just like the passionate night we shared together.

"Hey," I finally reply.

"Is everyone else headed out?" Brogan asks Maddox.

"Yeah, they're wrangling the kids," he tells his wife.

"And you two skipped out?" she teases.

"Not enough babies," Maddox grumbles.

"I thought you were working on that, Mad?" Lachlan teases his friend.

"Oh, he's working on it," Brogan blurts, slapping her hand over her mouth. We all crack up laughing at her outburst.

"My man." Lachlan leans over me and Brogan to offer Maddox his fist, which Maddox bumps while wearing a wide grin.

The rest of the gang, their kids, and with more blankets in tow join us. Everyone gets spread out on their blankets, and lie back staring at the night sky. The twins and Lilly chatter away, and Kane babbles as if he's carrying on a conversation with each of them. I can't help but smile. These kids may not be related to me by blood, but I will forever be their aunt Maggie.

When the first spark of color hits the sky, the kids *ooh* and *ahh*, as do their parents. Kane cries a little, but I can hear his daddy telling him how pretty the sky is, and that there is nothing to be scared of, which calms him down.

For such a small town, Ashby puts on an incredible fireworks display out on the lake, and this really is the best place to watch it. I'm lying as still as I possibly can, because Lachlan is next to me. On the other side, Maddox and Brogan are all cuddled up, and I envy what my friends have.

I want to find that.

I'm shocked when I feel Lachlan link his fingers through mine, giving them a gentle squeeze. I do the same in return, letting him know I felt him. It's weird, being here with him, acting as if the night we spent together six weeks ago wasn't the best sex of my life. Hell, the best night of my life with him.

I'm struggling and I didn't think I would be. I know I've never done the one-night stand thing, but I thought since I knew Lachlan, and that he would continue to be in my life, that the emotions wouldn't take hold of me, but I guess I was wrong.

That night is all that I can think about.

For years, my ex belittled me. He made me feel unwanted and unsexy. I was convinced that no man would ever find me desirable, but unless Lachlan was a good actor, he did. No, I know he did. He showed me with his touch and with his words.

Lachlan Noble is going to be a hard act to follow.

One night is all it will ever be. I knew that before he ever touched me. It was my idea, but now, there's a part of me that might sort of... kind of wish things were different.

Okay, a big part, but what's done is done. It doesn't help that Lachlan has been finding these small, innocent ways to touch me today. Like massaging my shoulders earlier, then whispering in my ear how soft my skin was.

So not helping.

The fireworks finale lights up the night sky, and I worry someone might notice my hand locked in his, but I know they're all wrapped up in each other, and their kids. As they should be. Once the show is over, everyone starts packing kids and blankets back to the house. I take my time, and to my surprise, Lachlan does as well.

It's just the two of us when he finally speaks. "You good?"

I smile at him, hoping that it looks reassuring. "Of course."

"You just seem quiet today."

"Oh, that. I think I ate something bad this morning. I wasn't feeling well, but I'm good to go now."

He nods. "Do you need anything?"

This time, my smile is more genuine. Lachlan is a great guy. "I'm good, but thank you for offering." I bend over to pick up the blanket, but he beats me to it.

"I've got this. Come on." He nods toward the back of the house where everyone has gathered, and I fall in step beside him. "Is this yours?" he asks, holding up the rolled-up blanket in his arms.

"Yeah." I reach for it. "I'll go put it in my car."

"I'll carry it," he tells me.

"You don't have to."

"Didn't think I did. Can't a guy just do something nice for a pretty girl?" he asks.

"You've already had the goods. You don't have to keep laying on the charm," I say, keeping my tone teasing as we reach my car. I reach in and pop the trunk so he can toss the blanket inside, before joining him at the back of my car.

"Maggie." The way he says my name has me looking up to find Lachlan still holding the blanket, his eyes locked on mine. "That's not what I'm doing. I truly wanted to help you. It doesn't matter that I know what it feels like to have your pussy choking my cock. I'd still have offered to help you." He tosses the blanket into the trunk and takes a deep breath, while my body aches for him. "That's what a man does, Mags. A real man. Not some shallow-minded small dick fuckface that had to put you down to feel superior. All I wanted to do was help you." He closes the trunk of my car and stalks off toward the house.

My heart drops to my toes as I watch him walk away. He's almost made it back to the house when I call out his name. "Lachlan!" I take off at a light jog to catch up with him. Thankfully, he stops. His hands are fisted at his sides, but it's his eyes that truly gut me. The sadness laced with hurt steals the breath from my lungs.

When I reach him, I don't know what to do, so I step in close and wrap my arms around his waist, burying my face in his chest. His now-familiar scent washes over me, and I allow myself a few extra seconds to just breathe him in.

"I'm sorry," I mumble against his chest. "I didn't mean to upset you or hurt your feelings. I'm just not used to men being nice because they want to be."

Finally, he wraps his arms around me and hugs me back, and it feels right, as if this is exactly where I'm supposed to be. I quickly dismiss that thought, pushing it out of my mind, because that's not what this is. Lachlan and I are friends.

Friends can hug, right?

"I hate that fucker for what he did to you."

"I'm a work in progress," I mutter.

I feel his lips press to the top of my head, and then he's leaning back, placing his finger beneath my chin, his blue eyes finding mine. "You are not a work in progress, Maggie. You're perfect just the way you are. Take everything that man said to you and erase it from your mind."

"That's easier said than done, especially after three years of almost constant ridicule."

He mumbles something about five minutes in a dark alley, and I place my forehead against his chest to hide my smile. One day this man is going to make some woman very happy and feel cherished. He just needs to find her.

It takes effort, but I force myself to step back from him. "Come on, stud. Let's go join everyone else." I'll miss the warmth of his arms and the false sense of security they offer. He's not that person for me, and that's okay. One day, there will be a man who will come along who loves me fiercely, and when he shows up in my life, I'll have worked through my shit with my self-esteem that Eric trashed, and I'll be ready for him.

"You think I'm a stud, huh?" He wags his eyebrows, and I crack up laughing. Lachlan is this macho guy with such a soft heart. It's a contradiction, and he's funny, fun to be around, and I'm glad he's also forgiving. He didn't deserve my words.

"What's so funny?" Briar asks as we reach the backyard.

"This guy"—I point toward Lachlan—"thinks he's a comedian."

"I'll show you, comedian." He lifts me into his arms, tossing me over his shoulder, and takes off as if he's going to the lake.

"Lachlan!" I half yell, half laugh. "Put me down." I smack at his back and his ass, but it does nothing.

"Say I'm the funniest guy you know." He stops walking and waits for me to comply.

"You're the funniest guy I know."

"That's better." Instead of putting me down, he turns on his heel and heads back to our friends. He doesn't stop until he's in front of a vacant chair. He lowers me to my feet and holds on long enough for me to get my balance. I swat at his chest, and he grins, his blue eyes sparkling in the light of the fire.

Yes, it's July in Tennessee, and we still have a fire. "Now I feel buzzed." I laugh, patting my hair that I'm sure looks like I just walked five miles in a windstorm from hanging upside down.

"You're welcome." Lachlan bows dramatically, and everyone laughs at him.

"Go over there." I chuckle, pointing to a chair on the opposite side of the fire.

"Uncle Lach, I want a ride," River says, bouncing on Maddox's lap.

"Me too!" Rayne declares.

"Isn't it past your bedtime?" he asks the girls.

"We're not tired," River says, covering her yawn.

"How about a story first?" Lachlan suggests.

"Oh, will you do the voices like Daddy does?" Rayne asks.

"I'm not sure I can do it as well as your dad does, but I'll give it a try. Why don't we go inside and pick out a book."

"I wead," Lilly tells him. She's sitting on Roman's lap and was half asleep until all the commotion. She raises her arms in the air, and Lachlan plucks her from her dad's lap, settling her on his hip.

"What about you, little man?" he asks Kane. The cutest baby boy ever just stares up at him, his eyes heavy. It won't take much for any of them to be asleep. Lachlan holds his arm out and tells Legend, "Baby me."

"You sure you want all of them?" Forrest asks. "I can help."

"Sit, your a— rear end back in the chair, Daddy Forrest. Uncle Lachlan is having story time."

"Aunt Maggie needs to come too," River announces. "She's going to be lonely."

"Oh, sweetie, I won't be lonely. I have all my friends here with me," I tell her.

"But you need someone with you," Rayne adds.

It's then that I understand what they're saying. In their little minds, because I'm not coupled up, they're worried I'll be all alone. My heart swells ten times its normal size. At least that's what it feels like to have their love and worry.

"I promise you, I'll be okay," I assure them.

"You might as well come with us," Lachlan tells me.

"I thought it was Uncle Lachlan's story time?" Forrest asks, smirking.

"It is. No parents allowed," he tells Forrest before turning his burning blue gaze my way. "Coming, Mags?"

I can't very well say no when the twins are bouncing up and down, begging me to come with them. "I guess it's safer if a responsible adult was with the kids," I tease, and Lachlan tosses his head back in laughter.

"Come on, trouble." Lachlan's face is lit up by his smile.

"Only if I get a baby out of the deal." I stand and move toward him, holding my arms open. I don't care who I get, but baby Kane reaches for me. I take him into my arms, and he rests his head on my shoulder.

"Smart man," Lachlan whispers.

I pretend not to hear him as I follow the four of them into the house. River and Rayne rush to a small bookcase in the corner that's filled with books. You would think that they still live here, but that just shows you how incredible this family is. They each pick out a book and climb up on the couch.

"We can sit in the middle," Rayne says.

"And baby Kane can sit with Aunt Maggie and Lilly with Uncle Lach, so the family is all close," River explains.

"Sounds like a plan, ladies." Lachlan sits beside River, which leaves me taking the spot beside Rayne. I shift Kane on my lap, and he stays snuggled up to my chest, which is fine with me. I love snuggles from adorable little boys and girls, especially the ones in this family. They feel like my family too.

With all four kids snuggled in, Lachlan begins to read. He speaks softly and changes his voice when the story calls for it, and I find myself just as captivated as the kids. There are so many sides to this man, to all of them, but Lachlan was never really separate from the others for me before. He's always just been one of the guys. All five are hot as hell, but they were always just my friends', husbands, and their friends. Something changed that night in the cabin.

I know exactly when that changed, and so does my body. I need to keep reminding myself it was my idea. One night, no strings, scratch the itch, that's what I wanted, but part of me wishes things could be different. I know that's not what he wants, and I'm not ready for that either. I still have a lot of self-reflection to do. I can't be in a relationship when I'm constantly second-guessing everything my partner says.

Does he really think I'm beautiful? Is he really working late? Does he think my ass looks huge in my new skirt? Too many scenarios flash in my mind of my insecurities. I know they stem from Eric and his mental and verbal abuse. Knowing it and training my mind to know he was wrong are two different things.

I've got work to do, but in the meantime, I'll have the memories of our night together to hold me over until it's time to really venture out into the dating world, and hopefully, I'll be able to find my forever love.

Shaking out of my thoughts, I tune back into the story and Lachlan's deep, sexy voice. He finishes the first book, closing it, and placing a tender kiss on Lilly's head, and that's when I notice she's sound asleep. They all are.

"We lost our gang," he whispers.

"Looks like it. I'll put Kane in his Pack 'N Play and come back and get Lilly to put her in hers."

"Okay, then I'll set the twins here on the couch."

We work quietly and efficiently as we get all the kids settled. "Should we stay inside and listen for them?" I ask.

"Nah, we've got this." He picks up a baby monitor I didn't notice from the end table and turns on both units. He keeps one monitor in his hand and places the other empty hand on the small of my back as he leads me back outside.

"Where's your entourage?" Roman asks.

"All conked out," Lachlan replies.

"Lilly and Kane are in their Pack 'N Plays and the twins are on the couch. I put lots of pillows on the floor in case they roll off," I tell them.

"Oh, they'll be fine," Briar assures me. "They're old enough now we don't have to worry about that."

"Thanks for that," Forrest says, nuzzling his wife's neck. All the wives are on their husband's laps, and I'm thankful for River and Rayne, whose big little hearts rescued me. I'm happy for my friends, but sometimes being the ninth wheel can be awkward. I guess at least it's not just me, since Lachlan is still single.

Lachlan grabs a couple of bottles of water, and hands me one before taking the empty chair next to me. We join the easy conversation with our friends, as if our night together never happened. I'm sure there will be a day when I'll look at Lachlan and not think about his hands and his mouth on my body, but I doubt it will be anytime soon.

LACHLAN 2

"YOU'RE ALL SET." I PLACE my tattoo gun on the small rolling tray, and wipe off the excess ink before standing and offering my client a handheld mirror to assist her in seeing her new back tattoo, in addition to the mirror hanging on the wall.

"I love it!" She smiles widely, and I nod.

Another satisfied customer. It's hard to believe this is how I get to make my living. Sometimes it feels like I'm living in a dream, but I guess in a way, I am. I'm living *my* dream, doing what I love, and it never feels like work.

"I'll walk you out. Lyra's working the front desk. She can get you all cashed out." The girl gives me a smile, one that says she's interested. I've been on the receiving end of those types of looks many times in my life, and normally, I'd flash her a grin or give her a wink, but not today.

She does nothing for me.

In fact, it's been almost two months since I've done either of those things. Not since the night I spent wrapped up in Maggie. It was supposed to be a one-off, and it was, but here I am, still thinking about my time with her.

Her high heels clack along the tile floor as I lead her back to reception. Who wears high heels, Daisy Duke cutoff jean shorts, and a tight-ass tank top to get a tattoo? Am I getting old and changing my mind about what I find sexy? Is it watching my best friends' wives and how they carry themselves that's changing my thoughts? Sure, high heels and booty shorts are sexy, but there is a time and place for that, and apparently, my old ass thinks this isn't the place.

I'm thirty-three, not seventy-three, but it still irks me all the same.

"Lyra, this is—" Fuck, I can't remember her name. I turn back to my client and she bats her eyelashes. Her very fake, very long, spider-leg-looking eyelashes.

"Sasha," she purrs.

I barely contain my eye roll when I turn back to Lyra. "Sasha." I hand Lyra the checkout receipt, and turn to leave, but squealing stops me in my tracks. Four other ladies join us one by one, each of the guys trailing either in front or behind them. It takes seeing all of them to remember they're all friends and booked the same appointment time, one with each of us. On a rare day, we're all five here at the same time. They all five got the same exact design in the same exact place.

The ladies smile and laugh and look at each other's tattoos, while Lyra rushes to cash them out. Legend gives me a look that says he's not impressed, which means his client must have hit on him. One way to piss him off—hell, piss off any of them—is to hit on them when they're all four wearing wedding bands.

"I struck out." I hear one of them say, and sigh. What is it about women and men who have no care that the other person is in a committed relationship, married or not? I mean, if they'll cheat on the person with you, then they'll cheat on you. At least that's my theory.

"Me too," the other three say, and I can actually hear the disappointment in their voices.

"Not me. I'm going for it," my client, Sara, no wait, Sasha says.

I kid you not. This woman lifts up her boobs, licks her lips, and saunters over to me in her high heels. I think it's supposed to look sexy, but I promise you, it's not. It's more like a newborn baby deer trying to find its footing. "Thanks again, Lachlan," she purrs.

Side note: the purr is meant to sound sexy, I'm sure, but instead, she's coming off sounding like a two-pack-a-day smoker. "Why don't we go celebrate with a drink, and then—" She shrugs. "—whatever else we can get ourselves into." She licks her lips and bats her spider legs at me.

"I'm working," I reply, deadpan. I'm happy to report that the eye roll is swiftly contained, but internally, I'm rolling my eyes hard at this chick. I mean, come on. Read the room, Sally.

"I can wait." She licks her lips again.

"I work until late." I'm showing no emotion. I'm not even really being nice to her, and she's not taking the hint.

"You have to eat, right?" she asks.

I blow out a heavy breath. I'm going to have to dumb this down for her, and I hate being a dick, but I'm just not interested.

"Lachlan, you're still coming to the house tonight for dinner, right?" Forrest asks. "You know the kids will be disappointed if Uncle Lachlan doesn't show up."

I smile at Forrest, making a mental note to offer to watch the girls for him soon. "Yeah, I have plans."

"Tomorrow night then?" she asks, just not getting it.

I hear one of the guys groan and mumble something under their breath from where they're standing behind me, but I can't make out what they're saying. "Look, Sandra."

"It's Sasha." She's still smiling at me as if I'm going to take her up on her offer.

"Sasha. Right. I'm not interested." I blurt the words because this girl can't take the subtle hints I've been giving her.

"Are you married?"

"No."

"Do you have a girlfriend?"

"No." She opens her mouth to, I'm sure, grill me even further, but I hold up my hand to stop her. "Thank you for coming in. Be safe getting home." With that, I turn on my heel and stalk toward the break room, removing myself from the situation.

I know it won't be long and the guys, and maybe even Lyra, will be on my heels wanting to know what's up. What's up is that I had the best sex of my life with their wives' friend, with my friend, and we promised it was a onetime thing.

I stalk toward the refrigerator, and I pull open the door. I grab a bottle of water, twisting off the cap and drinking the entire thing. The guys walk in as I'm tossing the empty bottle into the recycling bin.

They form a small circle around me, and I'm leaning back against the counter. "What?" I ask. I know what they want, but fuck me, I don't want to talk about it. I can't talk about it. I made a promise to Maggie, and I intend to keep it.

Roman crosses his arms over his chest. "What's up, Lach?"

"Just grabbing something to drink." My tone is clipped, and I take a deep breath and slowly exhale. I can't take this... frustration or whatever this is out on them.

"We can see that," Legend says.

"That back there." Forrest points over his shoulder. "That wasn't you."

"I don't know what you mean." The lie tastes bitter on my tongue.

"You've got more game than what we just saw out there," Maddox explains.

Running my hands over my face, I take a few seconds before dropping them and giving them as much as I can. "I'm over it," I tell them. "I'm over meaningless."

"You got someone in mind?" Roman asks.

I huff out a laugh. "No, but I've watched the four of you, and let's just say, I can see the appeal. That girl, she didn't want me. She wanted the bad boy tattoo artist she sees when she looks at me. She wanted one of the owners of one of the top tattoo shops in Tennessee. She didn't see Lachlan. Not in here." I tap my hand over my chest.

"Makes sense," Legend says.

"So, we need to find you a wife," Forrest adds.

"We should ask our wives to help," Maddox agrees.

"No. No. No. I don't need help. I'm just... in a funk, I guess."

"How long has it been?" Legend asks.

I don't need to ask him what he means. "Over a year," I confess. All four of them whistle. "Yeah," I agree. It's a little white lie because it's been less than two months, but that night was different. It wasn't meaningless, not to me. So yeah, it's been well over a year since my last meaningless hookup. From how my head won't forget about my night with Maggie, it's shaping up to be a hell of a lot longer than that.

"I don't miss it," Maddox tells me. "Not for one second do I miss random hookups."

"Agreed," the other three sound off at the same time.

"It's so much better," Legend chimes in. "You get to know her, and she you, and everything is just better."

"It's the love," Roman adds. He glances over at Forrest and smirks. "Makes the sex better."

"Ack." Forrest places his hands over his ears. "My baby sister," he says, and we all laugh. We'll be eighty, watching our grandkids, hell, our great-grandkids run around the yard, and Forrest will still react that way when it comes to Roman and Emerson.

"It's more than sex," Forrest adds, once he's removed his hands from his ears. "It's the connection that goes beyond... well, beyond anything I've ever known. I can't even explain it to you, Lachlan, but I promise you, brother, when you find it, you'll know and when you do, you're going to want to hold on tight with everything you've got."

"I'll find her," I agree. In the back of my mind, an image of Maggie with her long blonde hair splayed out on the dark sheets of my bed at the cabin filters through.

Could it be her? Could Maggie be my person? Is she feeling this... loss the same way that I am? I know I could just ask her, but we promised each other it would be one and done. I don't want to break my promise, but the idea that we could possibly be more, well, that sparks something inside me that's been dark for a long damn time.

The intercom beeps, and Lyra's voice comes through the speaker. "Legend and Forrest, your next appointments are here."

"You good?" Legend asks me.

"I'm good." I nod. He claps me on the shoulder and leaves the room. Forrest, Roman, and Maddox all do the same before leaving me to my thoughts.

Today has been one of the longest, and it's only a few minutes past five as I start my truck and head toward home. However, going home alone suddenly doesn't appeal to me. Not after opening up to the guys and the thoughts of Maggie running constantly through my head. So, instead, I turn right and head toward my parents' place. It's been a couple of weeks since I've stopped in, and I think some of Mom's home cooking is exactly what I need.

The house is all lit up when I pull into the drive. After grabbing my cell and my keys, I make my way to the front door. I rap my knuckles a few times before turning the handle and calling out. My parents assure me I don't have to knock, but there have been a few times I've walked in on them a little disheveled, and yeah, I don't want to see that, so I always knock, call out, and walk slowly through the foyer and into the living room giving them time to get themselves together.

"Hey, Lachlan, what brings you by?" My dad stands from where he's sitting in the recliner and pulls me into a hug.

"Just getting off work. Where's Mom?"

"She went shopping with Cassie. They're stopping to grab dinner and then heading home."

Cassie is Maddox's mom, and I love how our parents became friends because of our friendship growing up. "You had dinner yet?" I ask him.

"Nope. Have you?"

"No. Come on, old man. I'll buy you some pizza and wings."

"Don't tell your mother. I'm supposed to be watching my cholesterol."

I pause. "Everything okay?" Rodney Noble is not my biological father. That man I've never met. He found out my mom was pregnant and bailed. She met Rodney two years later. They married, and he adopted me. He is my father. It might not be his blood running through my veins, but this man raised me and loved me. Loves me like it is.

"Everything's fine. I had a checkup and my numbers were slightly elevated. I'm not even taking medication. Your mother is just taking good care of me."

There is a twinkle in his eyes that tells me he's loving every minute of Mom fussing over him. "All right, but if you get me in trouble, I'm telling Mom you gave me my first beer at fifteen."

"Hey! That's between men." He laughs. He holds out his hand. I place mine in his, and we shake on it. "Deal."

The drive to Dough Daddies in town is short, and Dad catches me up on how work is going. He owns a small plumbing company, and he's made quite a name for himself. Mom works for the city of Ashby in the title office. They've both had the same careers for as long as I can remember.

Once inside the restaurant, I lead us to a small booth in the back of the room. It's the middle of the week, so the crowd isn't nearly as heavy as it is on the weekends. The server rushes over, takes our drink order and scurries away with a wink in my direction.

"That still happens everywhere you go, huh? It's the eyes. The ladies love those eyes." He chuckles.

"Unfortunately," I mutter.

Dad's grin grows wider. "Getting old, is it? All the female attention?"

"You could say that."

"Does this mean your momma and I are going to get those grandbabies she's always asking for?"

Dropping my menu to the table, I sit back in my side of the booth and sigh. "One day, I hope so," I admit. "It was fun for a while, but watching the guys get married and have families, I can see the appeal."

"I was just like you when I was younger."

"What?" I'm shocked.

He nods. "I never wanted anything permanent. I had my heart broken in my early twenties, and I swore I'd never do it again."

"What changed your mind?"

"I met you and your mom. It took me a while to understand what I was feeling, but the minute I met her, and then you, I knew my life was changed. For the better," he adds.

"I didn't know that about you."

Dad waves his hand in the air. "Kids aren't necessarily supposed to know those things about their parents. Not until they're ready to hear it. Parenting is hard, Lachlan. You hope that you're giving your child the guidance and knowledge to make good choices in their lives, but ultimately, once they turn eighteen, it's all out of your control. Your mother and I got lucky. You were a good kid. Some foolishness from time to time, but we are so damn proud of the man you've become."

"I had a great role model." His face blushes, but his eyes soften with love. I've seen that look from him, directed at me my entire life. "Why didn't you ever have more kids? You and Mom together were a great team. I know the story you've told me repeatedly that I was enough, but there had to be another reason."

"It was my choice." He pauses to collect his thoughts, and I give him the time he needs. "I loved you both fiercely, Lachlan. I never wanted you to feel otherwise. I was worried that if your mother and I had more children, you might think I loved them more than you, which would never be the case. As you got older, we considered it again, but the age gap would have been too steep, and you were enough for us. You are our son, and we love you."

I blink hard a few times, because my own emotions are getting the best of me. "I would have known," I tell him, my voice cracking. "There wasn't a single day in my life that I didn't feel how much you loved me. I would have known."

He nods. "I know that now, but back then, the thought of you not feeling equal to a sibling, it gutted me. My buddies tell me I went soft when I met you and your mother, and they're probably right, but I'm telling you, son, there is not one single second of my life I regret. Loving you and your mother was as easy as breathing and just as essential for me. I want you to find that person for you. I want you to know what that feels like."

"I want that," I admit. "Hopefully one day I'll find her." My mind instantly goes to Maggie and the night we shared together.

"What's that look?" Dad asks, pointing at my face.

"What look?"

This time he's the one to fold his arms over his chest and freezes me with the intensity of his gaze. "You already found her."

"W—What?"

He smirks. "You already found her. You found someone to make you stop and think twice about the time you spent with her."

"We made a deal," I confess. "We promised one night, no strings. Our friends are friends, and it's a tangled mess."

His grin grows even wider and I realize my mistake. My parents know who I spend my time with, and they've met them all. It doesn't take a rocket scientist to figure out I'm talking about Maggie.

"It's okay to break a promise if that broken promise leads to more happiness."

"But will it? Or am I just hung up on her because she's forbidden?"

"She's only forbidden because the two of you made her that way. Change the narrative, Lachlan."

"You make it sound easy. I'm sure it's just me, and I'm in a funk. It will pass."

"Take some time to get your thoughts together, but don't ignore this in the process." He taps two fingers on his chest over his heart. "Pushing past my doubts led me to a life of love and happiness."

"Can I take your order?" the server asks, placing our drinks in front of us.

We order, and thankfully, the topic turns to a lighter subject. I've had more heart-to-heart conversations today than I have in my entire life. Okay, that's not true, but I'm mentally drained because of them, and part of that is all about me. I need to get out of my head and let this go.

MAGGIE 3

M Y KNEES WON'T STOP BOUNCING. It's annoying me, so I know it has to be annoying the other patients in the waiting room, but I can't help it. I'm nervous. I'm still holding out hope that the five tests I've taken over the last few days are false positives, but that hope is fickle, because I'm pretty sure the tests were right.

Not just because I took five of them, but because I've been nauseous for a couple of weeks now. My boobs hurt, and I'm late. As in two months late. Last month I chalked it up to working so many hours. The emergency room was short-staffed, and I picked up a lot of extra shifts. My schedule was all wonky, and I thought that was the reason.

I was in denial.

This month, specifically four days ago, when I didn't start my period, I knew. I drove straight to the pharmacy after work and bought a basketful of tests. Okay, just ten, but I've managed to only use five of them. All five were positive at different times of the day. All five were different brands.

That brings me to now. I'm sitting in the waiting room of my gynecologist's office for her to tell me what I already know.

I'm pregnant.

"Maggie," the nurse calls.

Pulling in a deep breath, I stand on shaky legs and follow her through the door to the back of the office. We stop at the scale, and I place my purse on the chair and step on. I don't look at the number. It doesn't matter. My hand lands on my flat belly. With those two pink lines, everything in my life has changed. Being here is really just a formality.

"Great, you're going to be in exam room three," she tells me. I follow her into the room and take a seat on the exam table. "So you're here for a possible pregnancy?" she asks. "You have at home positive tests, correct?"

"Y-Yes."

"Do you know the date of your last menstrual cycle?" I rattle off the date and the answer to the rest of her questions. "Perfect. Now, we'll need a urine sample, but we'll also draw blood as well. Do you think you can give us a sample now?"

"I can."

"Perfect. Just leave the cup in the little silver door behind the toilet. The restroom is directly across the hall." She opens the door, and points as if I can't figure it out on my own.

Honestly, it probably appears that way. I need to shake out of this funk. This wasn't how I planned to start a family, but this is how it's happening, and I can't change that. Well, I guess I could, but I won't. I've known for a few days, and already, this baby is a part of me, a part of my heart.

Quickly, I give my urine sample and settle myself back in the exam room, where I strip down and put on the gown provided before taking a seat on the examination table. I fist my hands in my lap as I let my mind wander over everything I'm going to need to do to prepare for this baby.

I also have to talk to Lachlan. Before I can let my mind go there and how that conversation might play out, something that I've thought about a lot the past few days, there's a knock at the door, and Dr. Holmes steps into the room.

"Maggie, good to see you." She goes to the sink and washes her hands before turning to face me. "I hear congratulations might be in order." She smiles kindly, and something about that smile eases some of my anxiety.

"Yes."

"Okay, tell me a little about what's been going on outside of the positive home tests."

I ramble on about my symptoms. "And I took five at home tests," I confess.

Dr. Holmes chuckles. "You are not the only one. I even took several with both of my kids. It's like you need to just really be sure."

"Exactly."

She instructs me to lie back, and she quickly and efficiently does her exam. She's stripping off her gloves when there's a knock at the door. She glances to make sure I'm again covered and sitting up before she answers. "Results," the nurse whispers.

"Thank you." Dr. Holmes shuts the door and turns to me and smiles. "Your exam and your urine results are both positive. Congratulations."

It's official.

I'm pregnant.

"Thank you." My voice is soft as I let this sink in. I already knew, but this moment makes it even more real.

Dr. Holmes starts to discuss the next steps, vitamins, and my next appointment. I'm only half listening because I'm going to be a mom.

Me. A mom.

The remainder of the appointment goes by in a blur, and I find myself sitting in my car, staring at the dash while the air conditioning blows full blast. It's a little after five. I was the last appointment of the day, and I know where my next stop needs to be. It's only right to tell the baby's father before I tell anyone else, but I'm dreading this conversation.

Digging my phone out of my purse, I shoot Lachlan a message.

Me: Are you home?

His reply is immediate.

> **Lachlan:** *Headed there now. Just left the shop.*
>
> **Me:** *Can I come by?*
>
> **Lachlan:** *Of course. Is everything okay?*

I've never asked to come to his place, and I can only imagine what he thinks my reason is now. I've been there with the group, but not on my own. "I'm sorry," I whisper because I'm about to change his life too.

> **Me:** *Yes. I'll see you soon.*

Tossing my phone back into my purse, I close my eyes and take a deep breath. I don't want to do this, but I know that I have to. It's the right thing to do, and I don't want to keep this from him. It's only fair he finds out. To be honest, I should have told him before now and asked him to come with me today, but I just couldn't do that. I needed to do this part on my own. I needed to let this truth sink in before talking to him.

No more excuses. It's time for the hard conversation. I've rehearsed this a million times, but that doesn't make this any easier.

I pull into Lachlan's driveway just as he's climbing out of his truck. I don't give myself time to stall, so I grab my keys and phone and climb out of the car.

"Hey, you." He comes over and wraps me in a hug. "What's going on?"

"Can we go inside and talk?"

"Sure." He places his hand on the small of my back and leads me onto the porch. With one hand, he unlocks and opens the door, guiding me inside. "Do you want something to drink?"

My stomach rolls. Whoever said *morning* sickness lied. It's all damn day. "No, thank you."

"Have a seat." I do as he says, and perch on the edge of the couch while Lachlan takes the recliner. His blue eyes are boring into mine, willing me to tell him why I'm here.

Placing my phone and keys on the table in front of me, I fold my hands in my lap, take a deep breath, and meet his gaze. "I've gone over this a thousand times in my head, but now that I'm here with you, it's all gone."

"It's just me, Mags. You can tell me anything," Lachlan says gently.

He's right. I need to just pull the Band-Aid off, so to speak. "I'm pregnant." I blurt it out and wait for his reaction.

Lachlan's mouth falls open, but he quickly closes it. "Okay." He nods and leans forward, resting his elbows on his knees.

He's not giving me anything else, so I keep going. "I'm keeping this baby. I want you to know you don't need to do anything. You don't have to do anything, but I want this baby." My hands go to my belly. "I just found out a few days ago, and I just came from a doctor's appointment, and I love this baby already, Lachlan. So, I'm doing this. I don't expect anything from you, and I'll tell the girls I don't know the father, that it was a one-night stand, and I'll keep my distance." I ramble on and then clamp my mouth shut when his shock turns to anger.

"Why the hell would you tell them you don't know who the father is?" He stands up and paces the small living room. He turns to face me, not stopping his pacing, and slaps his chest hard. "I'm the father, Maggie. Me. That's my baby."

"I didn't know how you would feel, and I wanted you to know that I can do this. I'm sorry it happened, but I love this little one, Lachlan."

He stops pacing and comes to stand before me. He stares down at me for several heartbeats before he drops to his knees and takes my hands in his. "Don't apologize to me. I was there. I was in that room, in that moment with you, Maggie, and dammit, to hear you say you don't want me in my child's life, that cuts deep."

"No. No, that's not—I didn't mean—" I stop and take a deep breath, and collect my thoughts. "I didn't mean that I didn't want you in this baby's life, just that I didn't expect you to be. I can handle this, and you have the choice to stay or walk away. Either way, it's your choice. Just like raising this baby is my choice."

"There is no choice, Maggie. I'm this baby's father." His eyes drop to my belly, and the look of longing I see on his face has tears springing in my eyes. I don't know why I do it, but I take one of his hands and place it over my still-flat belly.

When he finally looks up at me, there are tears in his eyes. "Can we try?"

I furrow my brow. "Try what?"

"To raise this baby together. I want to be there, Maggie. For you and our baby. I want to hold your hand at appointments. I want to help paint the nursery. I want to spend hours picking out names. All of it. I don't want to miss a single thing."

"Really?" I ask, my voice cracking as I lose my battle with my tears.

Lachlan wipes at my cheeks with his thumbs. "Yes, really. We're friends, Maggie. We shared a night together that I will always remember and not just because that night gave us our son or daughter. I could never forget you, and I want this with you. Sure, it's unconventional, but we can do this, Maggie. We can raise this baby together."

"You want to co-parent with me?" I ask, making sure that I'm understanding him correctly.

"Is that what it's called? I want to be this baby's daddy. My biological dad walked out on my mom when she found out she was pregnant with me."

"Oh, Lachlan."

"She met and married my dad, my father, not by blood but by love, and he's been there every day since. I know what it takes to be a good dad because I had the best example. Besides, I have four best friends who will be there if I need advice. And you. You and I, we can do this, Maggie. So, can we? Can we try this? I promise you we're going to kick ass at this co-parent thing."

"I'm sorry. You don't have to ask to be a part of our child's life. I'm just... you're not my ex, and that's not fair to you that I would assume that you would push me away. I'm sorry for doubting you. Yes, we can do this. We can raise this baby. Together."

I don't know what I was expecting, but it's not Lachlan to lean in and wrap his arms around me in a hug so fierce, it pulls the breath from my lungs. When he finally pulls back, he's wearing a smile that lights up his entire face.

"Okay, tell me everything."

So I do. I tell him how I've been nauseous, about my boobs hurting, and then the five at-home tests that I took, ending with the details of today's appointment.

"When do you go back to the doctor?" he asks, pulling his phone out of his pocket and tapping the screen.

"The second week of August." Reaching for my phone, I scroll to the appointment in my calendar and rattle off the exact date and time.

"I'll be there."

"You don't—" I start, then stop. "Thank you, Lachlan."

"This is my baby too. Do you need anything? I know you said you've been nauseous. What foods make it better or worse?"

"I don't really know if there is any one thing that triggers it. What I do know is that it's not just in the mornings. It seems to hit me at all hours of the day or night."

"Maybe you should move in with me so that I can be there for you when that happens," he muses.

"I'm a big girl and a registered nurse. I'm completely capable of taking care of myself."

"I know, but you're growing my baby in there. I should be there for anything you need."

"Lachlan, think about what you're saying. We're not together. If we were to live together, think about how confusing that will be for the baby, when either one of us meets someone. I promise I'll keep you as updated on my life as I possibly can."

"Fine, but I don't care what time it is, you text me. If you're up at 3:00 a.m. call me, text me. Hell, come over. Just... I don't want to miss any of it."

Reaching over the cushion that's between us, I rest my palm against his cheek. "You're a good man, Lachlan Noble. Our baby is lucky to have you as his or her father."

His blue eyes blaze. "We're having a baby! We need to tell everyone. Should we call them now?"

"Actually, I was kind of hoping we could wait until I'm out of the first trimester. If something were to happen, if I were to miscarry, it's more likely to happen in the first trimester."

"What? What do you mean? Is something wrong?"

"No," I'm quick to reassure him. "Miscarriages happen to many women, and I would rather just keep this between us for now, and once we're past the twelve-week mark, we can tell the world."

"How long is that?"

"I'm eight weeks along, so it's a month from now. Can you keep a secret that long?"

"I can try." He chuckles. "Can you?"

"Honestly, I'm not so sure I can. Especially with Briar being pregnant, and the others trying, or at least getting lots of practice in. We talk about babies and pregnancy a lot."

"We'll tell them together. You tell me when and we'll do it together. That's our new motto, Mags. You, me, and baby peanut." He rubs my flat belly again. "When can we find out? Oh wait, do you want to find out?"

"Do you?"

"Yeah, I mean, I think so. It would be nice to know so we can get his or her room ready, and pick out a name, and we'll need double of everything for my place and yours. Damn, I need a bigger house. I'll start looking."

"Your house is fine."

"It's a small two-bedroom, and the second bedroom is so small, it's almost like it's a large closet. Besides, the yard is also small, and we're going to need a swing set and room to play."

"Not for a while."

He shrugs. "Still needs to happen."

"Let's just get through the next four weeks, and then you can plan and buy until your heart's content. Deal?" I hold my hand out for him, and he places his in mine. I don't know how I expected this conversation to go, but it wasn't like this. Lachlan has calmed my fears and has accepted this pregnancy with open arms.

"Deal. Now, have you eaten?"

"No."

"What does my baby momma want?"

"Honestly, I don't even know what won't make me sick right now. I've been eating saltines, ginger cookies, and having ginger ale."

"Okay, how about we try a grilled cheese? I have some soup, tomato, or chicken noodle, I think in the cabinet."

"You don't have to cook for me, Lachlan."

"You said we could try, and this is a part of that."

"You're right, I did. Grilled cheese and tomato soup is my favorite."

His eyes sparkle. "Mine too."

That's how we spend the evening. Lachlan makes us dinner that I'm able to eat without incident, and we talk for hours about the baby, about life, and it's one of the best nights I can ever remember having.

I was scared to death to tell him, but he took those fears and spit them out, showing me the kind of man he is. He wants to try, and I want that too. More than anything, I want our baby to have two loving parents.

When I leave his place and head toward my own, a peace I haven't felt since I first suspected I was pregnant washes over me. Maybe we can really make this work. Maybe we can really give this a try.

LACHLAN 4

I CLEARED MY SCHEDULE FOR the entire day, but that just means I'm antsy as I wait for three o'clock to roll around. I'm excited, nervous, and scared as hell. I can't even hang out with Maggie before our appointment because she's working today.

Today, on the day we get to hear our baby's heartbeat, she's working. The woman works way too much, and I'm sure as she gets further along in her pregnancy, I'm going to have to stay on her about taking time and resting.

So, here I am, at nine in the morning, hours before we have to be at Maggie's doctor's office, and I'm too damn restless to stay in this house. After grabbing my phone, keys, and wallet, I head out to my truck. I'll go to the shop to work on some drawings or give the guys shit, maybe take a walk-in, which is something we don't do often. Our guest artist handles the walk-ins unless we have a no-show or cancellation, or days like today when I need a distraction.

It doesn't take long for me to get to the shop. As soon as I walk through the door, Drake furrows his brow.

"What are you doing here?" He looks down at his computer screen, worried he missed something on the schedule, I'm sure. "I thought you had the day off."

"I do. But I don't have anywhere to be until later today, so I thought I'd come in and work on some drawings."

"That defeats taking a day off," Forrest says, walking out of his room. He shakes his customer's hand before pointing toward Drake to take care of the cash-out.

"Yeah, well, I'm restless at home."

He nods. "Yeah, before Briar and the girls, I did a lot of the same on my days off. You need a good woman to help occupy your time."

It's on the tip of my tongue to tell him I have one, and she's having my baby, but I manage to bite my tongue. I promised Maggie I would wait until after today's appointment, and I never break a promise, especially to the mother of my child.

"Maybe." I shrug as if I'm not hiding this huge, life-changing secret from my closest friends. It's not just me anymore. Maggie and our baby come first, and I know the guys will understand that, but I still feel bad for not screaming from the rooftops that I'm going to be a dad.

"Forrest, your next appointment is here," Drake tells us.

"Go do your thing, brother. I'm going to be in here working on some mockups for a few customers. Get ahead a little."

"Don't work too hard," Forrest says, and there's a hidden message in his words. He knows I'm using work as an escape, but what he doesn't know is that after this afternoon, I won't need to hide what's on my mind.

Once in my office, I shut the door, put on my headphones, crank up my favorite playlist, and get to work. Thankfully, I'm able to get lost in my art, and before I know it, it's just after two o'clock, and I decide to drive to Maggie's work and pick her up. We can grab her car later.

Stepping out of my office, I can't hide my smile. Finally, the moment is here.

"Well, you're much more chipper than you were when you went in." Drake laughs.

"I wasn't not chipper before, just restless, but I'm heading out."

"Hot date?" Drake asks.

"Something like that." I smirk and walk toward the door, throwing my hand up in a wave on the way out.

The drive to Maggie's work is only five minutes, so I have time to stop and pick her up a ginger ale. She says it helps to settle her stomach. I buy some peanut butter crackers and a bottle of water for each of us, too, just in case she's not feeling the ginger ale.

When I reach the parking lot of the surgery center, which is connected to the hospital, I find her car easily. And today must be my lucky day because the spot next to her is open. I back my truck into the spot, so I'm sure not to miss her when she comes out. Not even two minutes later, she's walking across the parking lot. When she notices me parked next to her, she smiles, and I swear that smile twists something inside me.

I climb out of the truck, rush to take her bag from her, and lead her to the passenger door.

"What are you doing?"

"I'm taking you to our appointment."

"You know you're not the one being seen, right?" she teases.

"I do, but you and our baby are, so it's ours. Deal with it." I wink, and she grins, shaking her head. I wait until she's in the truck to hand over her bag. "I got you some snacks. They're in there." I point to the bag lying on the console. "Buckle up."

"Yes, sir." She salutes as she chuckles.

After rushing around to the driver's side, I hop back in, and make sure she's buckled her belt before I pull out of the lot. "So, we get to hear the heartbeat, right? This app I downloaded on my phone says he or she should be the size of an apricot." Reaching over, I place my hand on her belly. "So tiny," I murmur, keeping my eyes on the road.

"You downloaded an app?" she asks, popping a peanut butter cracker into her mouth. "Oh, these are good."

"I read that they help with nausea and the protein is good for you and the baby."

"Thank you, Lachlan. This was very sweet of you."

"I'm the daddy. That's my job."

"I can't believe we're going to be parents. It's so surreal."

I pull into the parking lot and turn off the truck before turning to face her. "It's here. Our little one will be here before we know it." I want to reach over and rub her still-flat belly, but I refrain. "Ready for this?" I ask her.

Her smile could light up the darkest of night skies. "I'm ready."

Nodding, I climb out of the truck and help her down, then lead her into the building with my hand on the small of her back. I stay with her as she checks in and then settle into the plush seats as we wait to be called back. My leg bounces because this is a huge moment, and I'm feeling so many things right now.

Maggie reaches over and places her hand on my knee. "You doing okay?" she asks.

"I'm... perfect, but this is big, Mags. Huge, massive, life changing."

Her eyes are soft, as is her smile. "It is."

"I'm nervous because I want to hear his or her heartbeat, and I want you and the baby to both be healthy, and I want to yell so everyone in this damn county hears that I'm going to be a daddy. I never thought about it. I mean, I did think about it, but never how I would feel, you know? And now this. You, me, and the baby, it's... everything." This time I'm the one that reaches over and places my hand on her knee. "Thank you for doing this with me."

"Lachlan." She breathes my name like a gentle caress, but before she can say more, her name is called.

I stand and offer her my hand, which she takes. I help her to her feet. Not that she needs it yet, but it's good practice for when she does, right? Regardless, I follow her back and she steps on the scale, turning to me and makes a silly face.

"Hate this part," she grumbles. "It's just going to get worse as the pregnancy progresses."

Before she can even step off of the scale, I move in close, and cup her face in the palm of my hands. "You're beautiful, Maggie. You're growing our baby. Fuck what the number says." Leaning forward, I place a tender kiss on her forehead before stepping back.

"You better lock this one down." The nurse laughs as she leads us back to a room. She takes some vitals and tells us Dr. Holmes will be right in.

Maggie smiles at me, and I wink at her. What else am I supposed to do? Tell her that the nurse is right? That she should lock me down?

Turns out that "right in," literally means right in. There's a knock on the door, and then the doctor steps into the room. "Maggie, good to see you." She moves to the small sink to wash her hands. "How are you feeling? How's the morning sickness?"

"Not terrible, but it's still lingering."

"Let me know if it gets worse, and we can help by giving you something to deal with it."

"Thank you, but I'm managing okay," Maggie assures her.

"Perfect. Any other concerns. How's your appetite?"

"Okay. No weird cravings or anything yet. I'm eating lots of fruits and vegetables, and I've cut down to one small cup of coffee a day. That's still okay, right?"

"Yes, that's perfectly fine. Do you have any questions or concerns to discuss?"

"Not that I can think of." Maggie's eyes find mine.

I clear my throat. "No. No questions. I've been reading a lot," I confess. I guess because I don't want her to think I'm some deadbeat dad who doesn't care about my child, because I don't have any questions. I'm a mess and need to get a grip. My nerves are getting the best of me.

The doctor smiles at me. "That's good. There isn't a manual once this little one is born, so being as prepared as you can for this process and the delivery is very helpful."

"I'm new to this dad thing." I laugh. "My friends have kids, and they're amazing, but this one is mine, so yeah, I need to learn everything."

"Don't stress too much. Babies are a lot of trial and error and learn as you go. They might be tiny, but they have their own personalities from the day they're born. You all will learn together."

"Thank you." Her words are reassuring.

"You're welcome. Now, why don't we get some measurements? Check on how your baby is growing. Maggie, if you'll lie back."

Maggie does as she asks, and when she pulls up her scrub top, my mouth falls open. There is a very tiny bump that was not there the last time I saw her without clothes.

"You're showing," I blurt without thinking.

"You missed that, did you?" The doctor laughs.

"Oh, we're not together. I mean, we're raising the baby together, but we're not... it was a one-time thing," Maggie says, her face growing hot with embarrassment.

"No judgement here. I'm glad the two of you are making it work, whatever is best for you and your baby." The doctor measures Maggie's belly a few different directions. "You're measuring right where you need to be for twelve weeks." She smiles kindly.

"That's good, right?" Maggie asks.

"That's perfect."

"Now, how about we see if we can hear the baby's heartbeat? Let me run out to get the doppler. I'll be right back."

She leaves the room and I'm on my feet. I rush to Maggie's side and stare down at her belly. "Can I?" I ask, the words gruff on my lips.

I don't need to explain. She nods her agreement, knowing exactly what I'm silently asking for. Slowly, I lift her scrub top, and there it is. Her small baby bump that I haven't been able to see due to her clothes.

"Damn, Mags." Unable to stop myself, I lean over and place a kiss on her slight bump. "Daddy loves you," I tell the bump, and I hear a choked sob. Lifting my head, I see Maggie with tears rolling down her cheeks. "I'm sorry. I didn't mean to upset you."

"Hormones." She smiles through her laughter.

"Don't. Tell me what I did, Maggie."

"Nothing, Lachlan. You just melted my heart. You're really here and in this. I mean, you've been incredible since the moment I told you about the baby, but... I guess I'm just happy that our baby gets a daddy who's going to love him or her unconditionally. I wasn't sure how you would take all this and you've been nothing short of amazing." She wipes at her cheeks. "I guess what I'm trying to say is that if this was the plan for me, I'm glad it's you."

I'd give anything to kiss her right now. To tell her with more than my words that I'm always going to be here for both of them. I want to tell her I can't stop thinking about her, and that the greatest night of sex of my life led to this tiny miracle. However, I just smile. "Me too, Maggie. Me too." I squeeze her hand just as the doctor steps back into the room.

"Sorry, we had one break, so we're passing this one around. All right, let's do this."

A loud, whooshing sound fills the room. "Holy shit, is that the baby?" Even I can hear the awe in my voice.

"It sure is. Very strong and healthy."

Reaching into my pocket, I pull out my phone, open the voice app, and hit Record, hoping to capture the sound. I want to bottle it and listen to it forever, at least until our little one is here with us.

"You know, you can buy these now. They're under a hundred dollars or so for a good one."

"What? Can you send me a link?" I ask the doctor.

That has her chuckling. "I think we have some literature and a coupon. I'll grab it for you before you leave."

"Yes, please."

"Thank you, Dr. Holmes," Maggie speaks up.

"You're welcome. Everything looks great. We'll see you back in four weeks, unless you need us before then. If you ever have any questions or concerns, don't hesitate to call us, or if you're truly worried, go to the emergency room. Keep taking your prenatal vitamins and growing a healthy baby."

"Thank you," Maggie and I say at the same time.

"I'll send someone in with that literature on the doppler." She disappears, and I beam at Maggie.

"I'm buying it today. We'll be able to listen anytime we want."

"You don't have to do that."

"I want to do that. You better get used to me dropping by just to hear the baby's heartbeat," I tell her. She laughs, but I'm being serious. This is the most amazing feeling. "When do we get to see the baby?"

"Usually at twenty weeks. That's halfway, and we'll be able to tell the gender."

"That's too long," I pout, and it makes her smile grow.

"You'll survive, Daddy."

"How about you, Mommy? How you feeling?"

"Relieved. Happy." Her eyes find mine. "I'm really happy."

"Me too, Mags. Me too." I wrap my arm around her and hug her where she's still sitting on the end of the exam table. The nurse brings in the literature on the doppler, and I thank her. "Man, Forrest needs one of these. I wonder why Legend or Roman never bought one of these things?"

"They probably didn't know that you could."

"I need to call Forrest." I pull my phone out and then remember he doesn't know. "When can we tell them?" I don't want to pressure her, but damn, this secret has been hard to hold on to.

"We made it past twelve weeks. We're twelve weeks and four days, so I'm okay with telling everyone, but we're going to have to tell them how this all happened in the first place."

"I think they have the birds and the bees covered." I chuckle.

"You know what I mean. They're going to know when and have lots of questions."

"We'll tell them when, and that the rest is ours to keep. All they need to know is that we're raising this little one together. You tell them as much or as little as you want. That's what I'm telling the guys, and they'll respect it."

"I guess we can tell them whenever we're all together again."

"Tonight?" I ask hopefully. "It's Friday night, and I can assemble the masses. Not at my place. It's too damn small," I grumble. "I'm working on fixing that, but I can make it happen. If you feel up to it."

"Sure, if you can make it happen, we'll tell them tonight. It's been hard keeping this from them."

"So hard," I agree.

I lead her out of the exam room, where we stop to make her next appointment. I check it's in my calendar, and shoot off a text to Drake, who is still at the shop, letting him know to clear my day that day.

Once we're in the truck, I call Roman.

"What's up?" he answers.

"How would you feel about getting everyone together tonight? My place isn't big enough."

"I say let's do it. I'll call Em. I'm leaving the shop now. We'll just order some pizza and wings or something. You need me to spread the word?"

"Yeah, if you can. Say seven?"

"That works for us. I'll handle it."

"Thanks, Rome."

"Anytime, brother."

I end the call and look over at Maggie. "Tonight at seven at Roman and Emerson's. We're doing pizza and wings. Is that okay for you and the baby?"

"That actually sounds really good."

"Perfect. I'll take you to your car. Then I'll be back at your place at six thirty to pick you up."

"I can drive."

"And I can pick you up. United front and all that."

She opens her mouth to argue but quickly shuts it with a nod. "Okay."

I glance in the rearview mirror, and my smile is blinding. I'm worried it might be permanent. This baby wasn't planned, but it's already so loved.

MAGGIE

L ACHLAN PUSHES OPEN THE FRONT door of Roman and Emerson's house. "Uncle Lachlan's here!" he calls out.

A loud squeal and then little feet come racing toward us. Lilly launches herself at Lachlan, and he catches her easily. "I missed you," he tells the little girl, hugging her tightly.

"Missed you," Lilly replies back. She eyes me behind Lachlan and reaches for me.

"Hey, sweetie." I settle her on my hip and kiss her cheek.

"Hey, you." Emerson comes into the living room, and gives me a one-armed hug, before pulling Lachlan into a hug as well. "Did you get here at the same time?" she asks.

My friend is very intuitive, and she knows something has been up with me lately, but she's given me the space I've needed. They all have, while letting me know they were here for anything and everything that I might need.

"We rode together," Lachlan explains.

"Really?" Emerson wags her eyebrows, and I chuckle because she has no idea. "Come on in. Forrest, Briar, and the girls are heading over soon. Monroe and Legend had to give Kane a bath.

He had a diaper blowout, and Maddox and Brogan are probably working in a quickie before they get here." She giggles. "Maddox is determined where this baby-making business is concerned. He's trying to get pregnant before anyone else does. He's trying to beat us, and Monroe and Legend."

"You're all trying?" I ask before I can stop myself. "I knew Maddox and Brogan were trying."

Emerson smiles. "Yeah, Lilly is over two, so it's time, and Kane is almost one. I don't actually think they're trying as much as practicing." Emerson laughs. "However, Maddox is still on a mission to have the next baby in the family."

Lachlan's eyes widen. I can tell he's trying really damn hard not to let his smile show. "Are you coming inside?" Emerson asks, backing up. "Rome's in the kitchen, calling in the pizza and wings."

We follow her into the kitchen and as soon as Lilly sees her daddy, she's reaching for him. Roman takes her out of my arms while continuing with his call to order dinner. Lilly lays her head on his shoulder and tucks into his chest.

"She didn't nap today," Emerson tells us. "She's getting at the age where she's trying to fight naptime."

"No nap," Lilly says, and we laugh.

Roman ends the call, tosses his phone on the counter, and rubs Lilly's back. "Lil, naps are good for you. You know Daddy likes to take naps."

"Wif Mommy. Mommy take a nap wif me?"

Roman's eyes heat as he winks at Emerson. "With Mommy," he agrees.

I can only imagine the naptime schemes you have to do when you have a toddler in the house. Not that I'll have to worry about sneaking around to hook up being a single mom and all that. I'll be too busy working and raising a baby. Sure, Lachlan is going to be there too, but we won't be sneaking around trying to find times to be intimate.

I'll have the memories of our night together to keep me warm, I suppose.

The door opens again, and this time it's Forrest, Briar, and the twins. I can tell by the patter of pounding feet and the "don't run in the house" hollered out by their parents.

"I didn't think we'd ever get here." Rayne sighs dramatically.

"Daddy's a slowpoke." River giggles.

"Take it easy on your old man," Forrest says, walking into the room with his hand laced with Briar's. "It's not my fault, I had to wash off my makeup." He smiles down at them and you can see it as clearly as a bright blue sky that these three ladies are his world. The new baby, too, obviously, when he or she gets here.

"Daddy, you looked pretty," Rayne tells him.

"I know, Dazzle, but Daddy told you he can't wear makeup outside. That's just for in the house when we're playing dress up."

"Oh, I don't know," Rome chimes in. "I'd like to see it."

"Uncle Rome! We can do your makeup too!"River exclaims.

"Yeah, Uncle Rome," Forrest jabs.

"Who's doing whose makeup?" Monroe asks.

"Me and sissy are doing Uncle Rome's," Rayne tells her.

"Maybe later, double squirts," Roman says, and the girls fall into a fit of giggles at the bizarre nickname. I get it, we all do, but to the girls, it's absolutely hilarious.

"Hand her over," Maddox says, walking into the room and straight for Lilly. She cackles as he takes her into his arms. "When will he wake up?" Maddox nods to where Kane is sleeping against Legend's chest.

"After the sh—dump he took, he's probably content for a while," Legend says, fondly staring down at his sleeping son.

"He's had some issues today, so we're letting him sleep. He only napped for about twenty minutes earlier," Monroe explains.

"Sounds like Lilly."

"We're big girls. We don't nap, right, sissy?" River asks Rayne.

"Nope. No naps for us big kids," Rayne agrees.

"Can we go play, Mommy?" River asks.

Briar looks up at Emerson. "Of course," she replies. "Lilly, do you want to go play?"

She nods and wiggles for Maddox to let her down, and the three of them take off to the corner of the living room, where Lilly has a little play area.

"Okay, did I miss someone's birthday?" Maddox asks. "I know I've been a little preoccupied, so if I did, I'm sorry." He furrows his brow like he's trying really hard to figure out why we're all here.

"Can't we all just get together randomly without a reason?" Roman asks him. His eyes flash to where Lachlan and I are standing.

"There is a reason," Lachlan speaks up. "And it's not a birthday."

"And that reason is?" Legend prompts him.

Lachlan reaches down and laces his fingers through mine. I squeeze his hand, knowing our friends are going to get the wrong idea, but I need his touch to keep me grounded for this.

"Maggie and I are having a baby." He says the words casually, as if he's talking about the weather, then lifts our joined hands to his lips, and kisses my knuckles.

"Rewind," Maddox says. He looks at Brogan. "Did he just say...?" His voice trails off as if he can't believe the news.

"How?" Monroe asks. "I know how, but *how*?" She chuckles.

"When?" Briar asks.

"Where?" Brogan chimes in.

"Are the two of you together?" Emerson adds.

I take in a breath and slowly exhale, preparing to tell them all the things, but Lachlan beats me to it.

"Mo, I think you know how babies are made. Briar, we had a night together at the cabin in Gatlinburg, and in case your question has a double meaning, we're due at the middle of March. Em, we're not together, not as a couple, but we are going to raise this baby together." He answers all of their questions quickly and efficiently.

The room is eerily silent for a few seconds, and then everyone starts talking at once. We're pulled into hugs and slaps on the back, kisses on the cheek, and congratulations all around.

"You did this to beat me," Maddox teases.

"I didn't." I hear Lachlan tell him. "But I gotta tell ya, man, I wouldn't change it even if I could." My heart melts, and the girls must notice because they all offer me watery smiles.

"Why's everyone being so loud?" Rayne asks.

Lachlan lifts her into his arms. "Well, you're getting a new baby cousin."

"Another one?" she gasps.

"Yep."

"Yay!" she cheers, wiggles to be let down, and races off to the living room. She announces very loudly to her sister and Lilly about their new baby cousin.

Lachlan moves to stand next to me and bends his lips to my ear. "You doing okay, Momma? Need anything?"

I turn to look at him over my shoulder. "I'm good. Thank you."

"We'll leave when you're ready."

"We just got here." I furrow my brow. Surely, he doesn't want to just drop the news and leave.

"I know. I also know you worked today, and we had a pretty emotional appointment, so when you're ready, say the word." With that, he walks back to the other side of the island.

"Forrest, come here, man. You've got to see this." His words have all heads turning toward him. "Look, you can actually buy the doppler to listen to the heartbeat anytime you want."

"What? No way. Why did I not know this?" Forrest turns his eyes to his wife. "Did you know about this?"

Briar chuckles. "No, but that's cool. I'm sure they're crazy expensive."

"No. Look, I bought this one, great reviews, and all that. It was only one hundred and thirty dollars."

"Only." Monroe giggles.

"Hey, this is daily listening to my kid. You can't put a price on that."

"What he said. Send me the link. I'm in."

"Forrest." Briar shakes her head. "I'm already halfway through my pregnancy."

He shrugs. "We can use it for the next one, or pass it on once our little one is here."

"Next one?" Brogan asks her sister.

Briar places her hand on her baby bump. "We haven't discussed anything past this one, but my husband seems to think that he needs to keep me knocked up."

"Brogan, baby, you think we should get one just to have it when we're ready?" Maddox asks his wife.

"Kind of what I was thinking," Legend chimes in.

"I'm going to need one too," Roman agrees.

"Guys, we're not even pregnant." Emerson shakes her head, amusement all over her face.

"Just being prepared, baby girl," Roman tells his wife, before going to his phone. All of them are tapping at their screens, all of them except for Lachlan. He's standing tall, proud as a peacock that he brought this world-changing news to his best friends.

"They really are something," Brogan muses.

"We got lucky," Briar comments.

"So damn lucky," Monroe agrees.

"We'd definitely be lost without them," Emerson adds.

"Lachlan has been great so far. I'm glad it's him. I mean, if this had to happen, I'm glad it's with a man who cares and wants to be a part of his child's life."

"How are you feeling?" Monroe asks.

"Good. A little morning sickness, nothing out of hand."

"Fourth of July." Emerson nods.

"Yeah, I didn't know then, but the nausea became a regular thing, and then the boob pain, and the missed period. It all just kind of clicked for me and I took five tests at home," I admit.

"So the two of you aren't together?" Emerson asks.

I expected this question. "No. Not romantically. I told him I didn't need his help, and that I didn't expect anything from him, but he said he wanted this. He wants to be in our child's life."

"Of course he would. This is Lachlan we're talking about. Has he told you about his parents?" Monroe asks.

"He did."

"Wait, what's wrong with his parents?" Brogan asks.

"It's not my story to tell," I tell her.

Emerson waves her hand in the air. "He doesn't care if people know. His biological dad bailed when his mom told him she was pregnant. She met his now dad who adopted Lachlan when he was two."

"The dad he didn't have to be," Briar says, tears in her eyes. "I understand that." Her eyes flash to the kitchen toward where the guys are standing, but we all know she only has eyes for Forrest.

"Yeah," I agree.

"He's going to be a great dad," Monroe tells me. "Maddox too." She winks at Brogan.

"What if I can't get pregnant?" Brogan asks, her voice soft and with a hint of despair. "We've been trying for a couple of months now, and nothing."

"These things take time," Briar tells her sister. "And emotions play a key role. Just enjoy trying, and it will happen when it's supposed to."

"He wants this so much," Brogan says, her voice cracking.

"What about you?" Emerson asks. "Is this what you want?"

Brogan nods. "More than anything."

"I know it's hard, but stay positive. It will happen," Monroe assures her.

"I'm sorry." I reach over and place my hand on her arm. "You've been trying, and here I am, tossing this pregnancy in your face. I didn't mean to do that."

"No. No, Maggie, not at all," Brogan is quick to reassure me. "I'm so happy for you. I know this is probably not how you planned it, but life tends to do that, tossing us curveballs when we least expect them."

"Like me." Emerson smiles.

"And me." Monroe waves her hand in the air.

"And me," Briar adds.

"All four of you have pregnancies that were not how I'm sure you planned them, and that's your story. I know I'll have mine. I guess, for me, I'm just worried that it's not going to happen because my life is… more than I ever could have imagined it would be. I never thought I'd find a man to love me, scars and all, and now that I have, I want everything with him."

"It's going to happen for you," Briar tells her sister. "I can feel it."

Brogan smiles. "In the meantime, I get to be Aunt Brogan and get lots of practice."

"Oh, are you ready to go home and practice?" Maddox asks, stepping up behind us. We all laugh because we didn't even see him there, and he's all for devoting time to practice.

"No, we're spending time with our family," Brogan tells her husband.

"But going home to practice is making a family," Maddox counters sweetly, kissing her cheek.

I can see the indecision on Brogan's face. Not that I blame her. If I had a sexy husband wanting to practice with me, it would definitely be hard to say no.

The doorbell chimes, and the kids start to cheer, chanting, "Pizza." I guess they're hungry. Roman gets the door, and we all trail behind him into the kitchen. The kids' plates get made first and then the rest of us dive in to do the same.

"How are you feeling? Need a ginger ale?" Lachlan asks.

"I'm good, thank you. Besides, I don't think Roman and Emerson keep that on hand."

"I brought some in a cooler in the back seat of my truck, in case you needed it."

I turn to look at him, and he shrugs. "I wasn't sure if baby Noble was going to play nice with Momma tonight, so I wanted to be prepared."

Not caring that our friends are here to witness this, I turn to him, wrapping my arms around him in a hug. His come around me, instantly holding me tightly. "Thank you, Lachlan. You take such good care of m—us." I almost said *me*, but I know it's the baby he's worried about.

"I'll always be here to help take care of both of you, Maggie. Today and twenty years from now. You and this baby, you're my family."

His words have tears springing to my eyes. I'd love to say it's the hormones, and that might be part of it, but the other part is this incredible man. He always knows exactly what to say, and I know he means every word. Lachlan is a "what you see is what you get" kind of guy, and what I'm getting is a man who was told his one-night stand and friend is pregnant with his baby, who steps up in a major way.

Pulling back, I smile up at him. "I'm glad it's you, Lachlan."

His blue eyes blaze with something I can't name. "Me too, Mags, me too. Come on. Let's get you something to eat." He releases me, picks up my discarded plate, adds a couple of slices of pizza and a few boneless wings, and carries it to the living room. I follow along behind him, like a puppy, and take a seat. I'm shocked when he bends and presses a kiss to the crown of my head once I'm seated, before heading back to the kitchen to make his own plate.

I don't dare glance around the table to see the curious looks of our friends, because I'm just as curious. Instead, I pick up a slice of pizza and start to eat. When Lachlan joins us a few minutes later, he places a bottle of water and a small bottle of ginger ale in front of me, before going to join the guys to eat in the living room.

"Maggie?" Monroe says.

I look up to find my friends watching me closely while the twins and Lilly munch away on their dinner. "I don't know," I answer her silent question.

"We're here," Emerson says.

"Thank you." I smile at them, and thankfully, the twins start asking us about our favorite pizza and ice cream, and the heat is no longer on me. However, I still feel the warmth of his arms wrapped around me.

—

LACHLAN 6

"I PROMISE YOU HAVE NOTHING to worry about," I tell Maggie. We're on our way to my parents' house to tell them about the baby.

"Are you not the least bit embarrassed to show up with me in tow and tell them, oh, by the way, we had a one-night stand, and now we're having a baby?"

She's telling me more than she thinks from that line of questioning. Reaching over, I lace my fingers with hers. "No. I'm not the least bit embarrassed to be having a baby with you. I'm not worried about my parents thinking less of me or you. You have nothing to worry about. What about you? Are you nervous about telling your grandma tomorrow?"

"No. She's always telling me her biggest worry is her leaving me in this world alone. She'll be happy to know I'll have family once she's gone." Her voice cracks. "I can't even think about her not being here anymore. I know that's a part of life, but I'm not ready for that. I don't think I'll ever be ready for that."

"Yeah," I agree. I don't know what else to say. She's right, death is a part of life, but that doesn't make it suck any less. "You have me and our baby forever, Maggie. You will never be alone. That's a promise I can make to you, your grandmother, and our baby. I'll always be right here."

"You're going to meet someone someday, and how you're feeling right now could change."

"Never. You are the mother of my child, Maggie. We shared an incredible night together, and now we're going to have a permanent reminder of that night. Whoever may or may not come into my life will have to understand that. There is no in between. I will always be there for both of you."

What I want to tell her is that we could be a family. I want to tell her that I couldn't stop thinking about her before I found out about the baby, but I know Maggie well enough to understand she'll assume my sudden interest in us being together is solely for the baby. That's not true, but only time and my actions will prove that to her. She's still dealing with some insecurities from her cocksucker of an ex-boyfriend.

All I need is time.

The remainder of the short drive is silent, and when I pull into my parents' driveway, I feel the atmosphere shift inside the truck. "Maggie, please don't worry. They're going to embrace you and this baby with open arms. I told you about my dad, right? About how he adopted me? Family is what you make it, Mags, and you and that baby are mine. They're going to love you."

She exhales and squares her shoulders. "Okay. Let's do it." She nods and reaches for her seat belt, and that's my cue to hop out of the truck to rush around and help her. "I can get in and out of this monstrosity on my own for now." She laughs.

"I know, but I want to help you. Pregnant or not, I'd be helping you. That's just how I was raised."

She eyes me suspiciously but doesn't say anything. Once she's out of the truck, I offer her my hand. She doesn't hesitate to take it, allowing me to twine our fingers together. I lead her up the porch and to the front door. I knock a few times, then push it open.

"Honey, I'm home!" I call out, and I hear my dad's deep chuckle coming from the kitchen.

"In here!" he calls back.

With Maggie's hand still locked with mine, I lead her down the hallway and into the kitchen. "Smells great," I tell my parents, who are standing side by side at the kitchen island.

"Stop." Mom laughs as she swats Dad's hands away from the garlic bread she just took out of the oven.

"See what I have to deal with?" Dad acts as though he's offended. "Maggie, it's good to see you."

"Yes, please ignore Rodney. I promise you he has better manners than that and he's not putting his fingers all over the food." Mom chuckles. "It's nice to see you," she tells Maggie. "I hope you two are hungry. I made lasagna, salad, and garlic bread. I even made Lachlan's favorite oatmeal and raisin cookies for dessert."

"You had me at cookie," I tell Mom, making them all laugh.

"How you stay so fit with all the sweets that you eat, I'll never know," Maggie says.

"He's always been that way," Dad tells us. "I eat one, and the doctor threatens to put me on cholesterol medicine."

"It smells delicious. Thank you for having me," Maggie says politely.

"Of course. Lachlan, grab us some drinks, and your dad and I will bring this to the table."

"What can I do to help?" Maggie asks.

"You're our guest. Supervise that one." Mom points at me. "He can be a handful," she jokes. Her eyes flash to our joined hands, but quickly avert back to our faces. Her smile says more than her words ever could.

"Don't I know it." Maggie chortles.

"Watch it," I say, tickling her side, which makes her squeal and take a few steps away from me. I wink at her, and she smiles. It's a genuine smile, not just one she uses to try and reassure me. My shoulders relax as relief washes over me. Everything is going to be okay.

❋

"That was delicious. Thank you. It's the most I've eaten in weeks."

"You're welcome. There are plenty of leftovers. I'll send you home with some. We've been eating a more heart-healthy diet recently, so this is a treat for us too."

"Yes, kids, thank you for coming so I can eat yummy food for once."

"Kids? I'm thirty-three, old man," I quip.

"And you'll always be a kid to me," Dad fires back.

"Yeah, you'll understand one day when you have one or a few of your own. They'll always be kids in your eyes, even when they are adults."

Reaching under the table, I reach for Maggie's hand and give it a gentle squeeze. "About that," I say, sitting back in my seat. "Maggie and I are having a baby."

My parents freeze, and then suddenly, they're both out of their chairs and rounding the table toward us. I stand and open my arms for my mom, but she ducks underneath and goes to Maggie, who is also barely standing before she's ambushed.

"Really? I'm going to be a grandma?" Mom asks, her voice cracking. "Lachlan Noble, this better not be a joke," she says, releasing Maggie and swatting my shoulder.

"Son?" Dad asks.

I step back and place my arm around Maggie's waist. "It's not a joke. We're thirteen and a half weeks. Maggie and I aren't together, but we are going to raise this baby together." I smile down at her, to find her already looking up at me. "Co-parents," I say, and she nods.

"Tell me more. Over thirteen weeks, have you heard the heartbeat?" Mom asks.

"We have. I even bought us a doppler to keep at Maggie's place so we can listen anytime we want."

"I, um, I brought it," Maggie says, her face flushing. "I wasn't sure if you'd want to hear."

"Yes. Yes. Yes!" Mom exclaims.

"Congratulations, son, Maggie. Being a parent is one of life's greatest joys. It's also one of the hardest jobs you will ever do."

"Thank you," I tell him, my emotions getting the better of me.

"I'll run out to the car to get the doppler," Maggie says.

"I'll go. Where is it?"

"In my purse. I left it on the floorboard."

"I'm on it." I squeeze her hip, a silent thank-you, before rushing out to my truck to grab the doppler. I'm excited about my parents getting to hear our baby's heartbeat, but if I'm being honest, I'm stoked I get to hear it again as well. I heard it Wednesday night, but that was a few days ago.

When I got home from work on Wednesday, the box was on my front porch, and I went straight to Maggie's so we could try it out. We sat on her couch for almost an hour, listening to our son or daughter.

"Mags!" I call out as I enter the house. "Get comfy on the couch," I tell her, walking into the living room.

She smiles and moves to sit on the couch. I lift up her shirt just a little, and put the doppler on her belly, mindful that my dad is also in the room. Not that it's nothing he wouldn't see if she were in a bathing suit. Even so, I want to keep her as covered as I can.

I kneel before her on the floor, turn on the machine, and move the wand around a little and there it is. The fast whooshing sound of our baby's heartbeat.

"Oh my goodness," Mom says, and I can hear the tears in the sound of her voice.

"That's really something," Dad says, who I can tell is trying not to let his emotions get the best of him.

"We made that," I whisper to Maggie.

"Bragging rights," she teases before Mom starts talking her head off about the nursery theme, if she's registered anywhere, and if she can help with the baby shower.

Dad and I are content to sit and listen to the women talk, and by the time we leave, Maggie and I both have to-go containers full of leftovers, and Maggie has set up a date to go window shopping with my mom to start looking at baby items.

With a round of hugs and the promise to do dinner again soon, we're headed back to her place.

"You were right," Maggie tells me.

"Say what?" I pick up my phone from the cupholder and hand it to her. "Can you bring up the voice recording app and say that again?"

"Stop." She laughs, swatting my hand away. "I mean it. Your parents are incredible, and your mom, she's offered to help so much."

"I hope you let her. This is her first and maybe only grandchild. I'd hate for her not to be able to be involved."

"When I found out I was pregnant, I just kept thinking that this baby won't have grandparents. Before you say anything, this was before I told you, and I was worried that you wouldn't want anything to do with this baby."

Her words affect me more than they should. I know she was scared, and that asshole ex of hers made her think all men are douche canoes, but I'd hoped she knew me better than that.

"Finding out made me miss my parents so much, but my mom, she was supposed to be here to take me shopping and to help me register, and to know that I have your mom who wants to do those things with me, that means more to me than you will ever know, Lachlan."

I pull into her driveway and leave the truck running but make no move to get out. "This baby makes us family. That means my parents included. They both gave you their numbers tonight for a reason. Not just so you can go shopping with Mom, but in case you need anything. Anything at all, don't hesitate to reach out to them or me. We're in this, Maggie. All the way in."

She nods. "I know you are. You've never wavered, and I'm sorry that I ever thought you would turn me away. I had a pregnancy scare with Eric. I was a week late and freaking out, and when I told him, he told me to handle it. I guess I just had flashbacks of that moment. Thankfully, my period came the next day, but I knew then that he and I would never work out. That very next weekend is when I walked into his apartment and found him naked on the couch with someone else."

If I ever see the guy, it's going to take a hell of a lot of effort not to kick his ass for treating her that way. I keep my face neutral, letting my anger for her simmer on the inside, because I don't want her to stop opening up to me.

"I'm sorry. You're not him, and I know that. I knew it then, but I let my past and fears take hold. Thank you for being an incredible man. Thank you for sharing your family with me. I meant what I said. If this was going to happen, I'm really glad it happened with you."

I've never wanted to kiss someone more in my life than I do at this moment. I want to, but I know that I can't. Instead, I lean over the console and press my lips to her cheek. "Me too, Mags. Me too."

"Anyway. I guess I should let you go."

"I've got nowhere to be." What I don't say is that there is nowhere I'd rather be than with her.

"Oh, well, I was going to run into town and grab some ice cream. You're welcome to come with me if you want."

"Why didn't you tell me you wanted ice cream? I could have taken you straight there."

"I didn't want to burden you with my ice cream craving."

I smack lightly at my chest. "I'm the daddy. You're doing all the hard work, so it's my job to satisfy the cravings."

"Fine, I'm really craving some butter pecan ice cream. The homemade kind that they sell at Pastry Heaven."

"Mags, you know they're closed, right?"

"I do, but did you know that Dough Daddies sells cartons?"

"What?" My mouth drops open. "How did I not know this? How, woman? You've been holding out on me."

"Do you not look at the menu?"

"No. I mean, not anymore. We've been there so much, I have it memorized. Besides, it's pizza. I always order my favorite. Who needs a menu for pizza?"

She's laughing so hard her body is shaking and those perfect tits of hers bounce, which is very fucking distracting. "Maybe you should start."

"Starting right now." I put the truck in Reverse and pull out of her driveway. "What kind of flavors are we talking about here?"

"Does it matter?"

"No, but I'm planning on what I need to order when we get there."

"I think it changes. They always have chocolate and vanilla. I hope they have butter pecan, but honestly, the homemade ice cream is so good, I'd settle for any of them."

"I wonder if the guys know this?"

"I'm pretty sure Forrest does. I saw a carton in their freezer when I got ice last weekend."

"And they didn't tell me either? This is a travesty, I tell you."

"You're too much." She giggles.

"I take my sweet consumption seriously, and do you know that I, too, have had a hankering for Pastry Heaven ice cream later in the day or night, and they close at like two in the afternoon, and I couldn't get it? I had to settle for the store-bought stuff. *Store-bought*, Maggie."

"The horror!" she gasps.

"Right?" I say. While I'm being serious, and I'm pissed that I didn't know this about my hometown, I'm also enjoying seeing her smile. Seeing her happy makes me happy, and that's just another reason I know we can be more. The more time I spend with her, the more of her time I want.

It's not just the baby, although it would be awkward if I wanted her and there was some other woman having my kid. Eww, no. Just no. The thought of anyone else carrying my baby, being a mother to my child, doesn't sit right with me.

It has to be Maggie.

It *is* Maggie.

Now, I just take my time and show her with actions that we are meant to be a family. I know we are. I can feel it in my bones and in my heart every time I have to go home without her.

At first, I thought it was just a good night of great sex; it's why I couldn't stop thinking about her, but I was wrong. It's Maggie. She makes everything better.

We make it to Dough Daddies and go straight to the takeout counter and ask for a menu. Sure enough, there is a bright pink piece of paper that lists the flavors of Pastry Heaven ice cream available.

"What kind are you going to get?" Maggie asks me, while I stare down at the list.

"They only have four flavors, and we're getting them all."

"What? We don't need four cartons of ice cream."

"Oh yes, we do. This will be our emergency supply." The server stops, and I order a half-gallon carton of butter pecan, cookies and cream, chocolate, and vanilla to go.

"The butter pecan stays with me," she says, reaching for her purse.

"You are not paying for your ice cream. And I already planned to leave them all with you. That way, if you get a craving for it, you'll have some on hand."

"I can't eat that much on my own. I'd be sick."

"Good thing your baby daddy will be there often to help. It'll be our thing. We can listen to peanut and eat ice cream, then maybe watch a movie or something."

"You don't have better things do to than watch movies and eat ice cream with me?"

"Nothing. There is nothing I can think of that I'd rather be doing than that." Okay, that might be a tiny lie, but I can't tell her that being inside her again sounds like a damn good time.

We're not there yet.

But we will be.

MAGGIE 7

AS WE DRIVE TO MY grandmother's house, warmth surrounds me. Her house was home to me for so many years. Grandma Doris was our saving grace, and then she was just mine.

The only family I have left.

I place my hands on my barely there bump and whisper a silent apology. This baby and Grandma Doris are the only family I have left.

"Maggie?" Lachlan's voice pulls me out of my thoughts. "You doing okay?" He reaches over and laces his fingers with mine.

"My mother died when I was thirteen."

"I'm sorry," he says, and I can hear the sincerity in his voice.

"Cancer of the liver. It was hell to watch her go through that. My dad was lost, and didn't know what to do without her, so we sold the house, and moved in with his mom, Grandma Doris. My mother's parents had already passed."

"That had to be hard."

"Losing her is a pain I still feel every day. So, we moved in with Grandma Doris, and we tried to find our new normal. And we did for a few years. We missed her every single day, but we were adjusting. Then, during my junior year, there was an accident. My dad was driving to work, and a semi didn't stop at the stoplight. He was pronounced dead on the scene."

"Mags." His voice cracks, and I squeeze his hand.

There is nothing that he could say that would make it better. "It was just me and Grandma Doris after that. She was my rock, and I was hers. We made it through losing them and until this baby, she was my only family."

I point to the road on the right, and without needing to say anything, he slows down to make the turn.

"Second house on the right," I tell him.

He pulls into the driveway and leaves the engine running. "Maggie, my heart breaks for you and everything you've been through."

"I need to get this out before we go in. When I met Eric in college, he said all the right things. He was charming and said he wanted to be my family. I fell hard and fast, and then he changed. He thrived on control and manipulation, and I was so lost in wanting a family that I let him." Taking off my seat belt, I turn to face Lachlan. "He made me feel a lot of things. He made me think a lot of things that I know now were just his need to control and manipulate, but I fell for it. All of it."

"Prick," he mutters.

I laugh, feeling instantly calmer. Telling him that story takes a heavy weight off my shoulders. "So, today, when you meet my grandma, don't worry if she's not as welcoming as your family was with me. We've been through a battle, and we made it out the other side, but she's a protective mama bear. I just needed you to know that."

"I can handle it. I'm ready to meet our baby's great-grandmother." He smiles. There's something in his eyes that I can't name, but I believe him. I hope like hell my gut is right this time. I've known Lachlan for a while, all of them, and I truly believe he's a good man. I thought that about Eric too. However, looking back, there were signs. Warnings that I didn't heed. This time, my eyes are wide open, and I already know without a shadow of a doubt that Lachlan isn't Eric.

"Ready?" he asks.

I nod. "Let's do this."

"Wait for me." He quickly climbs out of the truck and comes to my door to pull it open for me. "Practice, remember?" He winks, and even though I roll my eyes, I'm smiling. I just can't seem to help myself where Lachlan is concerned.

He helps me out of the truck and places his hand on the small of my back, allowing me to lead us to the front door. I don't bother knocking. Grandma knows I'm on my way, and I hate making her get up to get to the door. She doesn't move as fast as she used to. I've tried talking to her about assisted living, but she's stubborn.

"Grandma!" I call out. "Where are you?"

"In the living room, dear," she calls back.

"You ready?" I whisper to Lachlan.

"So ready." He grins and rubs his hands together as if he's truly excited about meeting my grandmother. What do I know? Maybe he really is. We're about to find out.

"There she is." Grandma smiles. "Oh, you brought a friend. A handsome friend," she coos.

"Grandma, this is Lachlan Noble. He works at Everlasting Ink with Emerson, Monroe, Briar, and Brogan's husbands."

"It's nice to meet you, ma'am," Lachlan says. He steps closer to offer her his hand.

"Oh, phooey, come over here." Grandma opens her arms, and Lachlan's muttered, "Yes, ma'am," has me smiling as he bends to hug her where she sits in her chair.

She never hugged Eric. Grandma is an excellent judge of character, and I can tell she likes Lachlan already. That's good. Maybe she'll take it easy on him, hell, on both of us once she finds out our news.

I take a seat on the couch, and once Grandma releases Lachlan from her hug, he takes the spot next to me.

"Tell me about this." Grandma waves her hands in the air.

"About what?" I play dumb, and she gives me a knowing look.

"I didn't know you had a man in your life." She tosses it out there. One thing about my grandmother is you never have to guess what she's thinking or where she stands on any topic.

"We're friends," I tell her. "Lachlan owns the tattoo studio with the girls' husbands," I remind her.

"Yes, so you've said. But this"—she waves her hands between us once again—"is more than that."

I nod. "You're right. Lachlan and I are friends, but um... we're also going to be parents together."

The look on her face never changes, but I can tell by the look in her eyes, she's processing my words. "You're pregnant?" she finally asks.

"I am. Just out of my first trimester."

"And Lachlan is the father. Your *friend*?" she says, emphasizing the word.

"Yes."

"Explain," Grandma says. Her voice is soft, and I know she's trying to understand, and I know I'm not doing the best job of explaining this to her.

"Maggie and I spent a night together," Lachlan says, speaking up. "It was one night, one neither one of us will ever forget. We remained friends, and when she found out she was pregnant, we decided to raise this baby together. We've not been romantically involved since that night, but we are both dedicated to being the best damn parents we can be to our son or daughter."

Tears prick my eyes because every damn day this man shows up for me. He knew without me telling him that I was struggling with this, and the way he described our situation was perfect.

"I see. So, when is the baby due?" Grandma asks.

"The middle of March," Lachlan says proudly. "Miss Doris, we actually have a surprise for you."

I turn to look at him, not sure what he's talking about. "You do?"

"The doppler," he reminds me.

"Oh." I brighten. How could I have forgotten about that? "We do." I turn back to my grandma and smile widely.

"Let me run out to the truck. I'll be right back." Lachlan stands and smiles at me before walking out of the room. It's not until the front door opens and closes that my grandmother speaks.

"You care about him."

"Of course I do. He's my friend and the father of my baby."

"Outside of that. You care about him."

"He's... one of the greatest men I've ever met. He spoils me and wants to take care of me and this baby. It's hard not to care for a man who puts you on a pedestal after accidentally getting you pregnant."

"He cares about you too. I can see it in his eyes."

"Yeah," I agree, because I know he does—not the way she's thinking, but he does.

"Are you ready for this?" Lachlan asks, stepping back into the room. He holds up the doppler, and his smile, it's radiant.

"What is this?" Grandma asks him.

"This little gadget will let us hear the baby's heartbeat."

"Really?" Grandma leans forward, her eyes brightening.

"Yes. We went to the doctor for our twelve-week checkup, and they used one, and when the doctor told me we could buy one to use at home, I ordered it that day."

Lachlan kneels before me, his eyes locked on mine. I nod, and he lifts my shirt and gets to work, placing the doppler on my bump. It takes a few seconds to move the wand around, but then, there it is. The sound of our baby's heartbeat.

"Grandma Doris, that's the heartbeat of your great-grandchild," Lachlan says proudly.

"Oh my word." Grandma places her hand over her mouth, and tears shimmer in her eyes. "Such a blessing," she says, and Lachlan grins up at me.

Something moves in my chest, and there is this overwhelming feeling of rightness that washes over me. This isn't the way I imagined becoming a mom, but I'm starting to believe this is how it was meant to be.

❧

I'm on the couch sipping some water. I'm out of ginger ale, and this morning, the nausea is intense. This is the second day in a row, and I'm not a fan. I rub my baby bump. "Take it easy on Mommy, huh?" I whisper just as there's a knock at the door.

A quick glance at the clock confirms it's just after six in the morning. Who could be knocking on my door at this hour? I remain in my seat, because what if it's someone breaking in? Rationally, I know a burglar wouldn't be knocking on the door; well, maybe a stupid one. I'm just tired and letting my mind run wild. I mean, no one I know would be on my doorstep at this time. What if it's a serial killer asking to use the phone or something? I'm a mom now, or will be. I have to think about these things. My phone chimes, making me jump. I move quickly to grab it from the side table and my stomach rolls. Morning sickness is a bitch.

> **Lachlan:** I'm at your door.

What? My heart starts to race. Why is he here so early? I look like hell, but I can't do anything about that now. Slowly, I stand and make my way to the door, willing my stomach to behave. Twisting the lock, I open the door, and a rumpled Lachlan greets me.

"I came bearing gifts."

"Gifts? Lachlan, what are you doing here?"

"Last night when we talked, you said yesterday morning was rough for you, so I brought reinforcements." He steps into the house, and I close the door behind him, slowly trailing behind him to the kitchen. "I brought a plain bagel and got plain and cinnamon cream cheese on the side, or I thought you might want to do peanut butter for the protein, but I got them just in case. I have two cans of ginger ale. I wasn't sure if you were out. I grabbed another box of saltines, so you can take them to work with you today, too, if you need them, and some peppermint and ginger candy. I read online that it helps with nausea."

I plop down onto a kitchen chair. "You did all of that before 6:30 a.m.?" I ask.

"No. I went out last night to get everything but the bagel."

"We talked after nine. Everything in town is closed."

"I know. I drove to the all-hours convenience store in Nashville after we hung up."

"You drove an hour away last night to get this stuff?"

He shrugs. "You needed it. This morning, I went to Pastry Heaven, so the bagel is fresh. I also have a loaf of wheat bread. I know that's your favorite, in case you prefer toast."

I'm stunned speechless. I don't know what to say. My stomach rolls again, and this time, I know it's not good. Standing, I slap my hand over my mouth and rush down the hall to the bathroom. I drop to my knees just in time. I groan once it's over, and that's when I realize my hair's being held back.

"What can I do?" Lachlan asks, rubbing my back with the hand that's not holding my hair.

"You can go. I hate you seeing me this way," I grumble. Tears spring to my eyes. The last thing I want to do is be a burden to him.

"I'm not going anywhere, and see you like what? Pregnant with our baby? I told you, I'm here for it all, Maggie. Tell me what you need."

"To brush my teeth."

"Fair enough." He drops my hair and climbs to his feet. The next thing I know, he's lifting me into his arms and carrying me to the sink. He sets me on the counter and starts adding toothpaste to my toothbrush.

"I can do it," I tell him.

"I know you can, Mags, but you're doing it all. You're doing all the work, and I feel helpless. Let me help you."

"I don't want to be your burden, Lachlan."

"What?" He rears back as if I slapped him. My toothbrush is dripping with water and the toothpaste is slowly slipping off the bristles. "You think you're a burden? To me?"

"You didn't sign up for this."

"And you did? Maggie, we did this together. It took both of us to make this baby. It's going to take both of us, and a damn village, to raise him or her. Those are the facts. What isn't is you being a burden." He pulls in a deep breath and heavily exhales.

"I know that's him talking. That bastard who made you feel like you weren't enough. Listen to me. You are enough, Maggie. You are everything. You're the mother of my child. You're not a burden. You're a fucking rock star. You're growing our baby. Keeping him or her safe and healthy until we're ready to meet them. That's not a burden, Maggie Ward. That's a fucking miracle."

My heart feels like it's too big for my chest. I know with absolute clarity that this baby might not have been planned, but without a doubt, I wouldn't want to be doing this with anyone but Lachlan. That's a scary revelation for me and for my heart. "You drove an hour last night after nine. That's easily a two-and-a-half-hour trip... longer depending on how long you were in the store, and now you're here bright and early to bring me food, and then you had to see that." I shudder as I nod to the toilet.

"I did that because I wanted to. Not because I felt obligated. That's what a dad does, Maggie. He shows up for those he cares about. He helps them in their time of need and goes above and beyond. I have a great role model, the absolute best. While I didn't ever see him take care of my mom while pregnant, I did watch him take care of both of us growing up, and it wasn't because we were his burden to bear. It's because we are his family. We were what was important, and that to me, is you and our baby."

Tears well in my eyes. "I'm sorry. Hormones."

"Don't push me away, Maggie. I know this is unconventional, but I promise you there is nowhere else on this earth I'd rather be than right there with you."

I nod, and wipe at my eyes. "Can I brush my teeth now?"

He chuckles. "Yeah, babe, you can brush your teeth now."

My heart stutters at the nickname he's never used with me before. It's so familiar and, in a way, intimate. He hands me the toothbrush, lifts me off the counter, and I turn to handle my business. Once I'm done, he laces his fingers through mine and leads me back to the kitchen.

"What are you thinking for breakfast?"

"The bagel, please. With peanut butter."

"Coming right up. Drink?"

"Just water for now. Let's see if I can keep that down."

"You got it."

I watch as he pulls two bagels out of the bag and rummages through my cabinets until he finds the peanut butter, which he slathers on before setting a plate in front of me and one right next to me. He gets us both a glass of water, and that's how I end up having breakfast after puking my guts up with my baby daddy.

That's not how I thought this morning was going to go, but even I can admit I'm glad he's here. His words race through my mind.

I'm not a burden.

He wants to be here with me. He believes that, and I believe him. I need to stop letting my ex and his words into my present-day life. He's in the past. I just wish it was that easy. The emotional and mental scars he inflicted run deep.

I was wrong, and my stomach twists now for an entirely different reason. "I'm sorry," I tell Lachlan.

He reaches over and places his hand on my arm. "No apology needed. We're both new to this, and there are going to be bumps, but I'm here for it all, Maggie. Good, bad, ugly, whatever it is, I'm all in where you and our baby are concerned. No matter what."

The sincerity in his eyes has warmth filling my chest, and suddenly, my appetite is back. I pick up the bagel and take a huge bite, making him smile.

We've got this.

LACHLAN

"FOUR WEEKS. WE HAVE TO wait four weeks?" I glance over at Maggie, who's sitting in the passenger seat. "I don't know if I'll make it," I tell her honestly.

"It will be here before you know it," she says, gently rubbing her baby bump.

"Four weeks, and we get to see our peanut." Reaching over, I place my hand just beneath hers on her growing bump. "Are we going to find out the gender?"

"Yeah, I thought we said yes to that already?"

"We did. Well, I assumed, but you're allowed to change your mind."

"You want to find out, right?" she asks.

I nod. "I really do."

"Me too," she says, relief evident in her tone.

"Do you have anything else to do today?" I ask her. It's just before lunchtime, and I have an idea I want to run past her.

"Nope. I took the entire day off."

"Want to spend the day with me?" I ask her. "We can go grab lunch, and then I have somewhere I need to be at two, and I was hoping you could come with me."

"Sure, why not? Wait, where are we going to lunch? That might be a deal breaker." She turns as much as the seat belt will let her to hear my answer.

"What are you and baby craving today? I don't care where we go." I just want to spend time with her. And I really do want her with me this afternoon.

"Pizza. Extra cheesy pizza."

"Done. Dough Daddies or something else?"

"Dough Daddies, obviously."

"How are we looking on ice cream?" I ask her. We've started hanging out a couple of nights a week, watching movies and eating ice cream. I spend a good part of that with my hands on her belly, and I'm grateful she tolerates me. We've gotten our money's worth out of the doppler too. It's a rush to hear our baby's heartbeat. I'm addicted.

"Well, we might need to pick up more." Her face turns an adorable shade of pink. "We'll swing by after my appointment and grab some more for tonight. That way, we don't have to rush lunch to get the ice cream back to your place."

Pulling out of the doctor's office, I point the truck toward Dough Daddies. It's only a five-minute drive at most, and soon we're seated at a booth, and a large extra cheese pizza is on its way with cheesy breadsticks with extra sauce.

"I'm glad the morning sickness is gone. I know I'm lucky that it was only a few really bad days," she says, taking a sip of her water.

"Me too. I hated seeing you like that and not being able to help."

"I hated you seeing me like that too," she grumbles. "So, where are we going after this? You have an appointment?"

"I do. With a realtor."

"What? You're moving?" Panic crosses her face.

Reaching across the table, I place my hand over hers. "Not out of Ashby, just to a bigger place. I need more room for the baby. My house is barely big enough for me." I laugh, but it's the truth.

"So, where is this house?"

"It's actually just down the road from Maddox and Brogan. Maddox knew I was looking and told me about it. I did a drive-by and called the realtor last night."

"So that's why you were out driving around when you called to check on me?"

"Not just to check on you. I like talking to you, Mags. I've gotten used to ending my day with your voice in my ear."

"Yeah," she agrees. "Which house?"

"It's the white cape cod, just down from them."

"No way!" she exclaims, leaning forward, which causes her breasts to rest on the table. Her "much larger than they were when I had my hands on them" breasts, and it's a battle to keep my eyes off them on a daily basis, and even more so when they're being offered up to me like they are now.

"Yes, way!" I laugh at her enthusiasm.

"Lachlan! I love that house." She's beaming.

"Honestly, I never paid too much attention, but the drive-by last night, I like what I saw, at least from the road."

"So, we're meeting the realtor?"

"We are."

"What do you know about it?"

"It's a three-bedroom, but has a full walkout basement with a game room, an office, and what could be a fourth bedroom downstairs. Five acres, so lots of room for a shop or for our little one to run and play."

"That sounds perfect. Our baby is going to want to spend more time at your place than mine," she jokes.

I want to tell her she can move in with me, but I bite my tongue. Baby steps. "That's not true," I say instead.

Our pizza is delivered, and we dive in. "Have you thought about names yet?" I ask her.

"No, not really. I was kind of waiting until we found out the gender, and then I thought we could sit down and talk about it. Have you?"

"No, not really. Like you, I thought we'd make a list together and do the process of elimination or something," I say, shrugging. "But I do think we need to consider nicknames."

"Oh, for sure. Kids can be cruel," she agrees. "In elementary school, there was a boy named Frank in our class. They called him Frankfurter. Not the worst, but no. Just no."

"Agreed. We definitely need to consider all possible nicknames."

"Look at us, already killing this parenting thing," she teases.

"You know it." I wink at her, and dive back into my lunch, enjoying her company.

"Come on in," Lana, the realtor, says as we follow her into the house. "The owners moved for work, so it's vacant. Lachlan, we talked on the phone about the specs. Do you have any questions?" she asks.

"Not currently."

"Great. I'm going to hang out on the front porch and reply to some emails. I don't like to hover so you can discuss. I'll be right outside if you need me."

"Thank you, Lana," I say, and turn to Maggie.

"I like her." She grins.

"Me too. I hate a pushy salesperson."

"Well, first impression?" she asks.

"I love the open-floor plan. It's bigger than it looked in the pictures online."

"You had an online listing I could have looked at? You've been holding out on me. I see how it is."

"I didn't even think about it." I laugh. "Come on, you." I hold my hand out for her, and she takes it.

Friends hold hands, right? We do, because she never turns me down when I offer her my hand. Maybe she's more ready for me to tell her I want for us to try to be more than I think.

"Wow, this kitchen is incredible. It's got a breakfast nook for a small table and a dining room. You could host everyone here for sure."

"It's crazy how you just read my mind," I tell her.

We walk through the house. The laundry room is a decent size, with a small counter to fold laundry, which is nice. I usually fold mine on the couch or my bed; that's if I fold it.

"I wonder where this goes?" She pushes open the door in the laundry room and turns to grin at me over her shoulder. "It's a huge closet."

"Go in. See where the next door goes," I tell her. I already know because I studied the images for far too long last night, but I won't tell her that. I like seeing the smile on her face as she discovers new aspects of the home.

"Lachlan! This is the primary bedroom. What a great idea to have them connected."

"Nice," I say, following her into the primary bedroom. "That closet is massive, and this room is too. It's the size of my entire house," I tease.

"Stop it." She chuckles. "It's not *that* big. That must be the bathroom." She points to another door, and I can't wait to see her face when she walks in. Even if I didn't already love the house and the location, especially since I'll be neighbors with Maddox and Brogan, this bathroom would have tipped the scales in the where do I sign direction.

"I feel like I'm on that *Cribs* show," she says. "Look at this."

"Much better in person," I tell her. It's gray-and-black tile, black fixtures, with a walk-in shower that has a rain shower head, and inside the glass enclosure is a clawfoot tub. It's all one glassed-in area of the room, and she's right—it reminds me of some celebrity home show.

"The owners bought it as a fixer-upper and completely remodeled it before a job change; at least, that's what Lana told me on the phone. They're motivated to sell too. Since they're paying two mortgages."

Maggie turns in a circle, and the smile on her face is captivating.

"Come on. Let's go check out the upstairs before we go to the basement."

"I think this is called a Jack-and-Jill bathroom," she says.

"It is. Two bedrooms that both have access to the bathroom from either side."

"This landing area is nice extra upstairs living space. It would be a good hangout with a TV, a small couch, maybe," she says, tossing out ideas about the upstairs landing area.

"Good idea." We step into each room and look at the closet size, as well as the bathroom. It has double sinks and a tub-shower combination.

"What's that?" she asks. She points to a small door on the wall; at least, it looks like a door.

"I'm not sure." I press it open and look in. "I think it's a laundry shoot. I wonder where it goes?"

"I don't know, but the previous owners really put their thinking cap on with that one. Now, if only there was a way to get it back up the steps the same way." She chuckles.

"Come on. I need to go back to the laundry room." We head back downstairs and to the laundry room. I open what I thought was just a storage cabinet by the washer, but it's clear that this is where the shoot ends.

"Sold." Maggie chuckles. "That's so cool, and the primary bathroom, and the kitchen. Lachlan, this place is stunning. You have to buy it."

"We still need to see the basement. That could be a deal changer," I tell her.

"Not likely," she mutters, but leads the way out of the laundry room and to the steps in the living room that lead us down to the basement.

"It's like a whole other house down here." She runs her hands over the small countertop in the mini kitchen.

"A giant rec room, a bedroom, a full bathroom, and another oversized room is how it was listed."

"And you remember that?" she asks.

"I might have spent a lot of time going over the listing last night when I got home from my drive-by."

"The walkout is a perfect spot to entertain, and the firepit has you and the guys written all over it."

"I happen to agree. I'd pretty much decided last night that if everything was as great as the pictures made it seem, I would make an offer. It's priced below market value because they just need to get rid of it. It's a rare find for sure."

"And you'd be neighbors with Maddox. It's perfect since Roman, Forrest, and Legend all live on the same street."

"Another good selling point." I nod.

"It's incredible, Lachlan. I can't believe you're buying this house because of the baby."

"It was time." I hold my hand out to her. "Come on. Let's go find Lana so I can put in an official offer."

"Every day should end with movies and ice cream," Maggie says, scooping a huge bite of pistachio ice cream into her mouth. "You sure you don't want to try this?" she asks.

"I'm pretty sure I'm not a fan."

"Oh, come on. Try it." She scoops out another bite, this one a little smaller than the one she just took and offers it to me.

Leaning in, I wrap my lips around the spoon and try not to grimace. "Not my thing," I say, swallowing and taking a bite of my chocolate to wash away the taste.

"Really? It's so good."

"That's the cravings kicking in," I tell her. "Didn't you say you've never liked pistachio ice cream before now?"

Her face lights up. "You're right. This little one must really love it." She rubs her belly affectionately.

"You're beautiful, Maggie. You're glowing, and I just need you to know, you're beautiful."

"You don't have to flatter me. The deed has already been done." She nods toward her belly. She takes her last bite of ice cream, and I take the bowl from her, placing it on the table to bring to the kitchen before I leave.

Discarding my bowl of ice cream, I move to the middle cushion that separates us on the couch. Slowly, I lift my hand and rest my palm against her cheek. "I'm not trying to flatter you, Mags, I mean it. At this moment, you've never looked more beautiful."

She opens her mouth to speak, but I trace the pad of my thumb over her lips to stop her. "I don't care what you're wearing or that you already washed off all your makeup. You don't need it, anyway. You're glowing. Your eyes are lit up with happiness, and you're carrying a part of me inside you. You're stunning." Knowing that I'm pressing my luck but unable to stop myself, I lean forward and press a kiss to the corner of her mouth.

She gasps, and when I start to pull away from her, she whispers one word, "No." Her hands grip my shirt, and her breathing picks up. "I need—" She cuts off.

"Tell me, Mags. We're in this together, remember?" My voice is soothing as I practically beg her to tell me what she needs. I have a pretty good idea. I've been reading the books, but I'm going to need her to spell it out for me.

"It's the hormones."

My hand moves to cradle the back of her neck, bringing her closer. "What about them?"

"They're... heightened. They're more, and nothing seems to help."

"I can help you." I lean in and kiss just below her ear. "Can we try, Mags? Can you let me show you that I can make the ache go away?"

"That's— Oh, god." She moans when I nip at her earlobe. "Blurring lines," she finally says.

"We're having a baby together. Neither one of us are seeing other people. I'm the perfect person to help you out with this. I'm here for anything and everything you need, Maggie. Even this. All you have to do is tell me what you need." I kiss down her neck, and her breath shudders.

"I need you to take the ache away."

"There's my girl," I say, pressing my lips to hers. I take my time tasting her. It's been too damn long since our night together, but her taste is everything I remember. Her lips are soft as they mold with mine. "Lie back," I whisper against her mouth. I stand from the couch and let her get situated, then reach down, tug her leggings over her hips, and toss them to the floor. Her panties are next. I should take her to her room, but I don't trust myself to not take this too far. She asked for relief, and that's what I'm going to give her.

Kneeling on the floor, I run my hand up her legs and settle between her thighs. "Open for me, Mags." She does as I ask, spreading her legs just a little, giving me enough room to explore her with ease.

"Is all this for me?" I ask as I slide my fingers over her clit.

"I—Yes." She nods.

"How long has this been going on, Maggie?"

"A few weeks," she confesses, covering her face with her palms.

With my free hand, I gently pull one hand and then the other from her face. "No hiding. Not from me. Not ever."

"Okay," she replies softly.

"My mouth or my fingers? Tell me what you want."

"You decide."

"My baby momma needs me to take care of her, but I can't do that if I don't know what she wants. Tell me, Momma. What do you need?" Bending my head, I place a kiss on her belly, over where our child grows inside her. I want to remind her that we've been here before, and fuck me, if I had my way, we'd be here often. She's so damn wet for me.

"Mouth. I want your mouth."

"Good girl. Turn my way." She does as I ask, and I settle between her thighs. "Move down a little," I instruct, and she wiggles until her ass is hanging off the couch. "I was craving something sweeter than ice cream," I say as I dip my head and take my first taste of the night. She moans, and the sound goes straight to my dick.

I start slowly, tracing my tongue through her folds, and when I reach her clit, I suck gently. Her hips buck off the couch. Her hands find their way to my hair, and she grips tightly. I welcome the pain, knowing it's only because of the pleasure I'm bringing her.

Over and over again, I bring her to the edge, only to back off, causing her to groan in frustration. I don't know if I'll ever be here again, like this with her, so I'm taking my fill, but I also know she needs this, so this time, when my tongue massages her clit, I don't stop until she's crying out my name.

When the last tremors work through her body, I stand and lift her into my arms. "What are you doing?"

"Putting you to bed." She doesn't argue as I carry her down the short hallway and step into her room. After placing her on the bed, I step back, adjust my cock, and smile down at the dopey, satisfied expression on her face. "Where are your sleep clothes?"

She points to a T-shirt at the end of the bed, and I freeze when I hold it up and realize it's mine. "My little thief." I chuckle.

"Something to remember that night," she counters.

My hand moves to rest on her belly. "You gave me something too." I kiss her lips, just a gentle peck. "I'm going to go clean up while you get changed. I'll be right back."

"You don't have to do that."

"I want to." Another peck to her lips and I force myself to walk out of her room, and clean up our ice cream mess. I turn off the TV, grab her a bottle of water, and head back to her room.

She's already lying under the covers and looks as though she's moments from sleep. "Here's a water if you need it. I'll lock up when I leave."

"Thank you, Lachlan." She reaches out and grabs my hand.

I give hers a squeeze, and because I can't fucking help myself, I kiss her one more time, this time a little longer, before turning out the light and walking out the front door.

MAGGIE 9

"I'M STUFFED," EMERSON SAYS, PLOPPING down on the couch next to me.

"You and me both. Legend is a master at smoked brisket," I tell Monroe.

"Shh." She shushes me. "Don't let him hear you. It will go to his head."

"Too late, wife!" Legend calls out, and we all laugh.

I glance over my shoulder to where the guys are all still sitting at the dining room table. We moved to the living room with the kids and more comfortable seating. Especially since Briar and I are both pregnant. Those hard dining room chairs are not where it's at.

Lachlan turns and catches me staring and winks. I smile and shake my head before turning back to the girls, only to find them watching me.

"So..." Brogan wags her eyebrows. "How's it going with the baby daddy?"

"It's... going," I say, my face heating when I think about last weekend and how he helped take the edge off before putting me to bed. I wanted to ask him to stay. Watching him leave was so damn hard, but my thoughts and feelings were confusing, and I needed time to process what happened.

"What's that?" Monroe points to my face. "What aren't you telling us?"

"Pregnancy hormones are a bitch, okay?" I blurt. It's more like a whisper shout, but they all hear me plain as day.

"Oh, don't we know it," Emerson chimes in.

"Is this something to look forward to or dread?" Brogan asks.

"You're definitely going to look forward to it," Briar tells her sister.

"Unless you're pregnant and single as a damn Pringle," I mutter.

"Why *are* you single?" Brogan asks. "Lachlan can't take his eyes off you. Are you not attracted to him?"

"What? You've seen him, right? Are we talking about the same guy? Lachlan Noble? The one responsible for this? Okay, half responsible? Yes, I'm attracted to him. That's the problem. He's too damn sexy, and he's doing all these super sweet things for me, and we're spending a ton of time together, and we're supposed to be friends."

"Are you not friends?" Monroe asks gently.

"We are, but then also this weekend, things... heated up a little. He... helped with the ache, so to speak, and then tucked me into bed. He didn't stay. He didn't even attempt to stay," I huff out.

"Did you want him to stay?"

I nod. "More than anything. We had a great day together, and I just... wanted all the warm and fuzzy feelings to be real, or at least pretend they were real just for a night. Gah!" I place my hands over my face. "It's as if a switch has flipped inside me. I feel like we've been dating, but we're not dating. He's there for the baby, but it feels like more, and my heart wants it to be more, but we're friends. We agreed that we were not together but just raising this baby together, and suddenly, he's all I think about.

Well, him and our baby." I clamp my mouth shut, having already said more than I intended to say.

My four closest friends stare at me, none of them saying a word. Brogan's eyes flash behind me, and I freeze.

Lachlan's hands land on my shoulders, something he's done a lot in the past, but since our night together, my mind reads more into it than I should be. "You need anything, Momma?" he asks. Leaning over, he rubs his hand on my belly.

"I'm good," I tell him, my body melting under his touch.

"Ladies, do any of you need anything?" he asks.

"Nope," all four reply.

Lachlan squeezes my shoulder with the hand that's still resting there before turning and walking away without another word.

"Please, for the love of butter pecan ice cream, tell me he didn't hear me."

"He didn't, but he stood up as soon as you stopped talking," Brogan tells me.

"I could tell from Brogan's facial expression it was one of the guys, so I stayed quiet." Emerson explains.

"We could see him too," Briar says, pointing at her chest, and then Monroe's.

I shudder and exhale, and Emerson places her hand on my arm. "It's fine."

"Okay, we'll go back to your speech, but first, can we talk about how he calls you momma?" Monroe asks.

"Forrest calls me that too," Briar tells us. "I think it's more because that's what the girls call me. But yeah, it hits you in the feels coming from them." Briar nods.

"It's sweet," Brogan comments.

"He's sweet. He's thoughtful and goes out of his way to do things for me. It's confusing me. That's all this is."

"He's into you," Monroe says, taking a sip of her water. "I say go for it. See where it takes you."

"It's not that easy. We have a baby to think about."

"He's always going to be there for the baby, and for you," Emerson assures me. "I've known these men all my life, and they're the good ones. All five of them. He's not going to let something as simple as an intimate relationship not working out keep him from taking care of you or his baby."

"I don't need him to take care of me."

"Sure." Emerson nods. "There's always the battery-operated version, but I much prefer the real thing."

I can't help it, I burst out laughing, as do the others.

"What's going on over here?" Legend comes strutting over with Kane in his arms. "You ladies are having too much fun." Kane sees his mommy and lights up, reaching for her. Monroe takes him from Legend's arms and smothers him with kisses, making him laugh.

There is nothing better than baby giggles.

"Just catching up," Monroe tells her husband.

"Uh-huh." He smiles, leaning down to kiss her. He takes Kane from her arms, and he's gone as quickly as he arrived.

"I want that," I confess. My words are quiet.

"I think you could have that. I think you're scared," Emerson tells me. "Your ex was an asshole, and I know there are some confidence issues, but Lachlan isn't your ex."

"There is so much at stake."

"But what if it all works out?" Brogan asks. "I know about being scared and letting your past hinder your present and future, and I had to take a leap of faith. Take things slow, feel it out. Maybe work things out in your head. Give yourself the freedom to picture life with him and then take it one day at a time."

Tears well in my eyes. "I love you. All of you. I couldn't do this without you. Lachlan, the baby, all of it. I'm so grateful to have each of you in my life."

"Same," the four of them respond.

I don't know what my future holds, but I do know that I have four incredible friends who will be there with me every step of the way.

"So, did you see the house?" Brogan asks.

"The house... yes, I saw it, and it's gorgeous. It's completely remodeled inside. Seriously, I can't wait for you all to see it." I smile when I think about how excited Lachlan has been all week. He put in an offer and it was accepted that day. He's already been back, taking his parents to look at it the next day. He asked me to go with them, but I was exhausted after working all day on my feet. He stopped by after with dinner, and he was so animated about all he wants to do with the house. He plans to build a shop, and paint, and his enthusiasm was contagious.

"Mad is pumped. We're going to be neighbors," Brogan tells me.

"Me too," Emerson chimes in. "The three of us all live close. I'm glad you and Maddox will have Lachlan close, and who knows, maybe our girl here will be living there soon too."

"I don't need you putting more thoughts inside my head," I tell Emerson.

"Come on, Maggie. Keep an open mind," Monroe teases.

"Really, guys, I'm so excited for him. He was like a little kid on Christmas morning after they accepted his offer."

"Well, driving by, it looks stunning. I can't wait to see it," Brogan replies.

I give her a grateful smile, and the conversation turns to Kane's first birthday, which will be here before we know it. It's hard to believe the little guy is already turning one. Time really does go by in the blink of an eye.

A little while later, I'm sitting on the couch, where I've been since we finished dinner, and my eyes are getting heavy. That's something else that's a side effect of growing a tiny human. I seem to always be exhausted.

Lachlan appears beside me and kneels next to me. He reaches out and pushes my hair behind my ear. "You ready to head home?"

"How do you do that?" I ask.

"How do I do what?"

"Always know what I need?" I reply softly.

His eyes do this thing where they look softer and even more blue. "Because I know you, Mags. I pay attention."

"I'm ready to go home," I say, because I don't know how to reply to that. He does know me. I'd wager a guess that this man knows me better than anyone. That includes the four women I've spent the night catching up with. They're my closest friends yet Lachlan knows me better.

"Come on, Momma." He stands and offers me his hand, and because I'm tired and pregnant, I allow him to help me from the couch. Except he doesn't stop there. He drops my hand and slides his arm around my waist. "We're headed out," he announces.

"Yeah, we need to go too," Monroe says. "Kane conked out a while ago."

We say our goodbyes, and Lachlan leads me out to the truck. He opens the door for me, like the gentleman he is, waits for me to be strapped in before he closes the door, and walks around the front of his truck to take his seat behind the wheel.

"I should have driven so that you don't have to take me all the way home, then back to your place," I tell him, covering a yawn.

"I don't mind."

"That puts you home late."

"I'm a big boy, Mags. I can handle it."

I don't reply because he's right. He's a grown-ass man; he doesn't need me worrying about him, but I do. He takes such good care of me and our unborn child, but who takes care of him?

I could be that person for him.

That's my last thought before I drift off to sleep.

I jolt awake to being carried up the steps of my front porch. I lock my arms around his neck and hold on tight.

"I've got you," Lachlan murmurs.

"You could have woken me up. I could have walked," I grumble—not because I'm mad that he's carrying me. No, I'm moody because he's confusing me and making me fall harder for him with every single interaction, and I don't know how to handle it.

"And I can carry you."

We reach the front door, and I dig my key out to unlock the door. "You can put me down."

"Just unlock the door, Mags," he says, chuckling under his breath.

I manage to get the door unlocked and turn the handle, and he steps inside, kicking it closed.

"Do you need anything from out here?" he asks.

"A water. I usually take one to bed with me every night."

"Let's get you in bed, and I'll come back for it." He takes off down the hall with only the dim shine of the lamp I left on while I was gone to light the way.

Finding his way in my dark bedroom, he carries me to the bed and lays me down gently. Reaching over, he turns on the lamp, illuminating the room in a soft glow. This time he doesn't ask where my sleep clothes are. He goes to the dresser but can't find what he's looking for as he digs around. I know he's looking for his T-shirt that I kept, but I've worn it the last few nights, and it's in the dirty clothes.

"Where's the shirt?"

"I have others."

He turns to look at me over his shoulder. "I like knowing you're sleeping in mine."

"It's dirty," I confess, putting him out of the searching game he's doing in my dresser drawer.

Calmly, he closes the drawer and moves back toward the bed. I watch him with rapt attention because he's empty-handed. I'm not wearing his dirty shirt just to appease him. I've literally slept in it every night for a week. It was time to wash it. Expecting him to go looking in the hamper, I'm shocked when he pulls his shirt over his head and hands it to me.

"Wear this."

"What are you going to wear?" I ask him as my eyes dart to his chest. I swallow hard to fight back my desire.

"I'll be fine. Besides, I'm sure I have another in my truck. If not?" He shrugs. "I'm going to let you change while I go get your water." He turns and walks out of the room.

The first thing I do is bring his shirt to my face and inhale. He smells so damn good—sandalwood and something uniquely Lachlan. I should give him his shirt back, but the idea of sleeping all snuggled up with his scent surrounding me is just too damn tempting to pass up.

He comes back into the room a few minutes after I'm finished changing and gives me a sweet smile. "Looks better on you," he says, placing the bottle of water on my nightstand. "Here." He hands me my purse. "I thought you might want to charge your cell phone."

"Thank you, Lachlan. You spoil me," I tell him.

His hand touches the side of my cheek. "I enjoy taking care of you."

"The baby," I remind him.

"You and the baby," he amends. "Do you have everything that you need?"

His words roll through my mind. *You and the baby.* Is he feeling this too? Is it possible that we can be more? I know the girls suggested I think about it and see what happens, but can we?

"Maggie? You okay?"

"Stay." The word is out of my mouth before I can change it, and it very well might be the one word that changes our relationship. For better or worse, that's yet to be seen.

"Are you feeling all right? Should we call the doctor?"

I place my hand over his that's resting against my cheek. "I feel fine. It's late, and I'll worry about you driving home."

"You really want me to stay?"

"I do."

He leans over, his lips mere inches from mine. "Where do you want me to sleep, Mags?"

I swallow hard. "Beside me." Two more words that have the power to make a huge impact.

He stares deep into my eyes, looking for what, I'm not sure, but he eventually nods. "Okay. Let me go lock up." He stands to his full height, and his hand falls from my cheek as he leaves to lock up my house.

I take the few minutes he's gone to internally freak out. It's not as if we've never shared a bed before. So it was one night, but we're having a baby together, and we can do this, right? I just really don't want to be alone tonight, and the thought of him here with me, well, maybe I'll be able to get a good night's sleep instead of lying awake thinking about how things seem to be changing between us.

He steps back into the room, and I scoot over to the other side of the bed. I watch as he strips out of his jeans and kicks them to the side before pulling off his socks. He's in nothing but his boxer briefs as he turns out the light and climbs into bed.

We both lie still in the darkness of the room until he finally speaks.

"Maggie?" His voice is gruff.

"Yeah?" Mine doesn't sound much better.

"If I'm staying here, then you're going to need to be in my arms. I can't sleep next to you and not hold you. If you'd rather I leave, or go to the couch, I can do that too."

"No," I rush to say, and move to the center of the bed. He meets me halfway. I turn my back to his chest, and he pulls me so that our bodies are flush. He places a kiss on my cheek, and then rests his large palm under his shirt on my bare belly.

"Better," he murmurs, and within minutes, we're both drifting off to sleep.

LACHLAN 10

M Y EYES SLOWLY BLINK OPEN, and I smile when I see Maggie curled up next to me. Her arm rests over my chest, and her leg is tossed over mine. I could definitely get used to waking up like this. I was shocked when she asked for me to stay last night, and even more so when she agreed to let me hold her. It would have been pure torture to sleep next to her and not be able to feel her warmth in my arms.

She starts to stir, and I can feel the moment she's fully awake. Her body stiffens slightly, and I trace my hand gently up her spine until she relaxes her body back into mine.

"Morning, Momma." I smile, because I could really get used to waking up like this.

"Good morning. Thank you for staying," she rasps, her voice still laced with sleep.

"No place I'd rather be." She starts to move, and I wrap my arm around her, holding her close. "Where are you going?" I keep my tone light.

"I'm crowding you."

"You're not crowding me. I'm holding you, Maggie. There's a difference."

She lifts her head to smile at me. "I need to pee too," she says.

"Fine," I grumble. "I'll do the same and meet you back here in five." She furrows her brow. "We're snuggling, Mags. Five minutes." I bop my fingers against her nose, and she starts to laugh, when panic crosses her face.

"Don't make me laugh." She scrambles from the bed, her baby bump pressing against my T-shirt. I don't take my eyes off her until she disappears behind the bathroom door. Only then do I climb out of bed and go to the bathroom down the hall. I detour to the kitchen and start a pot of coffee. I know she still likes her one small cup a day.

I grab a new bottle of water for both of us, go back to her room, and perch on the side of the bed, downing my water in one go. "What do you want to eat for breakfast?" I ask her when she steps out of the bathroom.

"Um, I don't know. I might just make some eggs and toast or something."

I think about it, but then I have a better idea. "Get dressed. We're going to my parents' for breakfast."

"We are? Was this planned and I forgot?" She wrinkles her nose as if she's trying to remember and can't.

"No. It wasn't planned, but it's about to be."

Leaning over, I grab my cell phone from the nightstand, unplug it from the charger, and call my mom. She answers on the first ring. "Hey, Mom," I greet.

"Lachlan, what's wrong?" she asks immediately, making me laugh.

"Nothing is wrong, but I'm craving some of your homemade buttermilk pancakes and some bacon."

She laughs. "What time?"

"An hour?"

"We'll be ready. Oh, and, Lachlan, bring Maggie."

"I was planning on it. In fact, I'm bringing two guests, and no, the baby does not count, so technically, I'm bringing three guests."

"Sounds good. Drive safe. I'll see you in an hour." I end the call and smile at Maggie.

"You just randomly call your mom on a Sunday morning and invite yourself to breakfast?" she asks in disbelief.

"Yeah. And I'm bringing you, peanut, and Grandma Doris." Speaking of Grandma Doris, I dial her number, and this time, I put the call on speaker.

"Lachlan? Did we have plans today?" she asks.

"We didn't, but now we do. Maggie and I will be there to get you in about a half an hour. We're going to my parents' for breakfast."

"Oh, dear, well, I'll be ready," she assures me. "See you soon." I end the call, and toss my cell to the bed.

"You called my grandmother."

"I did."

"Why did she think she forgot plans with you today?"

Well, damn, I didn't think this one through. "No reason."

"Lachlan." She tries out her mom voice as she crosses her arms over her chest. I bite my cheek to keep from smiling. She's going to be such an amazing mom. Not just because she's perfected the "talk now" look, but because she's amazing, and our kid gets to have that every day.

"Okay, I've been there a couple of times since we told her about the baby."

Her mouth falls open in shock. "You've been to see my grandma?"

"I have."

"Why?"

"Well, when we were there, I noticed the faucet in the bathroom was leaking and there were a couple of boards on the porch that were loose, and I didn't want her to fall, so on my day off a few weeks ago, I gathered everything I needed, picked up some lunch, and spent the afternoon with her."

"You spent the afternoon with her?" she asks. "You fixed things at her house?" Her voice cracks.

"I'm sorry. I should have told you, but I wanted to help, and I thought if I told you, that you would think it was just because of the baby that I felt obligated or something. That's not it at all. I wanted to help her."

"You wanted to help her?" she asks, wiping the tears that are coating her cheeks.

"I did." I nod. I start to stand because I can't see her cry, but instead, she starts to take slow, steady steps toward me. I decide to stay put and see what she's going to do.

"Is that all?" she asks once she's standing toe to toe with me where I sit on the edge of her bed.

"Um, no. I might have taken my dad with me one day too. The back porch needed some new shingles, and he helped."

"Your dad helped?" she croaks with a sob.

I can't take it any longer. I place my hands on her hips, and widen my legs, pulling her even closer. She comes willingly. "I did. I was able to help. *We* were able to help," I amend, "and we wanted to do it."

"I'm at a loss here, Lachlan. I don't know what to think about this."

"I'm sorry that I kept it from you. I was going to tell you. I knew you would find out."

"I talk to her every day and she never said a word."

"Maybe she assumed I'd told you. That's on me. I'll make sure she knows I kept it from you. Please don't be mad at me." I've never begged a woman for anything, but for this one, I'll beg every damn day. The thought of her being mad, of me being the reason for that anger, or worse, pain, twists my stomach.

"Mad at you?" Her brow furrows.

Lifting my right hand, I wipe the tears from her cheeks. "That's why you're crying, right? You're mad I didn't tell you?"

She shakes her head. "I'm not mad at you, Lachlan. I'm floored, flabbergasted, and touched beyond belief. Since losing my dad, no one— It's just been us."

"Not anymore." I want to kiss her. I want to show her with more than my words that she and this baby and Grandma Doris are my family, but I don't want to push her. "Now, you better get ready. We have to stop at my place so I can change and get a shirt before we pick up Grandma Doris."

"I can give you this one back," she tells me.

"Nah, it looks better on you, anyway. Go get ready." I tap her ass lightly, and she gives me a watery smile.

She rests her palms against my cheeks and leans in, kissing my lips lightly. It's way too fast, but I'll take anything she's willing to give me. "Thank you, Lachlan."

"Always," I tell her, and nod for her to get ready. We've got pancakes to eat.

"There they are," my dad says as he opens the door for us.

"Were you missing me, old man?" I tease. He's never at the door waiting for me to pull in.

"You? No. These beautiful ladies, most definitely."

"Mom!" I call, laughing. "Dad's trying to steal my girls."

My mom steps out of the kitchen with a dish towel slung over her shoulder. "Lachlan Noble, we taught you how to share," she scolds.

"See," Dad taunts.

"Mom, this is Grandma Doris. Doris, this is my mom, Amanda."

"It's so nice to meet you. Thank you for having us," Doris tells her.

"Any family of Maggie's is family of ours," Mom assures her. "Come on in. The pancakes are ready, and you better get to them before Rodney and Lachlan do."

"Hey!" Dad and I call out, and the three ladies laugh.

"Maggie, sweetheart, look at you. May I?" Mom asks with tears in her eyes as she stares at Maggie's baby bump.

"Of course." Maggie smiles.

Mom reaches out and rubs her belly, which makes Doris do the same. "Come, let's get you fed. Maggie, when do you have some free time for that shopping trip?" Mom asks her. I don't hear Maggie's reply, but I know she's in good hands.

"Your girls, huh?" Dad smirks.

"I mean, we could be having a boy, but yeah." I shrug.

"Does she know that?" He nods toward the kitchen.

"I'm working on it."

"Good." Dad nods and walks toward the kitchen with me right behind him.

When we reach the dining room, the ladies already have a plate and are digging into their breakfast. I go to Maggie, place my hands on her shoulders, and bend so my lips are next to her ear. "Do you need anything?"

She looks at the side to face me. She's so close I could kiss her, but I refrain. "No, your mom is taking good care of us."

"Good." I can't help myself when I peck a kiss on her cheek. "What about you, Grandma?" I stand to my full height. "Can I get you anything?"

"Oh, heavens no. This is plenty." She nods to her plate of pancakes, her side of bacon, and the steaming cup of coffee sitting in front of her.

"Mom?"

"Make yourself a plate, Lachlan. We're all good here." She smiles at me, and it's one of those mom smiles that tells me she can see right through me. I'm not just being nice; I want to be everything that Maggie needs, no matter what that looks like. It's that one look from my mother that lets me know she understands that. I expect a phone call later, unless she talks to Dad first. My conversation with him should clear up any confusion she might have.

Maggie isn't mine.

But I want her to be.

That's all they need to know for now.

"Have you kids thought about a nursery theme?" Mom asks.

"Not yet," I tell her, sitting next to Maggie with my plate piled high. I glance over at Maggie. "I think we want to find out the gender first, before we make any solid plans."

"Makes sense." Dad nods.

"Doris, Maggie and I are planning a shopping day soon. We'd love for you to join us," Mom tells Doris.

"That's sweet of you, but I don't get around as well as I used to. I'm glad she has you," Doris says.

"Grandma." Maggie sighs.

Doris reaches over and pats her hand affectionately. "It makes my heart happy that you're a part of such a loving family."

"Grandma, I'm not—" Maggie starts, but my dad speaks up and stops whatever it was she was going to say.

"You're both family now. Soon, we'll have a little one to add to that list."

Beneath the table, I reach for Maggie's hand and squeeze gently. She turns to look at me. "No matter what," I whisper, and she nods, blinking away her tears.

Dad starts telling a story about how I would beg for bread with sweet sauce when I was little, because I couldn't say pancake. Everyone laughs at my expense, but I'm okay with it.

"I'm thirty-three and still love the bread with the sweet sauce," I tell them.

"Maggie, if the baby has a sweet tooth like this one, you're going to be on constant watch. Lachlan is a terrible influence."

"What? Me?" I act appalled. "My son or daughter will know the finer things in life, like sugar." I chuckle.

"Oh, well, you better plan to stay up with them all night when he or she is ready to party at 2:00 a.m. and you both have to work the next day."

"Okay, so maybe we'll keep it to the nights where Mom or Dad are off the next day," I amend. Maggie's laughing, her shoulders shaking, and I love it. I love how well she fits in with us. How easily she's already a part of this family.

"You're going to have to learn to say no to sweets."

"Wait. Hold up now. I don't have to say no for me. Right? Mags? Say it isn't so," I say dramatically, and her shoulders shake harder as she covers her mouth with her hand.

"You can't very well eat cupcakes in front of your kid and not give them any," Dad explains.

"Yeah, but that doesn't mean I don't get them. I'll just wait until the baby is asleep. Problem solved."

"Yeah, until your son or daughter is old enough to know where you hide the goods. I remember when you were five or six, you wanted a Little Debbie cake, but it was so close to bedtime that I told you no. You pouted, but that was all. An hour later, I heard wrappers, and it wasn't a sound a mouse would make. Besides, it was coming from your room. I snuck into your room to find you under the bed with a flashlight and the entire box. You'd already eaten two by the time I found you."

That's how the rest of the morning goes. Mom and Dad share stories from my childhood. Maggie and Doris soak up every detail, even sharing memories from Maggie's childhood that include her parents.

I watch as they share a sad smile, but it's a good smile too. It's nice to talk about loved ones who are no longer with us. It helps keep their memory alive.

"Thank you so much for having us," Maggie tells my parents an hour later.

"You're both always welcome here," Mom tells her. She gives Doris a hug, then Maggie, and finally me. Dad does the same and they walk us to the door, waving us off.

"I could use a nap," Doris says from her spot in the passenger seat. "That's more action than I've seen in a long time."

"Grandma!" Maggie hisses out a surprised laugh from the back seat.

"What? I don't get out that often. This was a nice treat. Get your mind out of the gutter. You're about to be a mother," Doris says, barely keeping a straight face. "Lachlan, keep her in line, will you?" Doris asks me.

I glance at Maggie in the rearview mirror and wink. "Sorry, Doris, I can't say no to her. I'm pretty sure I'll never be able to," I admit.

"My goodness, you sure are something." She smiles and hums the rest of the short drive back to her place.

We get Doris settled back into her recliner and she's almost asleep before we're even out the door.

"Thank you for that. She's right; she doesn't get around as well as she used to. This was a treat for her."

"It was for me and my parents too. We got to know her better."

"I don't know how much time I'll have with her, and today meant everything, Lachlan. Thank you for including her."

"She's our family, Maggie." I wait for some type of reminder or comment about how we're not technically related, but it never comes. "So, what do you have planned the rest of the day?" I ask her.

"Nothing. I need to go to the grocery store for lunch stuff this week, but other than that, nothing. Why?"

"Well, I was hoping we could go furniture shopping. All of mine is secondhand, and I think with the new house, it's time to upgrade."

"Really? All new furniture?" she asks.

"Yeah, I mean, I've pretty much saved everything I've ever earned and I've made a few investments. My house is paid for, so when I sell that after moving into the new place, that will be a big chunk I get back. So, what do you say? Feel like furniture shopping? We can hit the grocery store on the way home for you to get everything you need for the week."

"On one condition."

"Name it." Nothing she could ask me to do for her would have me saying no, especially if it means I get to spend the day with her.

"Mexican for lunch." She rubs her belly, and something moves inside my chest, almost as if a fist is squeezing my heart.

"Mexican it is." I turn the truck toward Nashville. Glancing in the rearview mirror, I see the smile spread across my face. It seems to be permanent when the mother of my unborn child is around.

MAGGIE 11

"THANK YOU FOR TODAY, AMANDA. I've had the best time," I tell Lachlan's mom. We just finished a late lunch after shopping all day.

"Me too," she says, the excitement clear in her tone. "We needed another woman in the family. Just think, if this little one is a girl, we'll have them outnumbered." She cackles with laughter.

"We find out next week. I'm so excited. I'm glad Lachlan didn't want to wait. I mean, I would have waited, but it would have been torture."

Amanda laughs. "You have nothing to worry about. Even if he wanted to wait, I can't see him telling you no. He's a lot like his dad in that regard."

"What do you mean?"

"My husband is one of the rare gems of a man in this world. He was relentless in asking me out, and I was on the fence. At first, I was against it. I was a single mom, and my son's father abandoned us as soon as I told him I was pregnant. He told me to deal with it, and I never saw or heard from him again. I was a waitress at the time, living in a tiny one-bedroom apartment, barely making ends meet. I didn't have time for a man in my life. Then along comes Rodney. He sat in my section and flirted all night. Then the next night, and the next. Each night that he left, he would ask me for my number, and I turned him down."

"So, how did the two of you end up together?"

"I was with Lachlan at the restaurant where I worked. I was picking up my check. It was my night off and he was there. Lachlan was fussy, and he started making faces and playing with him, and asked for us to join him. I said no, of course, but then the skies opened up and it was pouring down rain, and I lived two blocks from the restaurant. I had to stay anyway, so I said yes."

"I love that story."

"That night he talked to me like I was someone, you know? I wasn't just this young struggling waitress and single mom. I was a woman. And the way he interacted with Lachlan, well, that sealed the deal for me. Once the rain finally let up, he asked me on a date again. Only this time, it was to the park. He wanted to bring pizza and let Lachlan play. I think that might have been the moment that I fell in love with him."

"Aww, I love that so much."

"So, you see, my son might not have his blood in his veins, but he does have his dad's heart. He wears it openly, and I don't need for him to say the words to know that you and your baby have a piece of it."

"Of course he loves his baby. He's already taking such good care of us."

"Not just the baby, Maggie." Amanda smiles, and it's genuine. Just like her son. He might have his dad's heart, but I can also see Amanda in him, and this is the family my child will grow up with. "Look, I know I'm his mom, and this might seem odd to talk to me about, but I promise you what you say with me will be between us. Unless you're hurt or unsafe, nothing leaves these lips." She gives me another kind smile. "I know you have Grandma Doris, but I also know you lost your parents far too young, and I'd never want to replace them, but I'd like to offer to be an additional support for you. To listen, to give you a shoulder, to babysit." She chuckles. "Whatever you need, I'm here for you. Rodney is, too, and well, you already know Lachlan would move heaven and earth or at least try if you asked him to."

"He's been great," I agree. "Thank you, Amanda. For your words and today. I miss my mother more on days like this."

"You're welcome, sweetheart. Now, tell me, are you all shopped out or do we have time to hit Marshall's before we head back?"

"There is always time for Marshall's," I tell her. We toss our trash, head out to her SUV, and make our way to the next stop.

"Did you know that Lachlan was going to be here?" I ask Amanda as we pull into her driveway, and I see his truck.

"No, but I'm not surprised. He knew you would be here eventually."

"You'd think he'd be sick of seeing me. We've been spending a lot of time together." Even saying the words, I know they're not true. "I shouldn't have said that. I'm sorry." I'm quick to retract my words. "He's made it clear he likes to spend time with me. I'm just... jaded from an ex." An ex that I'm sick and tired of hearing in my thoughts.

"Maggie, trust me, the jaded ex I understand. Just know that he's not worth your time. Maybe look at what's right in front of you." She nods toward what I assume is Lachlan's truck, but when I look up, it's him standing in front of her car, wearing a grin.

"Are you playing matchmaker, Grandma Noble?"

"Yes, and I love that more than you know. I'm going to be a grandma." She squeals in excitement.

"And we have the bibs to prove it."

"Right? They were gender neutral, and I couldn't pass them up."

"They are very cute," I say, as my door opens and Lachlan offers me his hand. I turn to look at Amanda, and she's too occupied placing her hand in Rodney's as he helps her out of the SUV. I didn't even see him outside.

I only had eyes for Lachlan.

Placing my hand in his, I allow him to help me out. "How was your day?" he asks, pressing a kiss to my temple.

"Good." I smile up at him. "Great, actually."

"I'm glad. Did you buy lots of things for the baby?" he asks, pressing his hand against my belly.

"A few."

"All the things," Amanda says as she and Rodney meet us at the back of her SUV. She opens the back and digs around in a bag, pulling out the bibs. They're a light shade of green and one says *I love my grandma* and the other *I love my grandpa*. "Look at these." She holds them up so that Rodney and Lachlan can read them.

Lachlan slides his arm around my waist, and I can't help but lean into his warmth. "Our kid is going to be spoiled, Mags. Just warning you now."

"Not spoiled, loved," Rodney tells us.

"And a little bit spoiled." Amanda chuckles. "Who am I kidding? A lot spoiled. Just wait until I know the gender." She beams at us.

"Good thing I bought a bigger house." Lachlan grins.

"You're going to need it with this one." Rodney pulls Amanda into his side and kisses her temple.

Just like his son.

"Amanda, thank you so much for today. I had so much fun."

"Oh, sweetheart, this is the first of many trips. Thank you for spending the day with me."

I reach into the back of the SUV to start grabbing my bags. "Which ones are yours?" Lachlan asks.

"The right side are mine. We tried to keep them separated to make this easy," I tell him.

"Beautiful and smart." He winks, grabs a handful of bags, and takes them to my car. There are only two for me to carry, and once everything is in my car, I turn to face him.

"Thank you for the help. I'll see you later?"

"What? You're leaving?" he asks.

"I need to get home and get off my feet. I'm exhausted."

"Shit. You're right. Why don't we go to my place? I made a big pot of chili. Are you still craving it?" he asks.

This man is turning my world inside out. "I am." I nod.

"Good. Let's go to my place. Are you okay to drive? We can leave your car here and come back later to get it. You can take a nap at my place."

"It's four. If I nap now, I'll never sleep tonight."

"Then we'll stay up all night." He grins at me. "Whatever you need, Mags, always."

"I can drive."

"I'll follow you." He leans in and hugs me tightly before escorting me to my door. I watch him walk to his truck, taking a piece of my heart with him.

The drive to his house is short, and I constantly look in my rearview mirror to make sure he's still there. He says he'll always be there, and I can say with confidence that I believe him. There are no red flags waving like there were with Eric. My eyes are wide open, and if I'm being honest, I like what I see.

When we pull into his driveway, he's out of his truck and to my door, pulling it open before I have a chance to. He offers me his hand, and I have no hesitation as I take it, allowing him to help me from the car. He keeps his hand locked in mine as he leads us inside the house. I'm getting used to my hand in his, and I don't hate it. I've come to crave his touch.

"Are you hungry now?" Lachlan asks as we enter his house. We both kick off our shoes and leave them by the door.

"No, we had a late lunch, but you can eat without me."

"Nah, I'd rather take a nap with you. I know you said you might not sleep tonight, but that's a bridge we'll cross if we come to it." He takes my hand and guides me down the small hallway to his bedroom. He doesn't bother turning on the light. "Do you need to change?" he asks.

I look down at the leggings and oversized sweatshirt I'm wearing. "No. With this growing belly, I dressed for comfort, which is my MO these days." I place my hands on my belly

Lachlan bends and lifts my sweatshirt and kisses my baby bump. "Tell Mommy she's beautiful," he says to my belly, and tears prick at my eyes. These damn pregnancy hormones are killing me. He stands back to his full height and motions toward the bed. "After you."

I'm too exhausted from a full day of shopping to argue how I won't sleep tonight. Instead, I slide into bed and beneath the covers. Lachlan takes his spot next to me and holds his arm out. I know what he wants, and I want it, too, so I slide next to him, curling against his chest as he wraps his arms around me.

We're both quiet for several minutes, and just as I'm about to doze off, he whispers, "One night. I slept with you in my arms for one night, and now, I can't seem to get a good night's rest without you next to me." I feel his lips press to my head. "Sweet dreams, baby."

He thinks I'm asleep, so I don't reply. Instead, I focus on my breathing, keeping it deep and even. And when I do finally drift off to sleep, I dream of him, of us, and our happily ever after.

When I wake later, the room is noticeably darker. The alarm clock tells me it's a little after seven. I didn't intend to sleep so long, but I was too damn comfortable. I know Lachlan is still asleep by the gentle rise of his chest with each breath. I snuggle closer, wanting to soak up as much time with him as possible. I breathe him in and sigh. He always smells so damn good.

"Did you just sniff me?" His groggy voice startles me, and I jump. "Hey, I didn't mean to scare you." He pulls me tighter into his chest.

"You smell good," I mumble.

He chuckles softly. "Are you hungry yet?"

"Yes, but I don't want to get up." I'm not ready to lose his warmth wrapped around me.

"I'll bring it to you," he offers.

"No. Just... let me lie here for a little while longer."

"I can do that," he agrees, holding me tightly. We've both been quiet for several minutes when he says, "You smell good too. Now my sheets will smell like you. Maybe I can get some sleep."

I lift my head. "Are you having trouble sleeping?"

"Not when you're here," he says, pushing my hair back out of my eyes. How he manages to do that in the darkness of the room, I'm not sure, but this is Lachlan, and I wouldn't be surprised if he has superpowers.

"Is there anything I can do to help?"

"Move in with me?" he asks.

"What?" I laugh nervously.

"I'm not sleeping because after one night of holding you, you've ruined me. This bed feels too small with just me in it, and as it turns out, I like to snuggle." He runs his index finger down my cheek. "I should amend that. I like to snuggle with you."

I still stare at him, even though I can't make out his features in the darkness of the room. That's probably what gives me the courage to say what comes out of my mouth next.

"Kiss me." The words are out before I can stop them. I'm ready to climb off this bed and rush out the front door when I feel his hand slide beneath my hair and cradle the back of my neck.

"Come here, beautiful," he mumbles.

Not needing to be told twice, I move up the bed, and then his lips are on mine. He kisses me once, twice, three times before his tongue traces my lips.

It's not enough.

I want more.

I *need* more.

It's me who pushes my tongue past his lips, taking the kiss deeper to a place I'm fearful I'll never be able to come back from, but I'm also not sure that I care.

Not when it's Lachlan.

He groans. It's a deep sound emitting from somewhere in the back of his throat, and it's so damn sexy. I nip at his lip, and he makes the sound again.

"Maggie," he warns.

"Lachlan," I counter.

He kisses me harder, deeper, and I melt into him. I've never felt this kind of attraction before. I've never been so consumed by another person that all I want to do is get lost in them.

"I need more," I pant as he trails kisses down my neck.

"Tell me what you need, baby, and I'll give it to you." He moves so that we're now lying side by side, facing each other on the bed.

"You."

"You have me, Maggie." His hand slides up under my sweatshirt. He pauses on my baby bump before venturing further. He cups my breast through my cotton bra. It has to be the least sexy one that I own, but I didn't expect to end up here, in his bed, in his arms like this.

Lachlan traces his thumb over my achingly hard nipple, and I moan. "More."

"Tell me how much more, Maggie."

"Touch me."

"I am touching you. You need more than this?" he asks, tweaking my nipple through the fabric of my bra.

"Yes."

His hand trails back over my belly and to the waistband of my leggings. He slides his hand beneath the fabric and over my panties, also cotton, unsexy, and completely soaked. "Is this for me?" he asks.

"You know it is."

"Is this where you want me to touch you?"

"Yes. Please," I murmur.

He moves to slide his hand beneath my panties, and this time he's the one sucking in a breath. "So warm and wet for me, Mags." He flutters his fingers over my clit before diving in blindly to explore more of me. "Are you going to come for me, Maggie?"

"I hope so," I taunt, and he laughs under his breath.

"My mouth's watering," he whispers. He removes his hand, and I hear him smacking his lips as he sucks on his fingers.

"Lachlan!" I was close. I *am* close.

"I'm sorry. I had to taste you." He moves his hand back to my pussy and slides one finger inside me while the palm of his hand moves over my clit. "Is this what you need? Is that better?"

"Yes," I moan.

His lips capture mine as his fingers work their magic to build the glorious pleasure between my thighs. I arch into him. So close. I'm so close to falling, but I need something. He adds another finger, and I moan like a porn star.

"There it is," he whispers. "That's what you need. More of me. Your pussy is squeezing my fingers. You're close, baby. I can feel it. Come for me."

"Lachlan!" I call out his name as my release barrels into me. He doesn't stop until I've slumped back into the mattress.

He removes his hand, and I hear his lips smacking once again. "You're my favorite treat," he tells me, and I can't help it. I laugh.

"What am I going to do with you?" I ask him. I feel relaxed and sated, and happy. Happy to be here with him.

"Keep me?"

Is that hope I hear in his tone? "At least for eighteen years," I tell him.

"A lifetime, Maggie. You're stuck with me for a lifetime." He kisses me again, only this time it's a soft press of his lips to mine. "Come on. Let's get you cleaned up so I can feed you." He rolls out of bed, and there's just enough light that I can make out his silhouette holding his hand out for me, but not before I see him adjust his crotch.

"What about you?"

"I'll be fine, Mags. This was for you."

"That could be for me too," I challenge him.

"Let's feed you, and then we'll see how you're feeling."

I'm ready to argue when my belly growls. "Fine," I grumble. Placing my hand in his, I allow him to help me from the bed.

"Go get cleaned up. I'll meet you in the kitchen." His lips connect with mine briefly, and then he's gone.

In the bathroom, I turn on the light and stare at my reflection in the mirror. My hair is a hot mess, and my cheeks are flushed, but it's my smile that gives me pause.

Have I ever been this happy?

He's not even mine, and the man has me smiling like a kid in a candy store. How would it feel if this were real? I know it's real. This baby is real, and my feelings for him are real, but how would I feel? How happy would I be if I really could call him mine?

LACHLAN 12

M Y PALMS ARE SWEATING. I'VE wiped them on my jeans at
least a dozen times, and they still feel clammy. I'm ready
to stand and pace this damn waiting room, but I remain seated
next to Maggie. Outside of wringing her hands together in her
lap, she appears to be calm, cool, and collected.

"I'm freaking out too," she tells me when she catches me
staring. "We get to see our baby today. We get to find out if we're
going to have a son or daughter." Her face lights up.

She's glowing, and I want nothing more than to kiss her, and
I'm considering it when the nurse opens the door to the back
office and calls her name.

We stop at the scale, and I turn my head. I don't give a fuck
what the number says, but I know Maggie is self-conscious
because of the dickwad she dated before, so I do the honorable
thing and don't look.

"We're going to take you to the ultrasound tech first, and then
you'll switch rooms to see the doctor," the nurse explains. She leads
us farther down the hall and to the right to another long hallway.
"Take a seat on the exam table. Sandra will be right with you."

I help Maggie up onto the table, not that she needs my help at this stage of her pregnancy, but it gives me a reason to get my hands on her, and that's something I will never pass up.

Bending, I press my lips to her forehead just as the door opens. I step back and wait for the ultrasound tech to enter.

"Hi, I'm Sandra." She offers her hand to Maggie.

"Maggie, and this is Lachlan." She nods toward me. I also shake Sandra's hand.

"Are you ready to see your baby?" Sandra asks.

"We are," we say together as we share a smile.

Sandra dims the lights and moves toward the exam table. "Can you lift your shirt for me, Maggie?" she asks, typing on the screen.

Maggie does as she asks, and I grin as she bares her baby bump. There is a tiny piece of us that's growing inside her, and that's the coolest fucking thing that's ever happened to me. To get to witness her body grow and change for our baby, it's truly a miracle.

"I'm going to use some gel. It's warm, but I still like to warn you." Sandra squirts gel all over Maggie's belly, and I move in closer, not wanting to miss a single second of what's to come.

She moves the wand all around, and the screen is still facing her. "I'm just going to get some measurements for the doctor." Sandra works quietly and efficiently while I stand next to the exam table with bated breath, waiting to see my son or daughter.

"All right, all the technical stuff is out of the way. Your baby is very active. Do we want to know the gender today?"

"Yes," we answer together, making Sandra laugh.

"Well, you're in luck because this little guy wants to be seen." She points to the screen. "Right there. Congratulations, Mom and Dad, you're having a boy."

A boy.

A son.

Tears well in my eyes as I let that news sink in. I reach for Maggie's hand and my knees hit the bed. When I look down, I find her smiling up at me with tears in her eyes. She's fucking stunning, and I have to kiss her.

I have to.

Bending my head, I press my lips to hers. "Thank you."

She laughs through her tears. "Why are you thanking me?"

"For our son. For being my favorite human. I have an entire list if you want me to keep going." I kiss her one more time, then move my forehead to hers. "A boy, Mags. We're having a boy."

"We are."

I take a minute to get my composure before standing and nodding to Sandra. She's smiling at us before she turns her attention back to the screen. She points out arms, hands, legs, his heart, and I'm overwhelmed with love for this tiny little man I've never met before.

I focus on everything Sandra is saying, and when she's done, she hands me some towels and I help Maggie wipe up her belly.

"This is for you." Sandra hands me a strip of images. "Baby boy's first pictures." She smiles.

"Thank you, Sandra." I hold the strip up to show Maggie, and tears form in her eyes again.

"I'll take you to your next room to see Dr. Holmes."

I lift Maggie from the exam table and crush her in a hug. My chest feels tight, like it could burst at any moment, for the love I have for my child and his momma. I freeze and step back, staring down at her.

"You okay?" she asks, her hand resting against my cheek.

I place my hand over hers and smile. "Perfect, Momma. Come on. Let's go see the doctor." I take her hand in mine, lead her out of the room, and follow Sandra to the next exam room, where Dr. Holmes will check over her to make sure everything is going great.

Meanwhile, I'll be sitting there in the chair, watching, listening, and wondering how in the hell I'm going to tell the mother of my child that I've fallen in love with her.

"Want to swing by my new place? We can pick up something to take back there and eat," I ask Maggie once we're in the truck after her appointment.

"Yes. I'd love to see it again. How was the closing?"

"Good. I wish you could have gone with me, but I know how dedicated you are to your job."

"I took a half day. I have paid maternity leave, but I feel bad that I'll be leaving them short while I'm off."

"They'll miss you, but they'll manage. They did fine when Emerson was off after having Lilly."

"I know, but that's just me, you know? I don't like to be a burden to others, even my coworkers."

"You're not a burden, Mags. You're having a baby. It's not like you're missing weeks of work to go backpacking across the world and leaving them high and dry." I laugh.

"You're right."

I want to tell her that I'm always right but think better of it. Instead, I pluck the key I made her after the closing this morning from the cupholder and hand it to her. "This is for you."

"What's this?" she asks.

"That's your key to my new place. I didn't have one made to the old one because I knew that I was moving."

"Is there a reason you're giving me a key to your new house?"

"You're the mother of my son."

Maggie chuckles. "That's your reason."

"Yeah. What if you need me or need to come in and I'm not home? What if our little man needs something at my place, and I'm not there?"

"Then we wait for you to get there."

"No. I want you and our son to have full access to me at all times."

"Lachlan, that might be nice right now, but what happens when you meet someone? When you move her in?"

"I won't." My voice is clipped. The thought of any other woman in my world besides her makes me ill.

It's Maggie.

She's my family. Her and our son.

If I thought she was ready to hear it, to accept it, I'd tell her, but we're not there yet.

"Just keep it, Maggie."

"Okay," she quietly agrees and slips the key into her purse. "A juicy cheeseburger," she says.

"What?"

"I want a big juicy cheeseburger, some onion rings, and a chocolate shake."

"You hate onions," I remind her.

She shrugs. "Order me fries, too, then, just in case I change my mind, but the breading on the onion rings sounds so good right now. I love the breading. Not the onion."

"You got it." I drive to the nearest fast-food joint and order our food.

"You got four orders of onion rings, and two fries. I can't eat all that."

"Well, one order of fries and a burger is for me. The second order of fries is yours just in case, and if you only plan to eat the breading, you're going to need more than one order."

"I can't eat all of that. I know I'm eating for two, but not that much," she rushes to explain.

"Then you don't eat it. We'll toss it or take them home and put them in the air fryer to warm them up later. I just want to make sure you get enough to eat."

"And you're worried about your mom spoiling him." She laughs, rubbing her belly. "Your daddy is going to take the prize on that one, huh, little man?"

That tightness in my chest is back. I'm beginning to think it's a feeling that will always be there as long as Maggie is in my life.

Once we have our food, I head off to my new place. I help Maggie out of the truck, then grab our food and drinks while she uses her new key to let us inside. "Shit, we don't have chairs. I didn't think this through." I set the bag and our drinks on the counter, then turn to face her. "Come here."

She does as I ask. I grip her hips and lift her to sit on the island. "There, at least you can sit and enjoy your meal. I'm sorry I didn't think about having somewhere to eat."

"We could have just sat on the floor," she tells me with a shrug.

"No. I'm not letting my—the mother of my child eat dinner on the hard floor."

"So moody," she teases.

I reach into the bag and hand her a burger and a napkin before setting out the onion rings and fries for her to reach, then I dig into my own meal. "I should have asked the guys to meet me after closing and I could have at least moved my bed here so we could stay here tonight."

"You mean you."

"No, I mean *we*. It's my first night here. You have to be here for that." What I don't say is that she has to be here for every night from tonight on.

"Are you afraid to be in this big ole house all alone?" she teases.

"No, I just like my bed better when you're in it." I lean over and kiss the corner of her mouth. "Eat your dinner. Our boy is growing." I wink and take my own advice and go back to my own dinner.

"So, how do you want to tell people that we're having a boy?"

"Can I not just scream it from the rooftops?"

This makes her smile. "You can, but we can also think of a cool way to tell everyone."

"How about we have our friends over here tomorrow night? Legend and Maddox are coming to help me start moving a few things. Roman and Forrest are at the shop until five, I think. We can have food, and maybe lawn chairs for enough seating, and we can tell them then."

"I like that plan. How about my grandma and your parents?"

"Um, we tell them first, obviously. Why don't we tell them tonight? Can we take them cupcakes with blue icing or something?"

"Pastry Heaven is already closed for the day, but we can stop at the grocery store and find something. Maybe a small gift bag with some blue fabric, or blue baby clothes or something."

"I'm in. Eat up, and we'll stop at Grandma Doris's first since she goes to bed earlier. Then we'll go to my parents'."

She peels some of the breading off an onion ring and pops it into her mouth. "We need to start thinking about names too."

"I have some ideas. Well, one really."

"Really?" Her eyes light up.

"Yeah, I was thinking we could name him after our dads. Yours in honor of him, and mine for the man he taught me to be, and the dad he taught me to be when he didn't have to be. Sean Alan Noble or Alan Sean Noble. Sean for your dad and Alan for mine's middle name."

Her bottom lip quivers, and tears race unchecked down her cheeks. "I love that, Lachlan. Either or both, I don't care, but I love that so much. Thank you."

"We'll let it simmer and decide. I kind of like Sean Alan better, but I'm easy."

She nods. "Sean Alan Noble." She looks down at her belly. "Mommy and Daddy love you so much, baby Sean."

"Did we just name our son, Mags?"

She nods. "Yeah, we did."

I move to stand between her legs and gently cradle her cheeks, wiping at her tears. "I—My heart is so damn full, Maggie."

"Mine too, Lachlan. Mine too."

I kiss her softly, knowing that my entire world is right here in this room with me.

"Oh, heavens, what are you two doing here?" Grandma Doris asks. She's in her recliner, with the TV on low and what looks like a hot cup of tea in her hands.

"We brought you something," Maggie tells her.

"You did?" Her eyes light up with surprise. "I have everything I need," she tells us.

"Well, you don't have this." I hand her the small white gift bag. "Open it." I step back and stand next to Maggie, wrapping my arm around her waist while we watch.

Doris pulls the small tissue-wrapped frame out of the bag and slowly unwraps it. "Is this the baby? Oh, goodness, look at that." She runs her fingers over the frame. "Wait, the frame is blue. You're having a boy?" she asks.

"We're having a boy," Maggie confirms.

"Oh, sweetheart." Grandma Doris goes to stand, and I rush to help her. She pulls me into a hug and waves for Maggie to join us. The three of us stand in a small circle, celebrating the life of our son.

"We have a name," Maggie says, pulling back.

"Tell me." Grandma Doris smiles.

"Sean Alan. After Dad, and Lachlan's dad."

"Oh, my." Grandma Doris places her hand over her mouth and tears well in her eyes. "He'd be so proud of you, Maggie. They both would be. He's smiling down on you right now." She wipes at her tears, then looks at me. "Lachlan, thank you for taking care of our girl, and that little one, the way you do. I know in my soul that my son and my daughter-in-law would have loved you. I'm so happy for both of you."

I swallow back the lump in my throat. "Thank you, Doris."

"That's Grandma to you, young man, and soon-to-be great-grandma!" she exclaims.

We spend another half hour with her before we say our goodbyes and head to my parents' place.

"What ya got there?" Dad asks, watching as I set the white gift bag on the floor next to where Maggie and I just took a seat on the couch.

"Just a little something we picked up for the two of you."

"Rodney, we don't care about what's in the bag," Mom scolds playfully. "You had your ultrasound today. I've been dying for your call. I was giving you time together, but I really want to know if we're having a boy or a girl."

"We did find out if we're having a boy or a girl," I say, placing my arm around Maggie's shoulders and pulling her close.

"Yeah, yeah." Mom waves me off. "Tell me. I can't take it. Wait, you are going to tell us, right? You're not going to make us wait?"

"We're going to tell you. In fact, the answer you've been seeking is right here." I bend for the bag and hold it up for her. Mom leans over from the loveseat, grabs the bag, and turns to my dad and grins.

"Are you ready for this?" she asks him.

"You know it. Open it, woman. You've been dying to know all day, and now that the answer is literally in your hands, you're stalling." He chuckles.

"Okay." Mom flashes us a smile as she reaches into the bag and pulls out the tissue-wrapped blue frame, just like the one we gave Doris, with a sonogram picture inside. Slowly, she unwraps the frame, and stares down at the picture. "Oh my goodness," she breathes.

"A boy!" Dad cheers.

"Wait, how did you—?"

"The blue frame, Amanda." Dad laughs.

Mom tosses her head back in laughter. "I was so focused on the picture, I didn't even register the color of the frame. A boy!" Mom hands the frame to Dad so he can get a good look, and then both stand and pass out a round of hugs.

"Congratulations, you two," Dad announces.

"Thank you," Maggie tells them.

"Maggie, we need to plan another shopping trip," Mom tells her. "Oh, this is going to be so much fun."

"We will definitely have to do that," Maggie agrees. "We decided on a name," she tells them.

"You did? Do we get to know or is that a surprise?"

Maggie looks over at me and nods. "Sean for the first name. That was Maggie's father's name," I tell them.

"Perfect." Mom bobs her head.

"Alan, for the middle name." That one doesn't need an explanation. I watch my dad as he swallows hard and blinks back tears. Alan is his middle name. "After the man who was the father he didn't have to be. Who taught me how to love freely and showed me how to be a good dad."

Dad stands, and so do I. I meet him in the middle of the room as he pulls me into a crushing hug. "I love you, son. I'm so damn proud of you."

"I love you, too, Dad."

He steps back and clears his throat. "Ladies, why are our arms empty?" he asks.

Maggie giggles while she and my mom join us in the middle of the room. Dad pulls Mom into his chest, and I do the same with Maggie. She wraps her arms around my waist, and I kiss the crown of her head.

I love you.

I want more than anything to say those words, and I will soon. We spend an hour with my parents just visiting before we say our goodbyes.

"My place or yours?" I ask Maggie.

"It's getting late."

"I know, babe. Where are we sleeping? My old place or yours?"

I'm waiting for her to tell me we need to sleep at our own places and I have my argument ready, but it never comes.

"I don't care as long as we're together."

Reaching over the console, I twine our fingers, and bring her hand to my lips for a kiss before resting our joined hands on her thigh. I point the truck toward my place because it's closer, and all I want right now more than anything is to hold my girl, and our son.

MAGGIE 13

I DON'T KNOW WHAT I expected to happen last night, but it wasn't that we would come back to his place and sleep. *Just* sleep. Lachlan held me in his arms all night long, and this morning he made me breakfast. The lines are blurred, and I, for one, am okay with that. We haven't really spoken about how things are changing between us, but it's there.

"The guys will be here soon," he tells me as we finish cleaning the kitchen.

"Oh, so you should probably take me home," I tell him.

"Why would I take you home?"

"Do you want them to know that I spent the night?" I hold my breath, waiting for his answer.

"Do you *not* want them to know that you spent the night?" he volleys back to me.

I don't have to think about my answer. "I don't care if they know."

He nods. "Good."

"I'm still in yesterday's clothes," I remind him.

"They didn't see you, and we're just going to be packing, anyway. You're not going to be doing much because you're carrying precious cargo," he tells me.

My belly flips and I gasp, because it wasn't my belly and his words that was the reason. It was the baby. "Oh my god, Lachlan!" I say excitedly as tears spring to my eyes. My hands go to my belly as I try to feel from the outside too.

"What?" He's next to me in an instant, his eyes full of concern and panic. "Are you hurt? Is it the baby? Talk to me, Mags." His voice quivers.

"I felt him. I felt the baby move."

"What?" The panic and concern are gone and replaced with wonder. "You felt him?"

I nod, smiling. I take his hands, place them on my belly, and we wait. "There. Did you feel that?"

"No," he says. He leans down and presses a kiss to my stomach. "Sean, it's Daddy, you need to take it easy on your momma in there," he tells our son. He glances up at me. "The book I read said that he can hear me. That babies can recognize voices when they're born."

"I read that too," I tell him.

"I can't wait to meet you," he tells my belly again. When he looks up, his blue eyes are blazing. I lean down and kiss him. This moment, it's so special and I'm glad I was here with him when it happened.

"If I keep kissing you, I'm never going to get moved," he murmurs against my lips.

"What's another week?" I ask, going in for another kiss. This is something we do freely now. We kiss all the time, and it's getting harder and harder to hide my true feelings for him.

"I want to be there and be settled." He nips at my bottom lip before standing.

"Fine. Where do we start?" I ask.

"Well, I was hoping you could help me pack, but you're not allowed to lift a finger. I'll have boxes made up for you and you can just add things to them. When they're full, let me know and I'll move it out of the way and get you another one."

"Yes, sir." I salute him.

"Mags." His tone is warning, and I smile cheekily.

"Lachlan?"

He points his index finger at me as he takes a few steps back. "You, my beautiful girl, are trouble." He winks, then turns to head to the garage to grab boxes he's been collecting since his offer was accepted on the house. I dry the dishes he just washed and lay them out on the counter to pack.

"What are those boxes?" I point to the corner of the living room when he's back in the house.

"On the nights I couldn't sleep, I started packing. Mostly dishes. I only kept out what I thought I might need."

I start opening cabinets, and sure enough, most of them are bare. "Wow, you've got a nice head start."

"I do. I think we might be able to get this all done today."

"Today?" My eyes widen.

"Yeah, I'm donating most of the furniture. The new stuff we picked out is being delivered today."

"How are they going to get in?"

"I have to meet them there at noon."

"Why don't you take me home so I can shower and get dressed, and I can go over and wait for them? Maybe you can bring those." I point to the boxes in the corner of the living room. "I can start unpacking for you."

"I don't want you lifting."

"I won't be. You can spread the boxes out on the floor, so I can access each one, and I'll unpack slowly, I promise. Let me help you."

He studies me for a minute, and I know he's going to tell me no. Reaching for my cell phone that's on the counter, I hit Brogan's contact, putting the call on speaker.

"Hey, you," Brogan answers.

"Hey. What are you doing today?" I ask her.

"Nothing much. Maddox is getting ready to head over to Lachlan's to help him start moving."

"Yeah, I'm here now. Listen, how would you feel about babysitting me today?"

"What?" she asks, laughing. "You need a babysitter?"

"Kind of. I want to start helping Lachlan unpack, but he's worried I'll lift something or that something will happen if I'm by myself."

"Oh, that tracks," she says. "If he's anything like his friends, he's got you up on a pedestal."

"I'm pregnant, not eighty," I say, irritated. I think he'd keep me wrapped in a bubble if he could.

"Yeah, but my guess is that you and that baby are his entire world. I can't imagine him being any different from the others. Maddox, I'm sure, will be the same way."

Lachlan steps around me and wraps his arms around my waist, pulling my back to his chest. He buries his face in my neck.

"Yeah," I agree. My heart skips a beat as I accept the easy comfort that he so freely offers.

"What time are we doing this?" Brogan asks.

"How about I swing by and pick you up in about an hour? I need to head home to shower."

"Oh, *really*?" she says.

"Yep." I hold back my smirk, knowing there's going to be an inquisition. "I'll see you soon."

"See you soon," she agrees, and I end the call.

Placing my phone back on the counter, I turn in his arms. "There, I won't be alone."

"Good." He kisses the corner of my mouth. "You and our baby are everything, Maggie. I know it seems over the top, but I can't help it where the two of you are concerned."

"It's nice to know I have someone looking out for me." It's nice to know that he cares as much as he does, and I know it's not just for the baby. He's proven that time and time again. "Now, take me now so you can get back here and get to work."

"Yes, ma'am." He laughs, releasing me, only to grab my hand as we lock up his place, and he takes me to mine.

"We made quick work of that," I tell Brogan as she breaks down the last box.

"We did. Now, what are we going to do?" The furniture delivery arrived right on time, and all set up, and these boxes are unpacked.

I glance down at my watch. "That only took us a little over an hour. I don't expect the guys to be here for a while yet. Why don't we run to the store, and I can stock his fridge, so that's one less thing he has to worry about."

"Oh, good idea."

"I also want to make something for tonight."

"Perfect. I know Lachlan said we could just order pizza, but I think some snacks, like dips would be nice too."

"Agreed." Grabbing my phone, I fire off a text to Lachlan.

> **Me:** We finished unpacking. We're going to run to the store just in case you get here before we get back.
>
> **Lachlan:** Thanks for doing that. Be safe.
>
> **Me:** Will do.

"Ready?" I ask Brogan.

"Yep." Making sure I have my key on my key ring, I lock the door, and we head to town.

"How was your appointment yesterday?" Brogan asks once we're in the car.

"Good."

"Just good?"

"Great," I admit. "We found out what we're having. We're going to tell everyone tonight."

"Ah, so that's the rush to have everyone over to the new place."

"I think it's a part of it. He's also really excited to be able to host everyone."

"Well?"

"I can't tell you. You'll have to wait until tonight."

"Boo." She laughs. "I get it. I think it's... I don't know." She shrugs.

"I felt the baby move this morning," I tell her, changing the subject.

"Really? Was it incredible?"

"Yes. I wish Lachlan could have felt it, but at least he was there for the moment."

"Won't be long, and he'll be able to."

"How are things with you all?" I ask her. "Still trying?"

"Yeah, and I'm late."

"What? Really?" I glance over at her before turning my eyes back to the road.

"Yeah, just a couple of days. Three to be exact. I haven't taken a test yet because I don't want to be disappointed."

"I understand that. I bought ten and took five of them. After all five came back positive, I stopped and made an appointment with my ob-gyn."

"Maybe I'll take one and not tell Maddox yet. He wants this so much. I hate to disappoint him."

"No, Brogan, you could never be a disappointment to him. He loves you, baby or no baby."

"I know. I guess I really want it too. He's given me so much, and I just want to give him everything he's ever dreamed of."

"He has that. A baby would just be icing on the cake." My heart goes out to her. I know how badly they both want this. I know they'll have a family of their own one day. It couldn't happen to a better couple.

"Thanks, Maggie."

When we get back to the house, Legend's, Maddox's, and Lachlan's trucks are all in the driveway. My car is barely in Park before the three of them appear and start carrying in bags.

"Gotta admit, it's nice to not have to lug all of that in," Brogan says.

"I'd have to agree." By the time we make it inside, they're already unloading all the groceries and laying them on the counter. "I can put those away. Go back to whatever you were doing," I tell the guys.

"We're taking a break. We have all three trucks unloaded. All that's left is the furniture to donate, and I have a company coming Monday to pick it up."

"I think I had them put all the new stuff where you wanted it," I tell him. "You might want to make sure before the guys leave."

"It's perfect, and they'll be back."

"I'm going to head home and shower. We'll be back at seven, right?" Legend asks.

"Yeah, that'll give Roman and Forrest time to get home and chill a little before heading over. Thanks for your help."

"Sounds good, and anytime. See you in a little while." Legend waves and walks out the front door.

"Mags, I think we're a little past these," Lachlan says.

I turn to see what he's talking about and see the pregnancy test I tossed in the cart for Brogan, just in case.

"It doesn't hurt to have one on hand," I say, my face heating. I don't want to out my friend in front of her husband.

"Is that for me?" Brogan asks quietly.

I nod.

"For you?" Maddox asks.

"I'm late," Brogan blurts.

"Late," Maddox repeats. "So, what do we do?" he asks. His eyes are full of hope, and his voice wavers.

"I have to pee on that stick Lachlan is holding. I'm sure it's nothing. Just stress."

"It might be something, and it might be nothing. Either way, I'm going to be right next to you when you find out." He takes the test from Lachlan's hand and slides his arm around Brogan's waist. "We'll see you guys later. Maggie, thanks for this." He holds up the pregnancy test as they head toward the door.

"I hope she's not mad at me," I say, worrying my bottom lip.

"She's not mad. She's the one who spoke up. That was a good thing you did for her."

"She's my friend. They both want this so badly."

"It will happen for them. Who knows, maybe they'll be announcing some news tonight like we are. Speaking of news, I called Pastry Heaven and had them make us cupcakes with a blue center. She worked me in, thankfully. They have white icing with blue and pink sprinkles, and I got white cake and chocolate."

"Really? I love that. The kids are going to love it too."

"Won't be long, and our son will be a part of that group."

His words fill me with joy, excitement, and most of all, love. For him and for our son.

"It will be here before we know it," he adds.

I smile. "Thank you for all of this. I'll give you some money."

"You're welcome, and no, you won't. You take such good care of us," he says, rubbing my belly. "I wanted to do this for you."

I look into his eyes willing him to understand how much all of his support means to me.

"Fine, I'll pay you like this." He steps forward, wraps his arms around my waist, and kisses me. Just as with every kiss and every touch, fire ignites between us. Lachlan lifts me to sit on the counter, knocking over some of the food in the process, but he doesn't stop kissing me. His palms rest against my cheeks, my legs wrap around his waist, and we're as close as we can get with my belly between us. He takes his time, tasting me, and I let him because I crave his kisses, crave his touch.

"Thank you, Mags." He slows the kiss, then rests his forehead against mine.

"You're welcome." He runs his hands up and down my back, before finally pulling away. I miss the heat of his body next to mine and his touch instantly.

"Let's put this stuff away. I'll then run out and get the cupcakes, and we're going to try out that new mattress and bed. We're taking a nap."

Maybe we can test the bed out for something other than napping? I don't say that though. Instead, I go with light and teasing to hide my desire for him—there's no time for that right now. "You tired, old man?" I grin. He's only nine years older than me, so he's far from an old man, but I still tease him about it. Our age has never come up. We're just Maggie and Lachlan, and I wouldn't have it any other way. I don't notice the years between us. Some might think that's too old, but I don't notice the age gap when we're together. It's just a number on a piece of paper.

"Not tired, but I know you are." As if his words give my body permission, I yawn.

"A short nap would be nice," I confess.

"You don't have to tell me, but did you take the test?" I ask Brogan, keeping my voice low so no one can overhear us.

"I did." Her blinding smile tells me what her words don't. "We don't want to ruin your surprise."

"Never. If you're ready to tell everyone, tell them. This baby is a blessing," I tell her.

"I know you're supposed to wait until you're out of your first trimester, but I don't know if Maddox can keep it quiet that long."

"Then don't. Announce it tonight. We're all here."

"I don't want to take away from you and Lachlan."

"We're family," I tell her. "You could never take away. Only enhance."

"Enhance what?" Maddox asks.

"Our lives." I smile at him.

"She figured it out," Brogan tells him.

"We're not going to say anything tonight, promise." Maddox holds up his hand.

"I want you to. You're family, and we're all here to celebrate new life. Your baby is a part of that."

"No wonder Lachlan is so smitten," Maddox teases.

"Smitten?" I laugh.

"Who's smitten?" Lachlan asks, joining the conversation.

"You are," Maddox tells him.

"Oh, that's not new news," he says, kissing my cheek. "Ready, Mags?"

"Sure, if you are?"

"I've been ready." He turns to the room and calls, "Time for dessert!"

The kids cheer, and everyone else just laughs. They're all used to Lachlan and his sweet tooth.

"For real, I need everyone in the kitchen. You're not going to want to miss this." He's got my hand in his, tugging me toward the kitchen as he speaks.

"Uncle Lachlan, we love the dessert," Rayne tells him.

"Of course you do. You're a very smart girl."

"Me too," River says.

"Yes, you too."

"Me." Lilly raises her hand.

"All of you. Geniuses, I tell you." Lachlan bops Lilly on the nose as we pass by Roman, where she's sitting on her dad's hip. "All right, here's the deal. Everyone gets a cupcake." He nods toward the box on the table. "Everyone has to bite into them at the same time."

"Hold up!" Emerson raises her hand in the air. "You had a doctor's appointment yesterday. Did you find out what you're having?"

"We did," Lachlan says proudly. "And you all are about to find out as soon as you take a bite of your cupcakes."

My friends squeal in delight, as do the kids. The guys are grinning and reaching for their cupcakes, just as Lachlan told them to.

"On the count of three. One. Two. Three!" he cheers.

Everyone starts calling out, "Boy!" and their congratulations. I smile up at him. "I think this is the first time I've seen sweets in your presence that you didn't have one."

"I'm too excited," he says, pressing his lips to my temple.

"One more thing," Lachlan says, holding up his hand. "We also have a name. Maggie's dad's first name and my dad's middle name. Sean Alan Noble."

Hugs and pats on the back start up, and my gaze catches Brogan's. She looks up at Maddox and the smile that lights up his face is one I see every time Lachlan looks at me. I know he cares about me, but could it be more? Could he be falling just as hard as I am?

"Also," Maddox speaks up, "with Laggie's permission."

I choke on the water I was drinking. "Laggie?" I sputter with laughter.

"Work with me here, Maggie." Maddox smirks. "As I was saying. With Laggie's permission, my wife and I would like to tell you all that we're also having a baby."

The room erupts in cheers and more hugs and smiles, and I know that this is going to be my future. These people, they're the best I've ever known. We celebrate our wins and our losses together. As a family.

My son is going to grow up with aunts and uncles, not by blood, but by love, and that makes my heart happy.

LACHLAN 14

A S SOON AS I'M THROUGH the front door, I kick off my shoes and pull my phone out of my pocket to video call Maggie.

"Hey, you," she answers.

"Hi." I sigh because it's been a long-ass day. "How are you feeling? How's our boy?" I make my way to the kitchen and pull open the fridge, looking for what I'm going to eat for dinner tonight.

"We're both good. He's really active tonight."

"I can't wait until I can feel him. That's a good thing he's been active, but I hope he's taking it easy on you. Have you had dinner?" I ask.

"Yeah, I heated up a can of tomato soup and made a grilled cheese. What about you?"

"Just getting home. My last client changed his mind on his design, so I had to make some modifications before I could make the stencil, and we both decided to just stay late tonight and knock it all out so he doesn't have to wait for it to heal and come back for the rest."

"Long day," she muses.

"Very long day." I grab the left-over Chinese we had Sunday when she was here. That was three days ago. It's still good, right? "This is still good, right?" I ask her what I'm thinking as I hold the box up so that she can see it.

"Yes, it's fine, as long as it's been in the refrigerator."

"Perfect." Propping the phone up on the paper towel holder, I pour the contents onto a plate and pop it into the microwave.

"How was the surgery today with the new doctor?" I ask her. She's been nervous about the new surgeon starting. Some of them can be real pretentious assholes. Her words not mine.

"Good, actually. He was really nice."

"Not too nice, I hope."

Her laughter fills the air around me from the small speaker of my phone, and I'm half tempted to drive to her place just to see her in the flesh.

"Not too nice. Besides, what man is going to hit on a woman who's big and pregnant?" She chuckles.

"First of all, you're a fucking knockout, Mags. And you're not big. You're all belly. Isn't that what Mom said? Hell, I was behind you the other day in the store and couldn't even tell you were pregnant from the back."

"Other than my waddle, you mean." She smiles.

"You don't waddle."

"I'm sure that time is coming."

I watch through my phone's screen as she stares down at her belly affectionately while rubbing over where our son is growing.

"Worth it though," she says, looking up and finding my gaze through the screen.

The microwave beeps, so I grab my phone, tuck my bottle of sweet tea under my arm, and retrieve it before sitting down at the dining room table, propping my phone up so I can still see her while I eat. "Do you want more kids?" I ask her, taking a bite.

"Yeah. As an only child, I always wanted at least two children, if not more. What about you? Do you plan on giving Sean a brother or sister someday?" she asks.

Not unless I do it with you. "Yeah, I could get behind that." I finish off my meal, while Maggie tells me Grandma Doris called and is knitting Sean a blanket.

"That's really sweet of her."

"It is. I love that I'll have something from her to hand down to him when he's older, maybe when he has kids."

"Hold up, woman. Don't go making us grandparents just yet."

"They say it flies by, Lachlan."

"I'm sure it does, but we're going to soak up every minute," I tell her as she stands and moves around her house.

"You getting ready for bed?" I ask.

"No. Don't judge me, but I want some peanut M&M's. I've been craving them all day and trying to be good, but I need my fix." She laughs.

"Me? Judge a sweet fix? Babe, did you forget who you're talking to?" I tease.

"Damn, I'm out." I hear bags crinkling. "I knew I forgot something at the store." Her expression falls. "Oh, well, I didn't need the extra calories anyway." She closes the pantry door and moves back to the couch.

"I should go so I can grab a shower."

"Sure. Get some rest."

"I'll call you before I go to bed," I tell her.

"You don't have to do that. You've had a long day."

"I want to hear your voice before I go to sleep."

She smiles. "Okay. Talk soon." She waves at the camera and ends the call.

Rushing to my room, I pull out a duffel bag and toss in some clothes for tomorrow, as well as everything else I'll need to shower at her place. Once I've locked up the house, I head to town. My first stop is the gas station. My girl needs her fix.

Twenty minutes later, I'm pulling into her driveway with two of the sharing size bags of peanut M&M's. I don't take my duffel in case she doesn't invite me to stay. Instead, I leave it on the back seat and march up to her door with the treat I bought for her. I don't want to knock and scare her since it's getting late, so instead, I text her.

Me: *Open your front door.*

Maggie: *What?*

Me: *I'm here. Can you let me in?*

Maggie: *I gave you a key.*

Me: *I know, but you didn't know I was coming, and it's not an emergency.*

Maggie: *Come in, Lachlan. I'm changing for bed. I'll be right out.*

Me: *I'll come help you.*

Maggie: *LOL. Be right there.*

Shoving my hand into my pocket, I pull out my keys and unlock her door, just as she comes striding into the living room, wearing my shirt and what appears to be nothing else. My feet carry me to where she's standing just behind the couch. I immediately caress her cheek. "You're beautiful." She blushes and tilts her head to the side against my hand.

"Is everything okay?" she asks, placing her hand over mine that's still resting against her cheek.

"I brought you something."

"At nine o'clock at night?"

I hold up the plastic bag from the gas station. "You were craving peanut M&M's."

"Lachlan."

"Come sit with me." Dropping my hand from her face, I lace our fingers together and lead her to the couch. I plop down and gently pull her onto my lap.

"What are you doing?"

"Holding you. Here." I hand her the bag so that both of my arms are free to wrap around them. "Hey, buddy," I greet my son. "Daddy loves you."

"He's moving," she says. She adjusts my hand to where she feels him, but I feel nothing. "Soon," she assures me.

"Soon," I agree. "This was really sweet of you." I turn so that I'm sitting sideways with my legs resting on the couch. "I hate that you came out so late just to buy these for me."

"Maggie, there isn't anything I wouldn't do for you."

"It feels like we're shifting," she tells me.

"Shifting how?"

"I don't know. Like I'm more than just the one-night stand you got pregnant."

"You've always been more."

"More than just the mother of your child?"

"Definitely."

"This is going to make me sound needy, but can you spell it out for me? What are we doing, Lachlan? Lines are blurred, and my heart's starting to take notice."

"Good. My heart took notice a long damn time ago. I've been waiting for you to catch up to where I am."

"And where is that?"

"I think about you all the time. Not just because of the baby. I hate sleeping at night without you next to me. So much so, that I have to call you every night before I go to sleep just to hear your voice. Earlier, you asked me if I wanted more kids, and my first thought was only if it was with you. That's where I'm at."

I want to say more, but I know how her mind works. She needs to process my words and how she feels about them. That asshole she was with before would tell her things just to bend her to his will. I'm not like that. I know she doesn't think that I am, but those scars are still there, so she needs time to sort out her feelings. And that's fine, because I'm not going anywhere.

"You look exhausted." She's changing the subject, and that's fine. I know that's what she needs right now. We'll get there. I know we will.

"I am."

"You should stay here tonight," she offers, just like I hoped that she would.

"Eat your snack so we can go to bed," I answer with a smile.

She chuckles, tears open a bag of her sweet treat, and pops a few into her mouth. "Want one?" she asks, placing her hand over her mouth as she speaks.

"Do fish live in water? Yes, I want one." I open my mouth, and she drops two in, and I chew.

"It's impossible to eat just a couple." She holds two more up to my lips, and I open for her.

"Agreed." She shares a few more with me as we sit quietly, just enjoying the fact that we're together, not needing to fill the silence with chatter.

"Okay, I can't eat any more. He's going to be bouncing around all night, and I won't get any sleep, but it was worth it."

"Let's go to bed."

She climbs off my lap, and goes around, turning off all the lights, and double-checks that the door is locked, and together, we make our way to her room.

She slides under the covers while I strip down to my underwear and take my spot next to her. She cuddles up to my side, and I wrap my arm around her, and within minutes, I'm drifting off to sleep.

"He takes after his uncle Lachlan," I say as I stand with Roman, Forrest, and Maddox, watching Kane smash through his own personal little birthday cake. He's shoveling it in by the handfuls.

"Looks like it." Roman laughs. "Remember when Lilly turned one? She didn't want to touch it, but once she did, it was game on. She had cake everywhere."

"She did," Forrest agrees. "I think Legend is wearing just as much of that cake as Kane is." He chuckles.

We bullshit for a little longer, and eventually, Legend joins us. "I can't believe he's a year old already," he says, smiling widely.

"Won't be long, and Lachlan and I will be a part of the dad's club." Maddox grins.

"Best thing ever," Forrest tells us.

"I'd have to agree," Roman says.

"How are things with Maggie?" Legend asks.

"Good. Really fucking good. She's been feeling the baby move. I can't wait until I can feel him too."

"It's a rush," Forrest says, running his fingers through his hair. "Unlike anything else." Legend and Roman agree with nods.

"I want her to move in with me."

"Does she know that?" Maddox asks me.

"No. Her ex tore her down, and I've been taking my time letting her see with not just my words but my actions that I want her."

"I don't think she'll turn you down," Roman says, nodding to where the ladies are sitting.

I turn to look to find all of them watching us. They smile and wave and turn back around. "How did five assholes who ink for a living get so fucking lucky?" I ask my best friends.

"Good question," Maddox says. "I know I don't ever want to know what life is like without them, so I say we just keep doing what we're doing."

"Amen to that." Legend bumps his fists with each of us, almost as if we're all in some kind of club and taking an oath.

"We've come a long way," Forrest says. "From those five guys who just wanted to pave their own way, to husbands and fathers. I knew it would happen one day, but I never dreamed it would look like this. I'm glad our wives are as close as we are."

"I'm working on it." I laugh.

"Oh, you're going to ask her?" Roman asks.

"Baby steps. I need to get her to agree to move in with me first. Then after that, all bets are off. Once I know she's mine, I'll pull out all the stops to get the three of us to share the same last name."

"Do you guys want cake?" Monroe calls out.

"Is that a real question?" I call back to her, and she grins, waving us over.

The five of us move toward the kitchen where Monroe and Emerson are cutting the larger cake and passing them out.

"Take your wives a piece. The kids are already handled," Emerson tells us.

Doing as I'm told, loving that they're already referring to Maggie as mine, I carry two small plates of cake and ice cream to the living room, handing her one.

"Thank you. I could have gotten that."

"I was already there," I tell her, taking a seat on the floor in front of her, resting my back against her legs where she sits on the couch.

"Monroe's passing out orders like a drill sergeant," Maddox teases, handing Brogan her plate.

Once all the adults have their cake, everyone finds a place to sit in the living room. We laugh and talk and play with the kids, and it's a great night. It's not how we started. We were just five guys, doing our thing. Now we're five guys who have found the loves of our lives, and we're all fathers, or going to be soon. This ending is way better than any of us could have hoped for.

"Pick whatever," I tell Maggie, handing her the remote. We came to my place after Kane's birthday party to watch a movie and eat ice cream. Not that I'll be paying attention to the movie. I usually spend more time watching her than I do the TV.

"What are you in the mood for?" she asks, pointing the remote at the TV, looking at our options.

"Do you want an honest answer?"

She stops and turns to look at me. "Always."

"You."

"W-What?" she asks.

"You heard me."

She looks down at her belly, and I know what she's thinking. She's too big, she's not sexy, but she's wrong. I've never seen a more beautiful sight. When her eyes find mine again, they're blazing with need.

I need to show her.

Standing, I take the remote and turn off the TV. "Let me show you. I know your mind is racing, and you think that there is no way I could want you, but you're wrong, baby. You are so wrong. You're sexy and beautiful, and I want to show you. I can tell you all day long, but I need to be able to show you for you to believe me."

"Okay."

"Okay." My heart hammers inside my chest, and I'm relieved at her easy acceptance. She feels this, too—I know she does—but she's not trusting my words. She needs to feel it in her heart, and against her skin.

She places her small hand in mine, and I lead her to the bedroom, turning on the small bedside lamp. There are so many things I want to do for her. So many ways I can show her how sexy she is. I move toward the bed and sit, pulling her between my spread thighs. My hands caress her belly.

"I know you think this baby bump isn't sexy, but you're wrong. Mags, this bump is a piece of us. There is a piece of me growing inside you, and that is the biggest turn-on."

"Show me," she breathes.

That's all the permission I need. I stand, working quickly and efficiently to strip her bare, then doing the same to myself. "On the bed, beautiful." She does as she's told and lies on my bed. Her hair fans out over the pillow, and her nipples pebble, begging for my touch.

My cock weeps to feel her warmth, but I told her I would show her, and that's what I plan to do. After climbing onto the bed, I pull the covers up over us. It's November in Tennessee, so it's cold, and I need her to be comfortable and relaxed.

She's lying on her back. While I'm on my side with my body propped up on my elbow, I begin to explore her. "These are so much bigger," I say, cupping one breast and then the other, testing their weight in the palm of my hand.

"Yeah," she murmurs.

I trace over her nipples with the pad of my thumb. One, then the other, giving them equal amounts of attention.

"Lachlan." My name on her lips in that breathy tone is like a warm embrace.

Bending my head, I suck one nipple into my mouth, nipping with my teeth, then soothing the ache with my tongue, before releasing her and moving on to the next. "Is this better?" I ask her.

"You're teasing me."

"I'm showing you," I counter. My hand moves to roam over her belly, and I bend my head to kiss her there. "Hey, little man. Daddy loves you," I whisper to my son. My hand continues its journey until I reach her pussy. She opens her legs for me and moans when I lightly graze over her without giving her what she needs.

"Please."

"Please, what, Mags?"

"Touch me. Please."

My hand flutters over her thighs. My touch is light, but the result is still the same. She shivers at the contact. "I am touching you."

"Lachlan." This time, there is a little bit of a warning, and a whole lot of need.

"Okay, touch you. How about here?" I ask, running my index finger through the wetness between her thighs. When I reach her clit, my thumb presses gently.

"Th—That works," she says.

Her hand reaches out, and she fists my cock. "Fuck," I rasp. She has no idea what it does to me to have her hands on me. "That's how bad I want you," I tell her once I've gained my composure. "I'm hard all the time just thinking about you."

I kiss her while sliding my middle finger inside her. She bites down on my lip, and I thrust my hips into her hand. I'm so lost in the sensation, I don't see her next move coming. She pushes at my chest, and I pull my hand from between her thighs. At first, I fear that I've hurt her, but then she straddles me, and all the blood in my body that wasn't already there rushes to my cock.

She rests her palms flat on my chest as I grip her hips. "What are you doing, Mags?"

"You said anything. That you would give me anything."

"I did." My hands roam from her waist to her belly. One stays pressed there, connected to our unborn child, while the other tweaks her nipple.

"I want you inside me."

"Lift this sexy ass," I tell her, smacking her ass lightly. She giggles and lifts up on her knees. "Now guide me inside." Reaching between us, she fists my cock and slowly lowers.

"Oh, damn," she mutters. "Why haven't we been doing this all along?"

"Good question," I reply, gripping her hips. I lift her off me, almost all the way off, then help lower her again. She finds a rhythm and I let my hands explore. Her baby bump, her tits, my thumb in her mouth. There isn't a single part of her body that I can reach that goes untouched by my hands.

"I'm close," she tells me. "It's so good. It's been so long."

"Take what you need, Maggie." It's as if my words set her off, and her moves grow faster, uncoordinated as she chases the high of her release. I feel it before she calls out my name. Her head is tilted back, her tits bouncing, and her pussy squeezes my cock like a vise, and I have no choice but to lose myself inside her.

Bracing her, I roll us to our sides, careful of our baby boy, and keep my cock nestled inside her. Her leg is tossed over mine, and I crush her to my chest in a fierce hug.

This woman is my everything.

Those three little words sit on my tongue, begging to be set free, but something still holds me back. I need to know what she's feeling, where she's at in her head about all of this before I go making it more complicated.

"You good, baby?"

She lifts her head. "I've never had sex without a condom. I don't know if that's what made it so good, or the fact that it's been a while, or maybe it's just us."

"It's us, Maggie. I've never, either, and I'm sorry. We should have talked about that first, but it's never been like this for me with anyone else."

"I'm already pregnant, and we're both only sleeping with each other, right?"

"No one since we made this little guy, and a hell of a lot longer than that before that night."

"Me too."

"You still want a movie and ice cream? I have your favorite."

"Too tired," she mumbles.

"Okay." I press my lips to her forehead before slowly pulling out and climbing out of bed. "I'll be right back." In the bathroom, I clean up, then wet a washcloth with warm water to do the same for her. When I turn, she's standing there. "I was coming back to take care of you."

She holds her hand out for the cloth. "I need to pee. Sean must be sitting on my bladder."

I smile. "Okay. I'll keep the bed warm for you."

A few minutes later, she's curled in my arms. Exactly where she's meant to be.

MAGGIE 15

"YOU'RE REALLY NOT GOING TO tell me where we're going?" I ask Lachlan.

"That would spoil the surprise."

"A hint?" I ask hopefully.

"My lips are sealed." He makes a move like he's zipping his lips and tossing away the key.

I spent the night at his place last night, something we've been doing since last Saturday after Kane's birthday party. If I'm not at his place, he's at mine. Every minute that I spend with him has me falling harder.

"We're here," he says, parking his truck outside a nondescript brick building just outside Nashville.

"And where is here?" I study the building, looking for clues, but I come up empty.

"Well—" He removes his seat belt and turns to face me. "—I booked us for an adventurous day together."

"Did you forget that I'm six months pregnant? What kind of adventure are we talking?"

He reaches over and places his hand on my belly. "I'd never be able to forget you or our son, Maggie. Maybe adventure wasn't the right word." He points to the brick building. "We're going in here to have a 3D ultrasound and then the next floor up, we're booked for a couple's massage. Yours is pregnancy accommodating," he adds.

"No way!" My mouth falls open. "How did you know I wanted to do that? The 3D ultrasound?"

"I didn't, but when we were at our twenty-week appointment, I saw an ad for this place on the table in the waiting room. I picked up a card. I was sure you saw me, but I guess not."

"No, I didn't. Lachlan, this is amazing! I'm so excited. Thank you." I lean toward him over the console, as far as my belly will allow me, and he meets me more than halfway to press his lips to mine.

"Today is our day. Just the three of us. Our little family," he says, smiling.

"Our family," I repeat. Our relationship has changed, but we haven't talked about it. Instead, we're just doing what feels right. For me, being with Lachlan feels exactly that.

I've let the insecurities of my past dictate my life for far too long. Part of me likes to think that I was waiting for Lachlan. That I needed his stubbornness to not allow me to push him away in order to break past the barriers my past had locked around my heart.

"Come on. We don't want to be late." Lachlan grabs his keys from the ignition, his phone from the cupholder, and exits the truck.

I know I'm supposed to wait for him to help me down. It's his thing. However, I'm too damn excited to wait this time. I have the door open and my foot on the running board to hop down when he lifts me from the truck, placing my feet on the ground.

"You didn't wait for me."

"Because we're going to see our baby today, Lachlan. In 3D!"

"We are." He bends his head and presses his lips to mine. "Come on. Let's go see our son."

I'm practically skipping all the way inside, where the warmth from the furnace greets us, masking the cool November Tennessee air.

"Welcome to Mommy and Me. How can I help you?" the young receptionist asks.

"Lachlan and Maggie Noble, we have an appointment at ten for a 3D ultrasound and then the couple's massage after," he tells her.

She replies, but I'm too busy running his words over in my mind. *"Lachlan and Maggie Noble."* I like the sound of that far too much.

"Perfect. You're with Clara today for your ultrasound. I'll take you back to her now. If you'll follow me," the receptionist says.

With my hand locked in his, Lachlan follows the receptionist down the long hallway and stops just outside the door. "Clara, your ten o'clock is here."

"Great, thank you, Ashley," Clara says as we enter the room. "Hi, Mom and Dad. I'm Clara, your ultrasound tech." She glances down at her computer. "My notes say you're having a little boy. Congratulations."

"Thank you," Lachlan and I say to her at the same time.

"Mom, we're going to have you get up on the exam table and pull up your shirt and your leggings down just past your belly." Her fingers fly across the keyboard of her ultrasound machine.

Lachlan helps me up onto the exam table and takes it upon himself to pull my shirt up and my leggings down, tucking them just beneath my baby belly. Not giving a single care that Clara is watching, he bends and places not just his hand but a tender kiss on my belly.

"Ready?" Clara asks, once he's standing to his full height.

I smile up at him. "We're ready." Lachlan squeezes my hand, and then it begins. Clara moves the wand around a little, then turns the screen so that we can see.

"There he is. Handsome little guy," she says, moving the wand around. "Don't worry, the package your husband ordered was the full deal, so you'll get lots of printouts as well as a video copy as a keepsake."

My husband.

"Really?" I ask, forcing my eyes from the screen to land on Lachlan. He nods and winks before his gaze goes back to the screen, watching our son.

By the time our session is over, I'm a crying, snotty mess, but it's happy tears. "I'll have everything ready for you to pick up at the front desk after your massage. Enjoy," Clara says, handing us back to Ashley, the receptionist.

"Now, the massage. You're going to be up on floor three. Nala and Amber are your massage therapists today."

"Thank you," I tell her.

"Go ahead and get undressed to whatever feels comfortable for you," Ashley says once we're in the couple's massage room. "Once you're ready, just hit the green button on the wall, and they'll give you five minutes from that point to get on the beds, covered, and face down. Obviously, the pregnancy table is for mom to be." She smiles.

"Thanks, Ashley," Lachlan tells her as she shuts the door, leaving us inside.

"Lachlan?"

"What's up, Momma?"

"Come here." I motion for him to come closer, and he does without question. His hands rest on my belly. "Thank you for this. That was incredible. I'll never forget today."

"The day's not over, Mags."

"I know, but I needed you to know what this means to me. Thank you." I stand on my tiptoes, and he meets me, because I can't get as close to him as I used to with my belly in the way. He kisses me softly.

"Come on. We have a massage to get ready for." He winks as he helps me strip down to my bra and panties. I'm not willing to go further than that. Then he strips to his underwear. He helps me onto my massage table, letting his hands roam.

"You have to stop that, or we'll never hit that green button," I mutter, feeling my body reacting to his touch.

"The idea has merit, but we can do that at home." He kisses my bare shoulder before pulling the cover up over me, going to the wall to hit the green button, and moving to his table, where he pulls the cover over himself. We're staring into each other's eyes, and the words that always come to mind when I think of him are on the tip of my tongue. A knock at the door stops me.

Soon. I'll tell him soon.

"Now, where are we going?" I ask Lachlan. I'm relaxed from the massage, my belly is full from an amazing meal at my favorite Italian restaurant, and I have 3D pictures of our baby boy, as well as a video in my hands. The man I've fallen madly in love with is sitting next to me.

I'm not sure life gets better than this.

"Well, I have one last surprise for you."

"Is it today's mission to make me a blubbering mess?" I'm only half teasing.

"No." He's quiet as he drives. "Today's mission was to show you that you're not alone. It was to show you that you are my family, and not just because we're having a son together. I wanted you to feel how special you are to me."

"Your mission *was* to make me cry," I tell him, wiping at my cheeks.

Reaching over the console without taking his eyes off the road, he takes my hand in his. "I promise you, Mags, it wasn't. I hope those tears are happy?" he asks.

"They are. Every moment of today has been incredible, and I don't know what you have planned next, but I'm certain it will be the perfect ending to our day."

Resting my head back against the seat, I close my eyes. I don't think I've ever felt this content in my adult life, not since losing my parents. It's a feeling I want to relish. That's my last thought as I drift off to sleep.

When I wake, it's to Lachlan running his index finger down my cheek. "We're here," he tells me.

"Where is here?" I ask groggily.

"At Grandma Doris's place."

Blinking a few times, I take in our surroundings. "Is that your parents' car?" I ask, seeing the dark blue SUV in the driveway.

"Yeah," he says, cupping my cheek. "I thought we could share the video and pictures from today with them."

"Is there anything that you don't think of?" I ask him.

"Not when it comes to my family. Come on. They're waiting for us." He flashes me a wide smile and climbs out of the truck. This time, I stay in my seat and wait for him. When he opens my door, I grip his shirt and pull him closer.

"Thank you for all that you do for us," I whisper against his lips before kissing him softly. I quickly pull back, not wanting his parents or my grandmother to be looking out the window and watching us. Not that they don't think we've been in this exact position before. I mean, we're having a baby together after all.

"You and our boy are my world, Maggie. I'd do anything for you."

Hand in hand, we walk into my grandmother's house. The sound of her laugh fills my soul as we make our way to the living room. Lachlan's parents are sitting on the couch, while Grandma Doris is in her chair, and they're laughing and talking like old friends.

It's been a long damn time since this house has heard that kind of laughter. After losing my mother, it was solemn and even more so after losing my dad. Lachlan Noble and his big heart has brought us back to life.

"There they are." Grandma smiles. "Can you tell us now?" she asks Lachlan.

I glance at Lachlan and he shrugs. "I wasn't telling them before you knew where we were going."

"We've had the best day," I tell them. I go to Grandma, bending to hug her where she sits, and then move to Lachlan's parents, hugging them tightly before taking a seat on the love seat. Lachlan follows my plan, passing out hugs, but he doesn't join me, not yet. Instead, he moves to the TV and inserts the flash drive into the back.

"So, I might have stopped by one day after work this week to make sure this would work," he tells us.

"Are we watching a movie?" Amanda asks.

"We are. Sort of." Lachlan nods. He grabs the remote and moves to sit next to me. "Today, Maggie and I had a 3D ultrasound done, and they made a video for us. We wanted to share it with all of you."

"Oh my," Grandma replies. She clutches her hand to her chest over her heart.

"We get to watch?" Mom asks, disbelief in her tone.

"You do." Lachlan hits Play, and the movie starts. Sean was very active today during the ultrasound, and he even waved at us. At least that's what I'm calling it.

"Oh heavens, he just waved," Grandma says, her voice cracking with emotion.

"See?" I lean into Lachlan, and he puts his arm around me, kissing my cheek.

The room is silent as we watch the full ultrasound. Once it's over, Lachlan stands and grabs the flash drive out of the back of the TV and shoves it into his pocket. "Thanks for meeting us here," he tells his parents. He turns toward my grandmother next. "Thanks for letting us use your place as the meeting point."

"You can surprise me like that any day," she says with a wide smile.

We stay for about an hour just talking and catching up. We make promises to all get together soon, and then we're on the road, headed back to his place.

"Thank you again for today," I tell him as we walk into the house.

"Stop thanking me. Today was for me too. I got to see our boy, got to make my girl and our family smile, got a massage, and a great dinner with even better company. Today was purely selfish on my part."

"I don't believe that for a second." I shake my head. This man is so giving and too humble to admit it. Never thought I'd see that from Lachlan, but I now know the man behind the smile. I know his heart, and I should because it owns mine.

"Ice cream and a movie?" he asks.

"Yes. I can't think of a better way to end the day."

"Go pick something, and I'll bring the ice cream." A quick kiss, and he's stalking toward the kitchen to get our sweet treat.

"I think Sean is going to have a sweet tooth like yours," I say a while later. "I've never craved ice cream like this before in my life." I hand Lachlan my now-empty bowl to place on the table because I'm too full, too comfortable, and too pregnant to move right now.

"Aww, my boy wants to be like daddy." Lachlan grins. He rolls over to his belly and lifts my shirt. "Daddy loves you," he tells my belly. He places his hand over my bump and smiles up at me. Sean kicks, and Lachlan's eyes widen.

"Was that? Did he just? Did that really happen?" he asks with reverence in his voice.

"He was telling you that he loves you back."

His voice is gruff when he says, "I love you so much, little man. I can't wait to meet you. Can you kick again for Daddy?"

Our boy does as his daddy asks and kicks hard.

"Holy fuck. I saw that."

"Yeah, he thinks he's playing soccer in there sometimes."

"Buddy, you have to take it easy on Mommy," Lachlan tells our unborn son. He kicks again, and the awe on Lachlan's face will be a look I'll forever remember.

This moment, seeing the wonder and the love in his eyes, will forever be replayed in my mind.

Lachlan sits up and takes my hands in his. He swallows hard, and the expression on his face tells me something big is about to happen.

"I love spending time with you. I love our nights with ice cream and movies. I love it when we're with my parents and your grandmother. I love it when we're with our friends or just the two of us. I love you here in my house." He brings my hands to his lips and kisses my knuckles. "Maggie, you make this place feel like home."

"I love our time together too," I tell him when he finishes his speech.

"Can we try?" he asks.

"Can we try what?"

"Us. This. Being a family. Can we try? I know you probably think this is because of the baby, but it's so much more than that. This is about me never wanting to be away from you. This is about me not being able to sleep unless you're in the bed next to me. This is more than just the fact that you're the mother of my son. Maggie, baby, you're the owner of my heart. I'm so in love with you. So in love with you that you're all that I see. I want this with you. This life. Nights hanging out on the couch, or with our friends and family. I don't want to co-parent with you. I want to raise our son together. In this house. In *our* house, because it feels like ours. I want you. I want our son, and I want a life with you. So, I'm asking you if we can try. Let me show you that you're my person."

Hot tears prick my eyes. He loves me. I can see the earnest look in his eyes. The man I've fallen madly in love with loves me back, and he's asking for a future with me, the one I've come to hope for the last few months. I can tell by the way his jaw is locked that he expects me to fight him on this, and he's right. Six months ago, I would have assumed it was because of the baby, but I know his heart, and I trust mine.

There is no question in my answer.

"Yes."

"I'll be—yes?" he asks, his mouth dropping open.

I nod. "Yes. I don't need to try, Lachlan." Leaning forward, I cup his cheeks. "I love you too."

"Move in with me. Make this our home."

Again, I don't need to think about my answer. "Yes." I want this. I want him and the life he just described for us. I want it all, and I'm not letting my past or my fears hold me back.

"Yes?" His smile could light up all of Ashby. "You said yes, right? I'm not just hearing things?"

"Yes. To all of it, yes."

"Sean, you hear that, buddy? We're a family. Mommy and Daddy love you so much, and we can't wait to meet you." He kisses my belly and then raises his lips to mine. The kiss is slow and easy. He shows me with his touch, with this kiss that I'm precious to him.

"I love you. I love how you put me and our son first. I love how you take care of us, and I love that you want this life with us as badly as I do. I don't know what the future holds, but I know that I want us to figure it out together."

Lachlan stands, and lifts me into his arms, making me laugh. "What are you doing?"

"Taking my girl to bed."

"Is this what I have to look forward to?" I tease.

"Yes. Every night for the rest of your life."

"Deal."

Just like that, every hope and every dream for us to be a family becomes my reality. This man, he's my future, and I'm his. There is nothing sweeter than knowing our hearts are on the same page.

MAGGIE 16

"STOP!" I'M LAUGHING SO HARD that I'm fearful that I'm going to pee my pants. We're having Friendsgiving the day after Thanksgiving—the latter we spent with Lachlan's parents and Grandma Doris.

"I kid you not. They both had shit all over them from head to toe," Monroe tells us, through her tears from laughing so hard. "Legend took it like a champ. He stripped them both down in the shower and bathed both himself and Kane at the same time, dressed them both and took care of the nasty poop-covered clothes."

"I've known these guys all my life, and it's cool to get to see them be dads. Forrest was always a father figure to me," Emerson adds. "But to see him with his daughters, to see all of them, it warms my heart. They were these guys with no attachments outside of me being Forrest's little sister, and now they're family men." She smiles wistfully.

"I'm certain Maddox and Lachlan are going to be the same way," Briar adds.

"Yeah," Brogan and I agree, and we all start laughing again.

"Ladies, are you ready to eat?" Lachlan calls out. "The deep-fried bird is ready," he adds.

"Say less," Monroe says. She's been talking about how good it smells since we got here.

We make our way to the kitchen, where the men are handling Friendsgiving dinner and taking care of the kids. We tried to help, but they kicked us out, telling us it was their day to spoil us. We didn't argue, but they take care of us every day. The girls and I already have a plan to do something special for them as a surprise.

Once the kids are set up at the small table I bought for them, now positioned in the corner of the dining room, well, minus Kane who is still in his high chair, the rest of the adults make their plates, and find a seat around the large dining room table Lachlan and I picked out after he bought this house.

Lachlan is at the head of the table, and I'm to his left. Instead of sitting, he stands, taking a minute to glance over at the kids, who are chatting and eating, to every person at the table. "Friendsgiving," he says with an easy smile. "Thanksgiving has always been a holiday to eat great food and be with the people I care about most. That's all of you in case you missed that," he jokes. "However, this year it's hitting a little different." He makes a fist and taps his chest over his heart. Then his gaze turns to me. "This year, I get to celebrate it with the love of my life. And in a few short months, our son will be here."

"Hold up." Maddox raises his hand. "What did I miss?"

"Have you not been paying attention?" Brogan asks. "They're together."

"I knew he wanted to be, but I didn't know that we'd reached the 'love of my life' confession stage." Maddox chuckles.

"We?" Lachlan asks.

Maddox shrugs. "Rome, Legend, Forrest, me, and now you. Through it all, we've been there for each other. We knew you loved her, but we didn't know if *you* knew that you loved her."

"Trust me, I know." As if he needs to prove his point, he leans over and kisses me. Just a quick peck, but it still has my heart tripping over in my chest. "Anyway. I love you all. Thank you for allowing me and my girl to host this year." He sits in his seat, and before we can start to eat, Maddox stands.

"This year has been insane. I got married." He smiles at Brogan. "And now, we're having a baby." He swallows hard. "I wouldn't want to take this ride with anyone else." He makes a fist and taps his chest just like Lachlan did, before sitting down and pulling Brogan into a kiss.

Forrest stands and clears his throat. "I think this might be our new thing," he says with a slight chuckle. He looks at Briar, and his expression softens. "I'm going to be a dad for the third time. Three babies, and a wife who brings so much love and light into my life, I didn't really know what I was missing until I found them. I'm thankful every single day that you and our daughters came into my life. I can't wait to have forever with you." Forrest makes a fist, taps his chest, and bends over to kiss Briar before taking his seat.

"I never could have imagined this is where we would end up," Legend says as he stands and locks eyes with Monroe. "This beautiful woman who offered to help me out ended up being the one person I can't live without. Then, she gave me a son, and now, another son or daughter to love. I don't ever want to imagine what my life would be like without you and our kids." He, too, makes a fist, taps it over his chest, and then kisses his wife.

My heart is so full, I feel like my chest could burst open as I listen to each declaration.

"Saved the best for last." Roman laughs as he stands. "First, Legend, Monroe, congrats on the new baby." Everyone around the table says the same. "Looks like the Everlasting Ink family is going to keep on growing." He smiles down at Emerson. "Lilly's getting a little brother or sister next year too."

"What?" Monroe screeches. "Really?" There are tears in her eyes.

Emerson nods, tears also forming. "Really."

"So, we're all pregnant at the same time?" Briar asks.

"We are," all the ladies, including myself, answer.

"They're all going to be the best of friends," Emerson says.

"Baby girl," Roman says, pulling Emerson's attention back to him. "I'm so thankful for you. You never gave up on me, on us. Now, we have this beautiful little girl and another baby on the way. You've given me everything I never knew I wanted. I love you." He makes a fist, taps it over his heart, and kisses his wife.

"Grown-ups are weird," River says.

"Yeah," Rayne agrees.

"Yeah!" Lilly echoes, and the entire room erupts in laughter.

"Happy Thanksgiving." Lachlan raises his glass of tea, and we all follow suit, raising our drinks.

"Happy Thanksgiving," echoes around the room.

We dig into our meals while talking, laughing, making plans, and making memories. This is our future. This is what my kids will grow up with. Something I didn't have. Family isn't just those you're born related to. It's also those you choose to love. Those people who come into your life at just the right time, and they stay for a lifetime. That's what we are. We're family. The Everlasting Ink family.

"Twenty-eight weeks and growing strong," Lachlan says, joining me on the couch.

We just got home from my doctor's appointment and are taking it easy. It's cold as hell outside, as it should be the week before Christmas.

"He'll be here for all of this next year." I point toward the tree and the presents beneath it.

"I can't wait," Lachlan says, leaning over to press his lips to mine. "Speaking of Christmas, I want to give you an early present."

"I can wait until next week."

"Yeah, but I can't." He chuckles. He stands from the couch and offers me his hand. "Come with me."

"I have to go somewhere for this gift?" I ask, not really wanting to move off this couch. I worked all day because we were able to get a late appointment and I'm beat.

"Yes, but not far."

"Okay." I place my hand in his, and he helps me from the couch.

"I'll carry you. I know you're tired." He lifts me into his arms, bridal style, and I lock my hands behind his neck.

"I could have walked. I'm just being lazy."

"No, Mags, you're not lazy. You're growing a human; that takes a lot out of you. Besides, we're just going upstairs."

My heart begins to race, because the only thing upstairs are the two spare bedrooms and a bathroom. The nursery. I bet he bought the furniture we were looking at. I bite down on my cheek to tamp down my excitement.

Once we're in front of the bedroom that we agreed would be Sean's, Lachlan places me on my feet.

"I'm going to place my hands over your eyes. Close them, too, and don't try to peek." He gives me a stern look.

"Yes, sir." His blue eyes darken and he licks his lips. "We'll get back to that," he muses. "Now, close those beautiful blue eyes," he tells me.

I do as I'm told, and he places one arm around my waist and the other shields my eyes. "Shit, I need to open the door. Hold on. Keep your eyes closed." I hear the door open, and then he's back with his arm around my waist, one hand covering my eyes, and we're moving. "Almost there," he tells me. We stop, and he drops the hand over my eyes. "Open."

I count to three slowly in my head and blink open my eyes. I blink again. Once, twice, three times as I take in what I'm looking at. It's not just the furniture we looked at. It's everything. The dark blue and cream contrasting walls, the wood nameplate above the crib, the cream and dark blue rug, the rocking chair, the changing table, and the art on the walls. It's everything. Every single thing I've shown him on my phone or while shopping, he's incorporated. There's a small end table and a bookshelf by the rocking chair for late-night feedings. Every little detail is perfect.

"Lachlan." My voice cracks. "When? How? When?" I can't seem to form a complete sentence.

"I've been working on it here and there since I moved in. Roman helped me paint on a day we both had off at the shop. Legend and Forrest both helped assemble furniture, and Maddox picked up the rocking chair for me while I worked on hanging the art and his name on the walls."

I stand in the middle of the room and turn in a circle, slowly taking in every detail. "This is better than I ever could have imagined it would be."

"Are you mad?"

I stop and turn to look at him. "Mad? Why on earth would I be mad?"

"I don't know. I thought maybe you wanted to do all of this on your own or something?"

"Lachlan, this is perfect. I couldn't have done better. I wouldn't change a single thing. You're his daddy. This is the perfect gift for both of us."

"Yeah?" He steps behind me and wraps his arms around my waist.

"Definitely. Thank you. I can mark this off my list of things that need to be done before our little man gets here."

"There's still so much that we need. I'll leave that up to you because I can't even begin to imagine what that list looks like," he admits.

"We'll do it together."

"I like the sound of that. Merry early Christmas, Mags."

"Merry Christmas."

"Have you thought about the nursery, any?" Brogan asks me.

We're sitting in her living room, us girls, the guys' moms, Monroe's mom, and Grandma Doris. We're all here for Briar's baby shower. She got so many cute things for their baby. The room is full of pink and purple for their baby girl.

"It's done, actually."

"What?" Emerson asks. "When did you do that?" She furrows her brow as if she's trying to remember me saying I was working on the nursery.

"I didn't. Lachlan did. He showed it to me last night. Your husbands helped him."

"Those sneaky little rascals." Briar laughs.

"It's perfect. Everything I ever could have imagined it would be. I can't wait for you to see it."

"Did he at least leave us some things to buy you at your shower?" Monroe asks.

"He did. He just bought the big stuff and the decorations. He said he knew there was so much more we would need, and he had no idea where to start."

"He did good with the room on his own, though," Brogan points out.

"He did, but it was everything I'd ever showed him. Either on my phone or when we were shopping. He paid attention to every detail."

"Yeah, they're good at that. I think it's their profession. Tattoo artists are all about the details. At least the good ones are." Monroe smiles.

"I'm so glad he finally showed you," Heather, Monroe's mom, speaks up. "He wouldn't show me pictures. He said you needed to see it first."

"Aww, really?" I ask. "I have some pictures I snapped this morning." Opening my phone, I pull up the pictures and hand them to her. My cell gets passed around as everyone takes their turn.

"That man, he sure does love you," Grandma Doris comments.

I nod. "I love him too."

"So, Briar, have you thought about names?" Heather asks.

"We have a few that we like. We want to stay with the outdoor theme. I think we're leaning toward Willow."

"I love that," Emerson says.

"I can't believe all five of you are pregnant at the same time," Cassie, Maddox's mom, comments. "They're going to all grow up the best of friends, just like their fathers were."

"More babies to love on." Sarah, Roman's mom, smiles. "I, for one, can't wait."

"Next Christmas is definitely going to be different," Brogan says.

"Oh, it's going to be so much fun," Grandma Doris tells us. "After you have children and they grow up, Christmas loses a little of its magic. At least it did for me. Little ones make it so special."

The moms nod their agreement, and excitement bubbles up inside me. I know it's a full year away, but I'm looking forward to all the moments and all the memories we'll make as a family. Not just Lachlan, me, and Sean, but our families and our Everlasting Ink family too. There is so much love to give. My heart is bursting with it.

We help Briar gather all of her gifts, carry them up to the baby's room, and help her get unpacked. The moms leave, and Amanda gives Grandma Doris a ride home. That leaves the five of us ladies. We sit for hours and talk and laugh and make plans for the future.

As I'm getting ready to leave, I take my now-empty glass to the kitchen and find Emerson at the sink, washing hers. "Thank you, Em," I say, feeling the emotions welling in my throat.

"What for?" She puts her glass away and reaches for mine, and I hand it over.

"For introducing me to your friends."

"You're my friend."

"I know, but we were work friends, and you brought me into the fold of your life. Those relationships have changed my life. So, thank you."

"I'd like to think that you and Lachlan would have found your way to each other, regardless. The chemistry between you was instant; we could all see it."

"It's not just Lachlan. It's the other girls, the rest of the guys. I only have my grandma, and now it feels like I have this huge extended family, and my heart—" My voice cracks. "It's bursting with love, and I'm going to be a mom, and it's just overwhelming in the absolute best of ways."

"Bring it in." She dries her hands, opens her arms for me, and I step into her embrace.

"Hold up," Monroe says from behind us. "Ladies, we got a group-hug situation. Your presence is needed." The next thing I know, Monroe is wrapping her arms around us, and then Briar and Brogan join in.

"I love you, guys," I tell them, not bothering to try and mask my emotions.

"Love you," they echo.

LACHLAN 17

FOR HOURS, I'VE BEEN LYING here awake, holding Maggie in my arms. The sun is finally peeking over the horizon, and I don't think I can wait another second to give her the gift. Technically, I'm asking her for one.

I've gone back and forth on whether or not I should do this today, but when it comes down to it, I don't think the day will really matter, because this isn't her gift. It's mine.

Needing her to wake up, I move my hand from her belly up under my T-shirt she's sleeping in, to her breasts. I gently roll her pebbled nipple between my thumb and index finger, and she moans.

I keep massaging her breasts, teasing her nipples, giving both equal amounts of attention, and when she presses her gorgeous ass into my hard cock, I know she's awake.

"Morning, Mags." I kiss her neck.

She turns her head to glance at me over her shoulder. "Why are you up so early?"

"I couldn't sleep." That gets her attention, just as I knew it would.

She turns in my arms and rests her palm against my cheek. "Is everything okay?"

I place my hand over hers. "Everything is perfect. Too perfect."

"That's a bad thing?" she asks.

"No, baby, that's a wonderful thing," I murmur against her lips.

"Is there something on your mind?"

"You." I kiss her again.

"Me?" She seems surprised.

"Maggie, there isn't a single second of the day that I'm not thinking about you. I even dream about you."

"Did you dream about me last night?" she asks, her tone teasing.

"I did." It's not a lie, I did, but I know it's because of my indecision of the question I need to ask her today. Turns out, that dream, and my early morning decision are going to play well for me today.

"What did you dream about?" she asks, snuggling closer.

I tuck her head beneath my chin and hold her tightly. "You were in a white dress, walking toward me. All of our family was there, but I couldn't tell you who for sure, because I only had eyes for you." It's true. I could feel their presence, but Maggie was all that I could see.

"Our wedding?"

"Yeah, baby, our wedding. We stood before everyone we love, vowing to love one another until the end of time."

"I think I like this dream."

"There were two people other than us that I remember clearly."

"Yeah? Who?"

"Sean and my dad."

"Tell me."

"I was holding Sean in my arms as you walked toward us. My dad, he was walking you down the aisle. When you reached us, we traded. He took Sean, and I got you." I kiss the top of her head.

"Do you think that's something he would want to do?" she asks hesitantly.

"Without a doubt in my mind," I assure her, knowing my dad would be honored to step up.

"Definitely a sweet dream," she murmurs.

Here goes nothing. "What if it wasn't just a dream?"

She pulls away so that she can look me in the eye. The early morning light is filtering through the blinds, giving us just enough light. "Not a dream?"

"It's *my* dream. The one I had last night and the one that I have for our future. Maggie, I love you. With each day that I get to spend with you, that love only grows. I want you here in this bed next to me forever. I want you, me, and Sean, and our future babies to all share the same last name."

"I like the sound of that."

Fuck yes! I let go of her and climb out of bed.

"What are you doing?"

"I have to get something." I move to my underwear drawer and pull out the ring box that's been sitting there since long before she moved in with me. Grabbing it, I make my way back to the bed. She's sitting up now, the blankets pooling at her waist.

"Lachlan?" she asks, tears evident in her voice.

"Come here, Mags." I offer her my hand, and she takes it. I help her stand, then drop to one knee. "Maggie Ward, you've changed my life. You've opened up a whole new world of love and happiness for me." Leaning forward, I press a kiss to her belly. "Love you, baby boy," I whisper. Then I open the box and hold it up for her. "You are my sun, my moon, and all the stars in the sky. Maggie Ward, will you do me the incredible honor of being my wife? Will you marry me?"

Tears coat her cheeks, and I start to worry, but then she smiles, so brightly that it rivals the early morning sun, as she nods. "Yes. Yes, I'll marry you."

With trembling hands, I pluck the ring from the box and slide it onto her finger. "Perfect." My heart gallops in my chest, and my legs are shaky as I stand, and pull her into a kiss. "Never letting you go, Mags."

"You promise?"

"With everything that I am." I kiss her again, and as my tongue slides against hers, I feel her hands go to the waistband of my boxer briefs and tug.

"Need these off," she says between kisses.

Pulling back, I discard my underwear, and she lifts her arms in the air. I pull my shirt she was sleeping in over her head and toss it to the floor. She shimmies out of her panties and I'm staring down at my future wife. My chest feels tight just thinking of her as mine for a lifetime.

"I need you, Lachlan."

I move to climb on the bed, so she can have me. Her belly is growing every day, and we have to get creative.

"No." She stops me, moving on the bed on all fours. She looks over her shoulder at me. "You coming?"

"I will be." I smirk and climb onto the bed after her. I press my hips and my hard cock against her ass as I grip each cheek. She moans and grinds back into me.

Pulling back, I grip my cock, ready to be inside her, when I see her hand go between her legs. She rubs at her clit, and moans, causing my cock to twitch in my palm. "Maggie," I warn her.

"You're taking too long. You were teasing me in bed, and then you asked me to marry you, and I'm dripping for you, Lachlan. I need relief, and if you won't give it to me." Her voice trails off when I push my hard cock inside her. She's so damn tight, and wet, and the warmth, it's like nothing I've ever felt before, and I know it's her. It's the love we share between us that makes every time with her better than the last.

"Mine. You are mine. Your pleasure is mine," I tell her.

"All yours, as long as you don't make me wait." She laughs and then moans when I pull out and push back in.

"I wanted to make love to you. Nice and slow."

"And I need you to fuck me nice and hard. We have forever, remember?" she asks.

"Who are you, and what have you done with my fiancée?" I ask her.

"I'm right here." She pants as I thrust into her.

"Am I hurting you?" I ask as I push into her again. My pace is frantic as I chase my orgasm.

"No. Oh, yes! Don't stop, please—" she moans, and fuck me, I'm ready to blow.

"Touch yourself," I tell her. I never come before she does, but this might be a first. I'm so close.

She slides her hand back between her legs, and within minutes, she's calling out my name.

"Thank fuck," I rasp as I still, releasing inside her. Not wanting to crush her or the baby, I pull out and help her lie back on the bed, taking my spot beside her.

"Merry Christmas," she says, kissing my sweaty, bare chest.

"Merry Christmas, my fiancée."

She wiggles around until she can lift her arm and admire her ring. "It's beautiful."

"Just like the woman who owns it." I pull her hand to my lips, kissing her ring. "Come on. Let's get a shower, so I can feed you and we can open presents."

"You gave me mine. The nursery and this ring."

"The nursery was more of a surprise, and the ring, that wasn't your present. I just couldn't wait a minute longer to ask you to be my wife. Come on." Climbing out of bed, I help her to her feet, and we shower together.

Best Christmas morning ever.

"Breakfast was great," I say, taking our plates to the sink.

"Thank you. It was a recipe I saw online. I was nervous last night when I was putting it together in the Crock-Pot. I wasn't sure if it was going to turn out."

"We should make it every year," I suggest.

"I guess we can add this to our Noble family traditions," Maggie tells me with a smile.

"Yep," I say, offering her my hand. "Come on, woman. We have presents to open." She takes my hand, and I lead her into the living room. Once there, I help her get settled on the couch with a pillow behind her back and her legs propped up with the reclining footrest.

"You first," she tells me. "Grab the big blue one."

Reaching under the tree, I grab the gift she pointed to, and bring it back to the couch. "What is it?" I ask her. It almost looks like a portrait of some kind with the way It's wrapped.

"Open it and find out."

Taking a seat opposite her on the couch, I carefully tear open the package. I turn it around so I can see and my breath stalls in my lungs. "Mags," I croak. I'm staring at an artist-drawn rendering of Sean's 3D ultrasound.

"You have everything, and I didn't know what to get you, so I was looking online, and this popped up. We can hang it here, or you could take it to work if you wanted to."

"This is incredible."

"You're an artist, so I was hoping you would appreciate it."

"Babe, this is the best gift I've ever been given." I lean over and press my lips to hers. "I love it. I don't know if I want it at work or in our office here."

"Either way." She shrugs.

"Thank you."

"Okay, your turn." I stand, go back to the tree, and grab the gift that I think she's going to love the most. I hand it to her and take a seat while she opens it.

"What? No way! A new Kindle? Mine is barely holding a charge," she tells me.

"I know. There's more on the back." She flips it over and sees the gift card taped to it. "I figured you could pick out your own accessories. You hadn't mentioned the case you wanted, so now you get to choose it on your own."

"Thank you. I love this. The girls are going to be so jealous." She shimmies in her seat.

"Nah, they're all getting them too. Roman saw me buying yours, so he bought one. Then Maddox walked in, and he ordered one too. Then Forrest and Legend found out and they both bought one as well. You ladies are all going to be reading in style." I laugh.

"You're the best." She tilts to the side, and I move in, kissing her softly. "I love you."

"Love you too."

We spend the rest of the morning opening gifts and snuggling on the couch. Maggie loved the earrings and bracelet I bought her, and I modeled the new jeans and long-sleeved button-up she got for me. By the time we're done, there's a pile of wrapping paper and we both have a stack of gifts.

"We went overboard," she says, laughing before taking a sip of the hot chocolate I just handed her.

"Just wait until next year. It will be all of ours and Sean's."

"Emerson said that Lilly liked the boxes and the bows more her first Christmas than she did the presents."

"Yeah, I remember that. I think this year that will change. Especially with the twins. Kane, on the other hand, he's probably going to be all about the paper and bows."

"I guess we'll find out tomorrow." She smiles.

"Yeah." I glance at my watch. We have a couple of hours before we pick up Grandma Doris and head to my parents'. "Christmas movie?"

"Is that a real question?" she asks, laughter in her tone.

"Pick a movie, woman." I hand her the remote.

She skims through our options and picks one, before moving to snuggle into my side. I kiss the top of her head and place my hand on her belly. My dad used to tell me that there was nothing he loved more than just spending time with Mom and me. As a kid, I thought he was just giving me a line, telling me that out of obligation, but I was wrong.

So very wrong.

This, right here, is my happy place. There is nothing I would choose over holding her, holding *them* in my arms. I didn't know that being in love would make me feel so... settled. So content. I can hear my dad saying, *"I told you, son,"* in my head, and it makes me smile. I'm going to have to confess he was right all these years, and I was wrong. He's going to love that.

Maggie places her hand over mine that's resting on her belly. "I love you."

"I love you, too, Mags. Merry Christmas."

"Merry Christmas."

LACHLAN 18

"THANKS FOR THE HOOK-UP ON the 3D ultrasound," Forrest tells me. "Briar loved it, so did the girls."

"Those things are bad-ass," I tell him.

"I'm going to need that information," Roman tells us.

"Go ahead and add it to the group text," Maddox tells us.

"Yep," Legend agrees. "Monroe can't stop talking about how you can make out the baby's features. She thinks he's going to have your eyes," he tells me.

"Did you see the drawing that Maggie got me for Christmas?" I ask them.

"Yeah, you showed us," Roman tells me. "That was a great gift idea."

"Right? I was going to hang it up in my office at the shop but decided to put it in the office in the basement at home."

"Good choice," Forrest tells me.

"Hey, do you and Briar have a name picked out yet?" Roman asks him. "You have a theme in your family." He grins.

"Yeah, we're naming her Willow."

"Nice." I nod my approval.

The ladies laughter catches our attention. The five of us stand here in the kitchen of Briar and Forrest's house, staring at our women in the living room like love-sick fools. I don't know how much time passes when Forrest clears his throat.

"Did you see the email our accountant sent?" he asks.

"No. Bad news? Good news?" I ask. The others shake their heads too.

"Good news. We almost tripled our income this year."

"No shit?" Roman asks.

"Yep. It has to be the extra space we added for the guest artists," Forrest explains.

"Our books have been packed," Maddox replies. He turns to look at Legend. "Thanks, man. We couldn't have done all of that without you."

Legend shrugs. "I didn't want the money. It felt dirty, but putting it into our business, investing in our future, our families, it felt right. It was my inheritance, after all. Hopefully, a few of our kids will want to work with us and carry on the Everlasting Ink tradition."

"He has some ideas for investing, and suggested bonuses for the owners," Forrest tells us.

"I like the sound of that," I tell him, and the others agree.

"Daddy!" Lilly calls out as she rushes over to Roman, and he bends to lift her into his arms.

"What's up, sweets?"

"Cookies." She points to the island that's covered in snacks and sweet treats.

"That's my girl." I hold my hand up to Lilly for a high-five, and she slaps her little hand against mine.

"Are you corrupting my daughter?" Roman mock glares at me.

I slap my hand over my chest, pretending to be offended. "I would never." After tossing my empty root beer can in the trash, I reach for Lilly. "Come on, girlie. Let's get you a cookie. You want a pink one?" I ask her.

"I wike pink." She nods.

"Pink it is." I grab a cookie and hand it to her.

"You know she's going to get that everywhere, right?" Roman asks.

"Don't worry about it," Forrest tells him. "Houses are meant to be lived in. Let my niece enjoy her pink cookie."

Lilly holds the cookie out to Forrest, who's standing next to me, and he pretends to take a bite. Lilly giggles. Her little body shakes in my arms as if Forrest is the funniest man she's ever known.

"Oh, Daddy, can we have a cookie too?" River asks.

"Of course you can," Roman answers, smirking at Forrest.

"I want a green one!" Rayne announces.

"I want a yellow one," River says.

Forrest gets to work handing them their frosted cookie color of choice, then hands them a blue one. "Take this to Aunt Monroe and tell her it's for Kane."

"Okay, Daddy." The twins rush off toward the living room, and Lilly wiggles to get down. Once she's on her feet, she races after her cousins.

"Go fish," Brogan tells Rayne.

"I can't believe they're still awake," Forrest tells me. We're sitting in the living room, on the dining room chairs we brought in, watching our wives, well, their wives and my fiancée, play Go Fish with River and Rayne.

"This one couldn't hang," Legend says, stroking Kane's back where he sleeps on his chest.

"You can take him upstairs and put him in the Pack 'N Play in our room. We set it up just in case," Forrest tells him.

"Nah, I got him. He won't be this little forever."

"Yeah," Roman agrees. "Lilly is two and a half, going on thirteen. God help me when she's a teenager." He chuckles.

"Where is Lilly?" Maddox asks him.

"She's conked out in the twins' room. I was sure with all of the cookies she consumed, she'd still be wide awake to count down the New Year, but she didn't make the call."

"You think Lilly is going to be bad at almost three going on thirteen? Try twin girls who are five going on fifteen. Fellas, I'm going to need some help when they start dating."

"You're fucked, bro." Legend laughs. "You can't tell them no now. How do you think that's going to work out for you?"

"If it's to keep them safe, I have no problem telling them no."

"Don't worry. They've got four uncles who've got your back," Roman tells him.

"She'll have Kane and Sean too," I remind him. "And who knows, Brogan, Monroe, and Emerson might all be having boys."

"Four women." Forrest shakes his head, but he's smiling. "I don't stand a chance."

"You would have been sunk with just Briar," I tease.

"Like you're not."

"Oh, I definitely am." I have no issue letting the world know how in love I am with Maggie.

"Girls, it's almost midnight," Forrest tells his daughters. "Are you ready to countdown?" he asks them.

"Yeah!" they cheer, climb off their chairs from the table set up in the living room, and race toward their dad. He gives them their New Year hats and glasses, and the glow necklaces they had on earlier.

Standing, I move toward my fiancée and kneel beside her where she sits on the couch. "How you feeling, Momma?" I rest my hand on her belly. I can't seem to stop touching her, and as her pregnancy progresses, the more that desire builds.

"Five-year-olds are about to out-party me," she says, placing her hand over her mouth to cover her yawn.

"I know. I can't believe they're still going."

"It's the cookies," Briar says, from where she's sitting next to Maggie on the couch. "All that sugar." She gives me a pointed look.

"Hey, don't blame the man with a sweet tooth." I chuckle.

"They'll crash soon," Briar says. "There's just too much excitement right now."

"Here we go," Forrest calls out. "Ten, nine, eight, seven," he starts the countdown.

Standing, I bend over the couch, slide my hand behind Maggie's neck, and guide her lips to mine. "Three, two, one," I whisper as our lips collide. Everything else fades away into the background. It's just the two of us in this room together. When I pull away, I rest my forehead to hers. "Happy New Year, Mags."

"Happy New Year."

This year is going to be incredible. We're so close to meeting our son, and if I have my way, Maggie will have my last name—sooner rather than later. We haven't talked much about our wedding, just that she doesn't want to be pregnant. Yeah, this is going to be a fantastic year.

After a quick round of celebration, we're saying our goodbyes, as is everyone else, and heading home.

"I'm so tired," Maggie says, climbing into bed.

"It's been a long day. I'm not used to these late nights anymore."

"I'm pregnant, but I know you've got some age on you," she teases.

"Hush it, woman," I say, nipping at her neck. She settles in my arms, and we quickly drift off to sleep.

I'm startled awake by a ringing phone. My eyes blink to read the clock. It's just after four in the morning. Reaching over to the nightstand, I grab my phone, but it's not mine. Cursing, I climb out of bed, careful not to wake Maggie as I rush to grab her phone.

"Hello?" I answer, stepping out into the hallway. It wasn't a number that was programmed into her phone, so if this is some kind of prank or scam call, I'm going to lose my shit on them. They could have woken her up, and she's exhausted.

"Hi, I'm trying to reach Maggie Ward," the woman on the line says.

"She's sleeping."

"I'm sorry to call at this hour. My name is Amy, and I'm calling from the Ashby Memorial Hospital. We have a Doris Ward who was brought in by squad about thirty minutes ago. We have Maggie as her next of kin."

"Yes. Is she okay?"

"Are you family?"

"Maggie is my wife." A little white lie that doesn't matter in this instance. My heart is pounding in my chest. "Doris suffered a heart attack. She was able to dial 911. We have her here in critical condition. Once she's stable, we plan to transfer her to the cardiac care center in Nashville."

"We'll be right there," I tell her. I don't wait for her to give me more information. I end the call and swallow back my own emotions as I prepare to wake Maggie and give her this news.

My feet feel as though they're full of lead as I make my way back into the bedroom. Easing myself down to the side of the bed, I watch her sleep. I know that I'm about to break her heart. Grandma Doris is everything to her.

"Maggie, baby, I need you to wake up for me," I say, rubbing her shoulder. She stirs, but doesn't wake. "Baby, I need you to wake up," I say again, this time louder, shaking her shoulder.

Her eyes blink open. "Lachlan? What's wrong?"

"We have to go."

"Go? Where?" she asks, confused. She moves to sit up, and I help her. "What's going on? What time is it?"

"It's just after four," I tell her, reaching over and turning the bedside lamp on.

"What are you doing up? What's wrong?" she asks.

I swallow hard. "It's Grandma Doris. She's in the hospital."

Her face goes ghostly white. "W—What?"

"The hospital just called your phone. I answered. She was brought in by squad. We have to go."

"Squad? Is she—?"

"She had a heart attack. She called 911, and they're waiting until she's stable to transfer her to a cardiac unit in Nashville."

"No." She shakes her head as tears race down her cheeks. "No. Lachlan, no." She sobs.

I pull her into my arms and hug her tightly. "We need to go to her," I tell her. I wish I could tell her that everything is going to be okay, that Doris is going to be okay, but the nurse didn't exactly give me that hope. Her voice sounded grim and uncertain, and I refuse to give Maggie false hope. "Come on. I'll help you get dressed."

I assist her in moving to the edge of the bed before going off to find her some clothes. I grab a pair of leggings and one of my sweatshirts, as well as some socks, and rush back to the bed to help her change clothes. When she moves to the bathroom to handle business and brush her teeth, I quickly slide into some sweats and a sweatshirt. I pick up both of our phones and meet her at the bathroom door.

"I need my phone."

"I have it." I hold it up to show her. She nods and allows me to lead her out of our room. I help her with her shoes, then slip into mine, make sure I have my wallet, and we rush out the door. "I should have started the truck," I say, cranking up the heat, hoping that it warms up soon.

"It's okay," she says meekly.

Reaching over, I take her hand in mine. "We'll be there soon," I tell her. She squeezes back but doesn't reply. All I can hear are her quiet sobs as she stares out the window.

Luckily, when we arrive, we are able to find a close parking spot. Hand in hand, we make our way to the reception desk. "Hi, we're here for Doris Ward," I tell the lady at the desk.

"And you are?"

"This is my wife, her granddaughter. She's Doris's next of kin." Maggie doesn't even flinch or look my way when I refer to her as my wife.

"One moment." She stands and walks away. A few minutes later, a nurse is calling us back. We follow her down the hall to trauma room three.

"She's weak and needs her rest. We're waiting to see if her numbers stabilize to determine if we can transfer her or have to admit her here."

"Thank you," I tell the nurse.

We push inside, and Maggie's choked sob has me swallowing hard. "Grandma," she cries as she moves to the side of the bed. Doris tries to open her eyes. It takes her a few moments, but she finally does it.

"My sweet Maggie," she says, her voice is hoarse and weak.

"What do you need?" Maggie asks her.

"Sweetheart, I'm just old," she says, giving her a half smile.

"Hey, Doris," I say, coming to stand behind Maggie. I place my hands on her shoulders, letting her know that I'm here. "You're looking beautiful as ever," I tell her.

"Oh phooey." She coughs, and I immediately regret my words when I see her struggling. "Such a charmer." She looks at Maggie, then back at me. "You taking care of my girl?" she asks. There is something in her eyes as she studies me that has me choking up.

"Always." I feel as though this is more than just a "yes, I'm taking care of her," and more of an "I'll always take care of her."

"Good. I like knowing she's in good hands."

"Grandma, I love you." Maggie's voice cracks.

"I love you, too, dear. I'm so proud of you, Maggie. Of the woman you've become, of the man you've chosen to share your life with. I know you're going to be an amazing mother."

"And you'll be an amazing great-grandmother," Maggie says.

"Honey, I don't know that I'll get to meet him," Doris says, closing her eyes. "Not from here," she rasps.

Fuck.

"No, Grandma. No, don't say that," Maggie cries.

"My dear girl, I'm old. I've lived such a good life. You've brought me so much joy. So much love," Doris says. She opens her eyes and looks between the two of us. "I love you both."

Leaning over the bed, I place a kiss on her cheek. "Love you too," I tell her. My lip quivers as I try like hell to fight the tears that are threatening to fall. I need to be strong for Maggie.

"You should let her rest," the nurse says as she quietly enters the room.

"I'm not leaving her," Maggie says, wiping at her cheeks.

"Can we stay?" I ask the nurse.

She looks at Maggie, then at her pregnant belly. "You can stay. Just let her rest."

"We will. I promise," I tell the nurse.

She checks Doris's vitals, and then she slips out as quietly as she entered.

"Tell me what you need, Mags," I whisper, pulling the extra chair over to sit next to her. I'd rather her be in my arms, but I know getting her to let go of Doris's hand even for a second is out of the question.

"I need her to be okay. She's it, Lachlan. I have no family left. I can't lose her. She's all I have left." She sobs, and I lean over and hug her as best as I can.

I want to remind her that she's not alone. That I am her family, that our son, my parents, and our friends are her family, but I know that now is not the right time. Instead, I hold her as she cries, and eventually, exhaustion takes over and she drifts off to sleep.

With my hand that's not holding her, I text my parents and the group chat, letting the guys know what's going on. We need them. I know that we can lean on them and that they will be here for whatever we need. I'm out of my depth here. I don't know what to do to make this better for her.

Eventually, I too drift off to sleep, only to be woken not long after to the sound of beeping. Maggie jolts awake as the room fills with doctors and nurses.

"What's wrong? What's happening?" Maggie cries.

I manage to lead her to the corner of the room, so we are out of the way to let the doctors and nurses take care of her. "Let's step outside, just right outside the door," I suggest, but she refuses.

"No. No. I can't leave her. I won't leave her."

So, instead, I stand with my arms wrapped tightly around her while we watch the medical staff do their jobs. Finally, after I don't know how much time has passed, the physician looks up at the clock on the wall and makes the call.

"Time of death, seven eighteen," the doctor says. He then steps toward us and bows his head. "I'm so sorry for your loss." He drops those words, and then quietly leaves the room.

Maggie wails as her grief takes hold of her.

The room clears out, and I guide her to a chair by the bed, and sit down, pulling her onto my lap. She cries, her body shaking from her grief, and I let my silent tears fall. Tears for an amazing woman, who helped shape the love of my life, and for my future wife who is heartbroken. I don't have the words she needs, and all I know to do is to hold her. Hug her tightly, and tell her that I'm here.

An hour later, I'm finally able to convince her to leave the room. She's a shell of herself as we walk out to the waiting room. My own tears fall unchecked when I see my parents, all the guys, and Brogan in the waiting room.

"The wives would have been here, but they're home with the kids," Roman says.

"Maggie." Mom's voice cracks as she pulls Maggie into her arms. I watch as Maggie grips my mom so tightly, I'm sure she's struggling to breathe.

My dad, the guys, and Brogan, all hug me and then take their turn with Maggie. I pull her back into my arms as soon as Brogan sets her free.

"Thank you for being here," I tell them. I knew they would be a pillar of support, but I didn't expect them all to show up. "I'm going to take Maggie home so we can get some rest," I tell them. "I'll call you all later."

"Of course, get some sleep. I'll make some dinner and bring it over later. I'll give you all a few hours to get some rest."

"Thanks, Mom."

"Thank you," Maggie whispers. "All of you."

I turn and lead her out to my truck. She's quiet on the drive home, and while we get ready for bed. I pull her into my arms, and she cries herself to sleep. It's not until her breathing has evened out that I let myself do the same.

MAGGIE 19

I DON'T WANT TO GO. I don't know how to say goodbye to her. She was there when we lost my mom and again years later when we lost my dad. She has been my constant in this world of pain. When I finally pulled away from Eric, my ex, she reassured me that everything was going to be okay. She was certain I'd one day find a man worthy of my time, of my love, and she was right.

She's gone, and I don't know how to get past this pain. I know that death is a part of life, but I've lost too many people who were important to me. I've lost my family. It's just me, all alone in this world, and that makes my heart ache.

Losing *her* makes my heart ache.

"Maggie?" Lachlan's voice pulls me out of my thoughts. I turn to look at him. "It's time to go."

I nod but make no effort to move. Instead, I stare at him. He's dressed in black dress pants, a black long-sleeve button-up, and his blue eyes, they're full of pain when he looks at me. I don't want his pain, and I don't want his pity. I'm the woman left in this world with no family and no connection to my roots, and that's just how it is.

Sean kicks, and I jolt at the movement as well as the unexpected pain because all I've felt since Lachlan woke me up and told me she was in the hospital is numb.

He comes rushing over. He slides one arm behind my back and the other rests on my belly. "Are you okay?" he asks gently.

"I'm fine. He's really active today."

He bends and kisses my belly through my black dress. "Be kind to Momma today, Sean. She needs our love now more than ever." He kisses my belly again, and then I feel his lips on my temple. "Time to go," he says, turning and guiding me out of our bedroom with his arm around my waist.

Before I know it, Lachlan is at my door, offering me his hand. We've arrived at the funeral home. I don't want to go in there. I don't want to do this. My eyes find his, and he nods.

"I know, baby, but I'm right here," he assures me. "This time is for family only," he reminds me.

We have an hour for the immediate family to say their goodbyes. I don't need an hour. It's just me, and since I'll never be ready to say goodbye, the time is pointless. However, I need to go in there and tell her one last time how much I love her, and how my heart will forever be missing a piece with her gone.

She would want me to be here.

I place my hand in his and allow him to help me out of the truck. He laces our fingers together as we make our way inside the funeral home. The funeral director we met with earlier this week greets us with a firm handshake and condolences. Lachlan handles that. I think I shake his hand, but I can't be sure.

Lachlan leads me into the viewing room. Is that what it's called? The layout room? Does it matter? No, not in the grand scheme of things. They should call it the heartbreak, goodbye room because that's what is happening.

My feet feel as though they weigh one hundred pounds as we slowly make our way to the coffin. I close my eyes, because I can't look. I just—a sob breaks free from my chest, and I feel faint, but Lachlan is there to catch me. He wraps his arms around me and holds me tightly to his chest.

"I'm here," he whispers. "I love you," he adds.

I don't reply, because I can't. I can't find my voice. This is it. This is the moment that I say goodbye to the woman who has been my rock throughout my life. The woman who helped me through the pain of losing my parents, her son, and daughter-in-law, and so many other moments of my life.

If she were here, she would tell me that this is a part of life. The circle of life, to be exact, and that I must live on with her in my heart. I know that because she told me so when we lost my mom, and again when we lost my dad. She'd tell me I need to be strong and let their love for me hold me up.

So, that's what I do.

I suck in a ragged breath and pull away from Lachlan's chest, wiping at my eyes. I take the final two steps to the coffin and stare down at her. Tears race down my cheeks, and I don't bother to wipe them away. I can't keep up with them, anyway.

"I love you so much, Grandma," I say, my voice raspy from tears, or maybe it's from pain. Probably a mixture of both.

I don't know how long we stand here, but I do know that Lachlan is with me. His hand around my waist, giving me his strength, is the only thing I feel outside of the pain.

I sway on my feet, and Lachlan steps closer. "Let's go sit. Get you off your feet for a few minutes. We'll be close, I promise," he assures me.

I don't know if I nod, but he turns us, and I close my eyes as I let him guide me where he thinks I need to go. "We'll sit here," he whispers.

I open my eyes, and it's not just a room of empty seats I'm seeing. My breath catches in my lungs when I see the room. It's not just us, as I suspected. Lachlan's parents are here. Roman, Emerson, Monroe, Legend, Forrest, Briar, Maddox, and Brogan. My eyes scan and I see Roman's parents, Legend's, Maddox's, and Monroe's, too, and my knees feel weak.

"I didn't know," I say through my tears.

I watch as Amanda and Rodney rise from their seats and make their way to us. Rodney reaches me first and engulfs me in a hug. "I'm so sorry for your loss," he tells me. "We're here for whatever you need." He steps back, and Amanda takes his place.

"Sweetheart," she says, her face crumpling. She, too, pulls me into a crushing hug. "We love you," she tells me, her voice cracking. "We're here for you. I'm so sorry, Maggie," she says. She releases me, and Lachlan is there again. His arm goes around my waist, and his lips land on my temple.

Roman and Emerson come next, then Maggie and Legend, Forrest and Briar, then Maddox and Brogan. Roman's and Monroe's parents are last, and they all hug me, telling me how sorry they are for my loss, that they're here for me.

That's what you're supposed to say, though, right? When you go through things like this? What else can you say? The family is standing before you, their hearts... well, in this case, my heart is torn to shreds. What else are they supposed to say?

Nothing.

Nothing they say will fix the pain I'm feeling.

No amount of hugs, and "I'm so sorry," will bring her back to me.

"Let's sit," Lachlan says once everyone has passed on their condolences. He helps me into a chair and wraps his arm around me. I lean into him, into his strength, because I can't seem to find my own. Time passes in a blur. The preacher steps forward, and I don't know how, but I missed the entire viewing. I vaguely remember some friends of Grandma's and her neighbors speaking to me, but it's all fuzzy.

The preacher talks about Grandma's love for knitting and working in the garden. He tells us how she's preceded in death by her husband, Grandpa Tom, her daughter-in-law, Kara, and her son, Sean.

"Doris leaves behind her loving granddaughter and the light of her life, Maggie Ward."

That's what does it. That statement, meant to be out of love, slices my heart wide open. My body shakes with my sobs, and I know I need to calm down. I know that I have the baby to think about, but I can't seem to stop. Lachlan's here. He's holding me, telling me how much he loves me, but it does nothing for the pain.

"Maggie, it's time to go," Lachlan tells me. He stands and helps me do the same. Everyone takes another turn hugging us before filing out. "Do you want to go see her again?" he asks.

"I—I can't."

"You can, baby. I'm right here. I don't want you to have any regrets." Carefully, with his arm around my waist, we go back to the casket.

"Hey, Doris, our girl is really missing you," he murmurs. "We love you. We miss you." His voice cracks, and that slices through me too.

Lachlan pulls me into his chest. "Talk to her, Maggie. If there is anything you need to say, please say it." He's pleading.

"I—I love you. I miss you, and I don't know how to do life without you," I say through my sobs. I bury my face in Lachlan's neck and let my tears flow. I hear him talking, but I don't understand anything he's saying.

Finally, he pulls away and lifts my chin with his index finger. "It's time to go," he tells me.

I nod, because I know we have to do this, even though I don't want to. Together, we make our way to the truck. Ours is first in line, and our friends and their families are right behind us, and there are a few other cars behind them. There are more people here than I ever thought possible.

The drive to the cemetery is short. Grandma will be laid to rest next to Grandpa Tom and my parents. We all gather round. Lachlan tries to get me to sit, but I refuse. Instead, he holds me up as the preacher says a few final words.

Thousands of memories flash through my mind, and she's in all of them. Lachlan leads us toward the casket and pulls out two flowers. One he hands to me, the other he keeps for himself.

"I love you," I whisper as I lay the flower on the casket. Lachlan keeps his, and I want to ask why, but I don't have the words. They seem to have escaped me. He takes me home, and I'm surprised to see everyone else here as well. Roman's and Monroe's parents came to get food ready for all of us.

"Thank you," I tell them. It's meek at best, but it's also the best that I can do.

Everyone stays; they ask how I'm feeling and how the baby is. I know they're trying to distract me, but it's not working. Everything is a haze, and I'm so fucking scared it will remain that way.

I'm in a room full of people, yet I feel more alone than ever.

It's been two weeks since we lost her, and my heart is still shattered. I haven't gone back to work, and I know that I need to. They've been lenient with me, probably because I'm pregnant, or maybe it's Lachlan telling them I'm not good. I know he said those exact words because I heard him.

"I can stay home. I can cancel my clients," Lachlan is telling me.

"I'll be fine."

"I'd rather be here with you," he says, trying to convince me that him not going to work again today is a good idea.

"You took two weeks off with me. You have clients who are depending on you."

"You are more important than any client, Mags. I love what I do, but that pales in comparison to you and our son."

"Lachlan." I sigh. I just need him to go to work. I need to be left alone.

"I'm staying," he says, starting to kick off his shoes.

"No. Go. JUST GO!" I scream. He freezes, and his eyes widen in shock. My voice is hoarse from all the tears I've cried, and my cheeks are wet from said tears. "I need time, Lachlan. I don't need you hovering. I just—I need some damn time," I say again. To be honest, I don't know what I need. I just know the guilt of taking up so much of his time, from taking him away from a job he loves is eating away at me. Just another bruise on my already broken heart.

The room is eerily silent, my anger hanging between us. I'm not mad at him. I'm just plain old mad. I'm sad. I miss her. Finally, he walks toward me. I expect him to fight back, but instead, he pulls me into a hug.

"I'll have my phone on me. You can call the shop too. I love you." He presses his lips to my forehead and lingers longer than usual. "I'll be home soon."

I don't say goodbye. I don't say I'm sorry, and I don't tell him I love him. I stand in the middle of our bedroom, a shell of myself, and watch him walk away.

I'm not hungry, but I know I have to eat for the baby, so I make my way to the kitchen to make some peanut butter toast. Just as I've taken the last bite, there is a knock at the door.

I almost don't answer it, but Lachlan has been buying stuff for the baby, and I don't want to miss a delivery, if that's what it is. He deserves that much from me. Pulling open the door, I suck in a surprised breath. "Amanda."

"Hi, Maggie. Is now a bad time?"

I step back, motioning for her to enter. I don't want company, but Amanda has been nothing but great to me. "Did he call you?"

"Did who call me?"

"Lachlan?"

"No. I did talk to him a couple of nights ago, and you've been on my mind. Can we sit?"

"Sure. You want something to drink?" I ask, remembering my manners.

"I'm fine. Thank you." She takes a seat on the couch, and I do the same on the opposite end. "Why did you think my son called me?" she asks.

With a loud exhale, I close my eyes and prepare myself for my future mother-in-law to hate me. "We fought. Well, I fought, yelled actually, and he was the amazing man he is, and let me."

Amanda smiles, which is not what I was expecting. "I have one of those. In fact, I'm certain that's where Lachlan learned it."

"I'm not mad at him. I'm just plain old mad. He wanted to stay home with me today, and the thought of him putting his job or life on hold for me... I don't want that."

"Been there, done that. I think I might even have the T-shirt to prove it." She smiles softly.

"Really?"

She nods. "I was a single mom when I met Rodney. Lachlan's sperm donor told me to handle the situation and skipped town. I never saw him again. I was doing it all on my own, and Rodney, he was persistent. He kept showing up, even after we'd been on a few dates, and I was sure he would leave. He never did."

"And you fought?"

"Oh, sweetheart, we argue, just like every couple. It's natural to do so. I can still remember the first real fight we ever had. Lachlan was sick, and we were supposed to go to dinner. I was stressed from missing so much work, knowing money would be tight, and Rodney he showed up at my place, anyway. He had food in hand, and things he thought Lachlan might like. I screamed and yelled that we weren't his problem. That I had to figure it out on my own because when he was gone, when he decided we were too much work, I'd still be alone."

"What happened?"

"He pulled me into a hug and let me cry. He then came into the house, picked Lachlan up, snuggled him and told me to go take a bath, and take some me time."

"Yeah, I'd say he gets it from his dad."

"He does." Amanda smiles fondly. "How are you doing, Maggie? Really, no bullshit."

"I—wasn't expecting that," I say, giving her a half smile.

"Us women, we have to stick together, so whatever it is, lay it on me."

"My grandma, she was there when we lost my mom, and when I lost my dad. She was there for me while I was in college, through past bad relationships, and now this." I look down at my belly, my hands resting there. "There isn't a single moment of my life that I don't remember without her in it. The good, the bad, and the in-between. I don't know how to do this without her. I feel so... alone. I know that's not the case, but I have no family." I rub my belly. "Sean, he's my family now."

"What am I?" Amanda asks. "What about my son, and the ring he put on your finger? Is he not your family? Rodney? Is he not your family? Your friends?" She raises a finger with each new name or group she calls out.

"Yeah, but it's different," I say. I don't know how to explain it to her.

"It's only different if you let it be different."

Tears well in my eyes and I furiously wipe them away. "I'm so sick of crying."

"Technically, I'm not a grandmother yet, but I am a mother. I know the love a mother has for her child, and I can only imagine that love being just as strong for your grandchild. For all the moments you mentioned that she was there for you, you were there for her too. She lost her son, but she had a piece of him with her in you. I didn't know Doris long, but I knew her well enough to know she'd hate to see you this way. She'd want you to enjoy the final few months of your pregnancy. She'd want to know that you were living the life you deserve." She reaches over and places her hand on mine. "I can't replace her or your mother. What I can do is love you and love this baby for all three of us. And Rodney, that man, he's going to spoil his grandson endlessly, for him and for your dad."

I not only listen to her words, I feel them in my soul. "Lachlan, he's been so amazing through all of this. I love him so much," I say, tears coating my cheeks. "I can't lose someone else that I love. I won't make it."

"You will. I wish I could tell you that the pain of losing a loved one is over for you, but I'd be lying. But I know you have it in you to fight through the pain. You have to live for them now, Maggie. For this little one." She places her hand on my belly. "Let him help you. Let all of us help you. You don't have our blood in your veins, but you are our family. I couldn't be more proud of the woman you are. The woman my son chose to give his heart to. The woman he's spending his forever with and starting a family with. You are my daughter too."

I'm crying so hard now that I'm unable to speak. Amanda slides over toward me and hugs me tightly. She doesn't say a word; she just lets me cry in her arms—the comfort of a mother, something I never thought I'd gain.

When my tears have run dry, I sit up and blow out a heavy breath. "I love your son with everything that I am. I love you and

Rodney too. Thank you for being there for me through all of this. I promise I'll get myself together."

"Just don't do it alone, Maggie. Whatever you need, we're here. We don't want to hover, but just know there isn't anything you could ask us for that we wouldn't do for you if it's within our control." Amanda gives my hand a gentle squeeze. "Now, how is this little guy? How are you feeling? Have you been eating?"

"He's great," I say, wiping at my tears. "Growing as he should be, and I've been forcing myself to eat."

"Good, but we're still going out to lunch. You need some fresh winter Tennessee air. It's good for your soul."

"I'm—" I look down at my faded hoodie and leggings. "—a mess."

"We've got time. Go get ready. I'll be right here." She reaches into her purse and holds up her Kindle. "I got this for Christmas. Thanks to you, I hear." She laughs.

"Best gift ever." I smile, feeling some of the weight and sadness on my heart lift.

"Oh, I couldn't agree more. Now, go on. Lunch is waiting."

"Thank you, Amanda."

"You're welcome, sweetheart. That's what family is for."

With a nod, I head to the bedroom to get ready for a lunch outing with my future mother-in-law. She's right; I know she is. I was too deep in my pain to see the blessings I have. I see them now, and I won't take them for granted ever again.

LACHLAN 20

I T'S A LITTLE BEFORE FIVE, and I've just wrapped up for the day. I'm cleaning up before heading home. I haven't heard from Maggie all day, and I'm worried about her. I don't know how to reach her. My heart breaks from the pain she's in, and I'm afraid I'm going to lose her to it. I'm worried the grief is going to suffocate her.

"He's in the back." I hear Lyra say.

I don't know which one of the ladies is visiting, but it could only be one of them for Lyra to tell them to come on back. I keep doing what I'm doing so I can get out of here when there's a knock at my door. Turning my head, my mouth drops open.

"Hey, is everything okay?" I ask, moving toward Maggie. She's showered and dressed and looks more alive than she has since the morning we got the call about Doris.

"I'm fine. I was hoping you could give me a ride home?" She bites down on her bottom lip.

"How did you get here?" I look her over. "Did you break down? Where is your car?" I rattle off as I check for injuries with my eyes.

"Your mom brought me."

"My mom?"

She nods. "She showed up at the house. We talked, I cried, and then she demanded I shower and go to lunch with her." She points to the bags at her feet that I missed in my exploration of her for injuries. "We did some shopping, and then I asked her to bring me to you."

I smile down at her and open my arms. This time, I wait for her to come to me, and she does. I wrap my arms around her and breathe her in. Relief washes over me.

"I'm so sorry, Lachlan. I know I've been hard to live with. I'm sorry I yelled at you this morning."

Her words pierce my heart. She's been struggling. I don't know what it feels like to lose your only blood relative, but she has me. We'll make it through this. As I pull away, I grab her bags and motion for her to step inside. I close the door, drop the bags on my desk, and take her hand in mine, leading her to the table. I lift her and settle between her legs. My hands rest on her cheeks as I stare into her blue eyes.

"I missed you, but you don't owe me an apology. I know what she meant to you. I know how much you loved her, and it's okay to be sad."

"I lost myself for a little while. I got in my head that I have no one, but your mom, she helped me realize what I was doing. In my grief, under the pain, I was pushing everyone who loved me away. My family."

"We *are* a family," I tell her, brushing my lips lightly with hers. "You scared me. I didn't know how to reach you."

"I think it had to be her, your mom," she clarifies. "I'm not sure I would have listened to anyone else. Your mom, she's incredible, Lachlan. I'm honored that you chose me to be a part of your family."

"Baby, my heart chose you, and there was no contest. It's only ever been you." I kiss her again, and she melts into me. This woman is my home and watching her struggle the last couple of weeks has been unbearable.

She pulls out of the kiss and smiles up at me. "Want to see what I got?"

"Most definitely." I pick up the bags and hand them to her.

"This." She holds up a small blue outfit with footballs all over it. "Is this not the cutest?" she asks.

"Very cute. Tiny," I tell her. She shows me a few more outfits, a few blankets, and some books she bought today while shopping with my mom. "Did you buy out the store?" I joke.

"Hey!" She playfully smacks at my chest, and some of the heavy weight on my chest from the past two weeks lifts a little more. She's coming back to me. "You've been buying, too, mister."

"Did you see how awesome that swing was? He had to have it."

"You know our friends are throwing us a shower."

"I know, but I couldn't help myself. How about we don't buy anything else until after the shower? We'll see what we still need, and then we can both go crazy."

"I don't know about going crazy. We might need a bigger house," she teases.

There's still sadness in her eyes, but her light is coming back, and I have my mother to thank for that. "Are you hungry?"

"Not yet. We ate so much at lunch. I'm stuffed."

"Well, let's get out of here. We can unpack this stuff in Sean's room, then a movie and ice cream are calling our names."

"Yeah?"

"It's what we do." I shrug, kiss her softly, then lift her from the table, placing her feet on the floor. I shove everything back in the bags, grab my phone and keys from my desk, and we head home.

"Are you sure you're ready for this?" I ask Maggie. "There's no rush."

"I don't think I'll ever be ready, but I know that I can do it with you by my side. Keeping the house is just costing money, and it's time to go through her things and put it on the market. It's time for another family to make memories there."

"Okay. We'll head over there after we leave the hospital."

"I can't believe she's here." She smiles. "I feel like both Briar and I have been pregnant for five thousand years." She laughs.

"Maybe four thousand," I tease.

"Brogan texted me and said River and Rayne are already in love with their baby sister."

"I bet. They have a real-life Barbie doll."

"Forrest and Briar are definitely going to have their hands full."

"They wouldn't want it any other way."

"Yeah," she agrees. "How soon until you think we'll have another one?" she asks, turning to face me in the passenger seat.

"You tell me when. It's your body that does all the work."

"What if I said I want them to be Irish twins?"

"What's an Irish twin?" I ask.

"Two kids born within a year of each other. Twelve months," she adds.

"That seems like that would be hard on you. Not that I don't love you pregnant." To prove my point, I reach over and rest my hand on her belly. "But don't you need time to heal?"

"I do, and I don't want them that close."

"Then why did you ask?"

I glance over before turning my eyes back to the road to see her shrug. "I still struggle sometimes that I have choices. That you're not dictating my every move. I know you're not my ex, but after years of living that way, sometimes, well, I like to hear you tell me that you're going to love me no matter what."

"I'm going to love you no matter what. Irish twins, twenty babies, or just Sean... I'll love you no matter what."

I pull into the parking lot of the hospital, and she's so excited to meet baby Willow that she's pushing open her door and trying to climb out of my truck on her own. "Hold up, Momma," I tease. "Let me help you." I rush to her side and help her down, making sure she's steady on her feet.

"Thanks!" She smiles up at me, takes my hand and pulls me toward the hospital doors.

She's come back to herself since her talk with my mother. I texted Mom and thanked her, but she's got a big-ass hug coming from me the next time I see her.

After taking the elevator up to the fifth floor, we don't stop at the nurses' desk. Maggie seems to know exactly where she's going. We stop outside a room, and she knocks softly, but it's Forrest's gruff, "Come in," that has us pushing inside.

"Oh my goodness," Maggie says, smiling at Briar, who is sitting up in bed, holding Willow. "How are you feeling?" She leans down and gives Briar a hug as best as she can with her belly in the way.

"Perfect." Briar smiles down at her newborn baby girl. "Want to hold her?"

"Can I?" Maggie asks.

"Of course you can," Forrest answers. "You're her aunt Maggie." He meets my eyes, and I give him a subtle nod to thank him. The guys know the struggle she's been having since Doris passed.

Maggie glances at me with tears in her eyes. "You better take her before I do," I warn her. Maggie's mouth drops open, and she hurries to bend down and take Willow into her arms.

"Hey, sweet girl, I'm your Aunt Maggie." She looks up again, and she's lost her battle with her tears. "She's perfect," she says, wiping at her eyes with her free hand.

Briar and Forrest tell us how the twins had to sit in a chair and hold her at the same time because they are both the best big sisters, according to the twins, but we all happen to agree with them.

I get my turn at holding baby Willow, and my excitement for our son to be here is off the charts. I can't wait to meet our little man. I snuggle the sweet baby while catching up with our friends. My eyes glance at the clock a little while later, and I know our time is up. "We should get going," I tell Maggie. "We're heading over to Grandma Doris's place to start packing up," I explain.

"I wish I could be there to help you," Briar tells Maggie.

Maggie's smile is soft. "Thank you, but you are exactly where you are supposed to be. Get some rest and enjoy that new baby girl." Maggie leans over and hugs her.

"We'll stop by to see you when you get home," I tell them. With a wave, we are out the door and headed to start packing up the life of a woman who will forever live in our hearts.

"I don't know where to even start," Maggie says as we step into the house.

"We start slow. Take your time going through it all and keep anything you want. We're not going to get this done in a day. We'll do this a little at a time." I don't know if she's truly ready for this, and I worry about her and the baby, especially if she gets really upset again. However, I also know she needs to do this, and I'll be damn sure I'm here for her through it all.

"Maybe let's start in the living room? That should be the easiest, and I want to donate all of her furniture."

"That sounds good. I'll grab some boxes out of the truck."

"You have boxes?" she asks.

"Yeah, I've been keeping them from the supply deliveries at the shop. I knew we would need them eventually."

"You're one of a kind, Lachlan Noble."

"Right back at ya, fiancée." I wink, and head outside to my truck to grab the boxes. As I'm unloading them out of the bed of my truck, I hear a car pull in. Looking over, I see Roman, Legend, and Maddox climbing out of Roman's truck.

"What are you all doing here?"

"We all had a slow day, so we decided to let the guest artists handle things." I know they're lying. I saw the schedule last night before I left.

"How did you know?"

"I talked to Forrest," Roman answers. "We're here for you, for both of you, but we want Maggie to know she's not alone."

Not going to lie, my best friends get me choked up. "Thanks," I say, nodding.

"Forrest wanted to be here, but he's with Briar."

"He's where he should be. Really, you all didn't have to cancel clients."

"It was nothing," Legend tells me. "We each had someone cancel, so we just moved our afternoons to our next day off. We told them we had a family emergency."

"Appreciate it," I tell them. They each grab an armful of boxes as we make our way inside the house. "Mags, we've got company," I call out.

"Who?" she asks. Her mouth drops open when the four of us walk into the living room, arms loaded with boxes. "What are you guys doing here?" She places the picture frame she was holding down and moves to pass out hugs.

"We thought we could lend our muscles."

"Thank you." Maggie smiles at each of them. "It means so much to me that you're all here."

"Forrest and Briar would be here if they could," Maddox tells her. "Emerson is working, and so are Monroe and Brogan. Perks of owning your own business."

"Right. Where do you want us?" Legend asks.

"Let's start making boxes, and Maggie can tell us what needs to be packed and what gets donated."

"On it," all three of my best friends say as we get to work.

We work for a solid hour, making good progress, when I hear Maggie gasp. I drop the roll of tape and turn to her to see she's not in pain, not physically. She's holding a blue gift bag in her hands.

She reads the outside of the card, "It says, *Maggie, Lachlan, and baby Sean.*"

"Hey, we're going to run and grab some lunch. We'll bring you all something back," Roman tells us before leaving quietly out the front door, no doubt sensing this might be something my girl wants privacy for.

"Are you going to open it?" I ask her.

"It's not the baby shower yet."

"I think this is a special circumstance. Go on, open it."

We both navigate to the couch. First, she runs her thumb over the writing on the card, then she turns it over and carefully opens it. She reads the outside, then opens and quickly closes it. "I don't think I can read it. Will you read it to me?"

She hands me the card and moves to settle against my chest while I read.

Maggie & Lachlan,

I am so proud of the two of you. You've handled a surprise situation with so much grace. I think maybe your mom and dad had a little something to do with it. They knew you needed someone in your life who would stand beside you and support you. Lachlan is that man for you. I'm so excited to see you both become parents. A great-grandchild, heavens, that's something. I bet your mom and dad are smiling down at you. They're proud of you, Maggie. Both of you. Lachlan, my son would have given you a hard time at first, but he would have been proud to call you his son with the way that you love Maggie. That's how he loved her momma, and my Tom loved me. You were meant to be a part of this family. Thank you for bringing yours into our lives.

Congratulations to both of you.

I can't wait to meet baby Sean.

Love,

Grandma Doris

I drop the card on my lap, my own emotions feeling haggard. I don't know what I expect from Maggie, but it's not for her to sit up and give me a watery smile. "She's here with us," she says.

"Always," I assure her. "See what's in the bag?"

She reaches into the bag and pulls out what looks like a knitted blanket in a variety of shades of blue. "There's more," she says, and she pulls out another one of the exact same. "There's another card." This time she opens it and starts to read.

My dearest Maggie,

I know life doesn't always work out the way we want it to, so I thought this second card for an explanation would be nice, just in case. I know my time here on earth is growing smaller every day, and I want you to understand why there are two blankets.

I know you, my granddaughter, and if my time on earth has passed, I know what you're thinking. You're already thinking you can't use this blanket because it's the last gift to you and the only one from me to your son. You want to preserve it, and me, I want both. So, you have one for you to preserve and one for you to use every day for that beautiful baby boy.

If you're reading this, that means that I've gone to be with Grandpa Tom and your parents, so I want you to know I have another gift for you. There are two pink blankets just like this one in the hall closet. In case you have a little girl in the future. I want both of your children to be wrapped in my love.

You're going to be the best mommy, and with Lachlan at your side, I know your kids are going to be something special.

I love you, my sweet granddaughter.

Grandma Doris

I'm holding my breath for her reaction, but again, she surprises me with a watery smile as she wipes the tears from her cheeks. "She knew I would need this."

"Yeah," I agree.

"I miss her so much."

"I know, baby. I do too." I give her a side hug, and then she stands.

"Okay." She blows out a breath, even as her smile wobbles. "We've got work to do.'"

"Maggie, we can stop for the day."

"No. I want to do this. I *need* to do this. This is what she would want. I know that she would want me to keep on living for her. For all of them. I know that I'm not alone, that I have you and our friends, and your parents, and this little one." She rubs at her belly. "I'm okay, Lachlan."

"I love you."

"I love you too."

MAGGIE 21

S TRONG ARMS WRAP AROUND ME from behind, and I know it's him.

"A little birdie told me you helped plan this." I wave my hands around our living room. Amanda was tasked with getting me out of the house while everyone else set up for my baby shower.

"Maybe," Lachlan says, dropping a kiss on my neck. "I just wanted today to be perfect. I wanted it to be here, so you didn't have to worry about lugging your gifts home, and it's a memory for us."

"So many memories," I say, leaning into him.

"Our little man got spoiled today, huh?" he says, looking at all the opened boxes and gift bags. Among them are the pink and blue blankets that Grandma knitted for us. Lachlan made sure they were on display with a card that read *Made with love by Doris* on them.

"He really did. I don't know that there is a single thing we're going to have to buy. Our friends went above and beyond."

"You mean, other than all the stuff we've already bought," he teases.

"Hey!" I turn to look at him over my shoulder. "You're the one who kept ordering online."

"It's the ads. You scroll through social media and something cool pops up, and your kid needs it. It's a crisis among dads," he tells me, trying like hell to hold in his laughter.

"True story," Forrest says, coming to stand next to us with baby Willow in his arms. She's two weeks old today, and the most precious baby.

"What's a true story?" Briar asks. She looks amazing for just having a baby. She settles onto the couch, props her feet up, and smirks at Forrest. She knew he was going to tell her to rest.

"That the ads on social media and the late-night purchases are a crisis among dads."

Briar's body shakes with her laughter. She winces, but it doesn't stop her from laughing still. "Shall we tell them, my dear husband, about your latest purchase?" she asks Forrest.

"Babe, it had to happen," Forrest defends himself.

"This I've got to hear," I say, moving out of Lachlan's arms and going to sit on the couch next to Briar. I also prop my feet up because they're swelling, and I know Lachlan is going to remind me to do it. "Let's hear it," I say, once I'm settled.

"So, this guy orders a robot vacuum. You know the little circle vacuums that do it all on their own?"

"That's not so bad. It actually sounds kind of helpful," I tell Briar.

"Oh, I agree. However, that's not why he bought it."

"It was the baby riding the sweeper, wasn't it?" Lachlan asks. "I almost did the same thing, but I knew it would be months before Sean can take a ride on his own."

Briar turns to look at me, and she's grinning like crazy. "See what I live with."

"Babe, it's like her own personal amusement park ride, right in the house," Forrest tells his wife.

"I'm doing it," Lachlan says, pulling his phone out of his pocket.

I watch them with a smile on my face. "It could be worse," I tell Briar.

"For sure," she agrees. "He's the best man I know, aside from the other four. They're all amazing men, and if this is what they want to do for fun, something that whole-heartedly involves our children, who are we to stop them?"

"My thoughts exactly."

"Time for cake!" Monroe calls out.

"This can wait," Lachlan says, shoving his phone back into his jeans pocket. "Mags, cake." He steps in front of where I'm sitting on the couch and offers me his hand to help me up. Together, we make our way into the kitchen to start passing our cake to our guests.

"Save me that corner piece," Lachlan tells me. "It has more icing."

"Why not take the bear and the blocks?"

"That's the center."

"Yeah, but it will have more icing on top."

"Not as much as two sides, and the piping around the bottom." He licks his lips, and I can't help it, I crack up laughing.

"You're too much," I tell him as he leans down and presses a soft kiss to my lips.

"I'm yours."

"And I'm yours."

"Hey, now, none of that," Legend says. "That's what got you that." He points to my belly.

"And you this," Monroe says, pointing to her belly. I'm sure she has a tiny bump hiding under there.

"We're really good at it," Legend tells his wife.

"So are we," Roman says, pulling Emerson into his arms.

"Don't let Forrest hear you say that," Maddox jokes.

"Hear him say what?" Forrest asks, as he joins us to get a piece of cake for the girls, himself, and Briar.

"Rome and Emerson are good at making babies," Lachlan tells him.

"Really, man? Really? You had to go there? Today is special," he says, before he bursts out laughing. "I tried. I couldn't pull it off," he says, pointing to his own face. "My niece is adorable, and I'm sure this next one will be as well. Outside of acknowledging that you are, in fact, the father, I don't want to hear how he or she got here, *K*?" he says, grabbing three plates of cake and ice cream before heading back toward the living room.

That's my family. The ones who have chosen to love me and be there for me through all of life's ups and downs. It's always like this when we get together. I miss Grandma Doris so much, but these people, my people, they make it easier. They're here for me. They love me, and I love them too.

I've been aching all day. Braxton hicks are no joke. I was just at the doctor's yesterday for a checkup and baby boy isn't ready to make his arrival just yet, but my body, on the other hand, is getting ready.

That basically means I can't get comfortable. I'm not sleeping well at night, and today, I've been up and down from the recliner to the bed, to pacing the floor. I'm miserable, but all of this will be worth it.

"Mommy loves you," I tell my baby bump. Well, it's way larger than a bump. I'm due any day now, and the waddle is in full effect. Everyone tells me that I'm still "all belly" and it's out there. It's a good thing I'm due soon because Sean is definitely out of room in there.

The dryer buzzes, letting me know that it's finished its cycle. I know Lachlan will give me a hard time about doing laundry, but I'm not lifting anything heavy. I'm folding the clothes as they come out of the dryer and placing them in stacks for him to carry when he gets home. Besides, keeping active is good for me, and maybe, just maybe, I'll be lucky, and it will trigger labor.

I'm excited to meet my son.

It takes me a few moments to lift from the couch and make

my way to the laundry room. I'm slow moving, but at least I'm moving. I bend over to grab the last item out of the dryer and feel wetness rush between my legs. I look down to see my light gray maternity leggings are soaked. It takes me a solid minute to realize that I didn't just pee my pants.

My water just broke.

Staying calm, I grab a towel from an earlier load of laundry and toss it to the floor. Then I grab another for myself and make my way to the bedroom. I change my clothes through the contraction that hits and then waddle back to the living room. I don't want to call the ambulance, and I know Maddox is off today because Lachlan told me fifteen times before he left for work, to call Maddox if I needed anything.

Apparently, he knows he's on baby watch. The perks of being best friends, neighbors, and scheduled to be off the same day Lachlan is working. I'm pretty sure they planned it this way, but I'll never ask them. I love how he takes care of us. His heart is larger than life.

Grabbing my phone, I call Maddox.

"Hey, Maggie. Everything okay?"

"Yes, but could you come over here and see me?"

"Sure, what's up?" he asks. I can hear him moving around.

"I'm pretty sure my water just broke."

"What? Holy shit, woman, you should have started with that. Stay there. I'm on my way."

"Not going anywhere." I chuckle.

"Did you call Lachlan?"

"No. Not yet. I want to be on my way to the hospital before I do."

"Okay. I'm walking out the door."

Taking my towel and my phone, knowing my bags and the baby's are already in my SUV that we bought last week, I open the garage door, and pull my car out. I'm walking around the SUV to get into the passenger side when Maddox comes roaring into the driveway.

"What are you doing, Maggie?"

"We need to take my car. It has the car seat and all the bags. I was pulling it out of the garage for you. Besides, I don't want to mess up your truck." I wrinkle my nose.

"The truck can be cleaned, but come on." He places his hand on the small of my back, while holding my arm with the other, and helps me to the passenger side.

"I need to put this down, just in case."

"On it." He quickly places the towel over the seat, helps me inside, and fastens my seat belt before rushing around the front of my SUV and sliding behind the wheel.

Once we're out of the driveway, I call Lachlan.

"Hey, Mags. How ya feeling?"

"Well, Maddox and I are on our way to the hospital. My water broke," I rush to say before he freaks out. Who am I kidding? He's going to freak out. Briar, Emerson, and Monroe already warned me about the full-on daddy-to-be panic mode that would set in.

"Are you okay? How are the contractions? Sorry, bro, my wife just went into labor. I can have one of the guys finish you up, or we can schedule again. I hate to run, but it's my wife. My son," Lachlan rambles.

I hear his client tell him to go, and they can finish up in a couple of weeks once he's healed and to take care of his wife and baby. Technically, we're not married yet, but I don't think this is the time to correct either one of them.

"I'm fine, Lachlan. Just breathe."

"I should be telling you that. Let me talk to Maddox."

"You're on speaker," I tell him.

"Maddox, brother, you have my entire world in that truck right now."

"I got this," Maddox replies. "Drive safely. We're in Maggie's SUV, so we have everything we need but you. Don't drive like a maniac. Her contractions are not close together. In fact, she's not had one since I've been with her."

"How far apart?" Lachlan asks.

"The last one was about ten minutes ago. We have plenty of time. Drive safe. We'll see you there."

"Maggie, I love you. We're having a baby."

"I love you too."

"Maddox." Lachlan's voice cracks.

"I've got them, brother. See you soon." He reaches out and ends the call on the dash.

"This is good practice for me anyway," Maddox says, making me laugh.

By the time we reach the hospital, I've yet to have another contraction. I get checked in and go straight up to the maternity ward. A nurse offers to help me change, and Maddox steps out in the hallway to call Brogan.

I'm barely in my gown when Lachlan comes racing through the door. "I'm here. Is he here? Did I miss it?"

The nurse laughs. "You must be dad?"

I swear his chest puffs out. "Yes. Me. I'm the dad." He slaps at his chest, and my heart melts as I laugh.

"Come here." I hold my hand out for him, and he comes to me, kissing my forehead, and holding my hand while the nurse gets me hooked up to an IV, and the baby monitor on.

"The doctor will be in soon. Can I get you anything?" the nurse asks.

"No, thank you."

The nurse nods and steps outside.

Maddox knocks. "I'm going to go to the waiting room and start calling everyone. Lach, did you call your parents?"

"Shit. No. Can you do that?"

"I'm all over it, brother." Maddox smiles and leaves the room.

"How are you?"

"I'm fine." I rest my hand over his heart. "Calm down. It could be hours before he gets here. We're both okay."

"We're having a baby, Mags." He kisses me softly as another contraction hits.

Lachlan holds my hand and tells me how great I'm doing and how much he loves me. He's my rock and fills my heart with so much joy.

"You know you're going to spoil him," I tell Lachlan.

"That's my job."

"Your job is to teach, love, and protect him."

"And spoil. I'm certain I read that somewhere," he says, smiling down at our baby boy sleeping in his arms.

"Sure you did." I laugh.

"How are you feeling? You didn't sleep long," he tells me.

"I'm perfect." I smile up at him. "What time is it?"

"Just after eight."

"A few hours."

"The waiting room is full, everyone is here, and they're excited to meet him. I told them they had to stay put until you were awake."

"You made them wait?"

"Yeah, you needed rest."

"Well, go get them." I sit up in the bed, wincing a little, before I hold my arms up for Sean. My heart is so full of love for our son and his daddy, it feels as if it could burst wide open.

Lachlan brings him to me and kisses us both on our heads. "He's perfect, Mags."

"He is. He looks just like his daddy." I pull off his little hat, and run my fingers over his soft hair, the same dark shade as his daddy's.

"I don't know... I think he has your eyes."

"We'll see, won't we, sweet boy?"

Lachlan moves to the opposite side of the bed and snuggles close. "I can't leave yet. I don't want to take my eyes off either one of you."

"What's going on?"

"My heart feels like it's going to explode. I've never loved someone more than I do the two of you. I didn't know it could be like this. I didn't know," he says again.

"Didn't know what?" I ask, smiling down at our son.

"That having a wife and a son would change my life so much."

"We're not married, yet," I remind him.

"Can we try?" he asks.

"Can we try what?"

"To get married? I'm sure I can make it happen. Have them come here to sign the marriage license and all that stuff."

"You mean that, don't you? You'd marry me today, right here in this hospital room?"

"Anytime. Anywhere. I need you to be my wife. I need the three of us to have the same last name."

"I already said yes," I remind him.

"Soon?"

"Soon," I promise.

"Best day ever," he says, closing his eyes.

"Yeah," I agree. "Best day ever." Reaching for the blue knitted blanket, I place it over Sean, even though he's wrapped up like a burrito in the provided hospital blanket and close my eyes. She's here with us, my family.

MAGGIE EPILOGUE

Two Months Later

"THANK YOU FOR WATCHING HIM," I tell Brogan as I pass Sean to her.

"Are you kidding me? I love my baby Sean time. Besides, I need all the practice I can get."

"We both know that's not true," I tell her.

She snuggles Sean into her chest, and it warms my heart knowing my son has so many people who love him. "So, does he know?" she asks.

"No. I had Lyra schedule me under a fake name, and made sure it was his last appointment of the day."

"He's going to flip. They love putting their work on us." She smiles, and I know she's thinking of when she got her first tattoo from Maddox.

"Yeah," I agree. Lachlan is going to be pumped to give me my first tattoo. Especially since he has no idea that I'm his last client of the day. "I'll be back to get him as soon as we're done," I tell her.

"Go on. We'll be fine. In fact, Maddox is on his way home. Don't worry. I swore him to secrecy, but he's just as excited as I am to be watching Sean for a few hours."

"Thank you. I really appreciate you."

"Go. And I want to hear all about it."

"You got it." I lean over and kiss Sean's cheek one last time before heading back out to my car and making my way toward Everlasting Ink.

As soon as I walk in the door not long after, I see Lyra's smiling face. She places her hand to her lips, telling me to be quiet, then waves for me to follow her back to Lachlan's room. When we reach his door, I stay a few steps back out of sight.

"Lachlan, your two o'clock is here," she tells him.

"Thanks, Lyra, send her in. The sooner I get this done, the sooner I get home to my family."

"Missing them, are you?" she asks, not bothering to hide her smile.

"Every day, Lyra. Every day," he says.

Lyra steps back, gives me a high-five, and walks away. I step into the room, and Lachlan still has his back to me. "Be right with you. Just texting my wife," he tells me.

Oh, how I love this man. He's been calling me his wife a lot lately. I guess he can get away with that since our wedding is in a month. He sends his message and places his phone back on his desk. Mine chimes before he has a chance to turn around. Pulling it out of my purse, I read it and reply.

"I miss you too. Sean is fine. He's with Brogan for a few hours."

Lachlan whips his head around to look at me, and his mouth falls open. "Mags, what are you doing here? Is everything okay?" His eyes roam over me as if he's looking for an injury.

"I'm fine. Sean is fine. As I said, he's with Brogan. I'm here for my two o'clock."

"What? Wait? You're my next client?" He furrows his brow and turns to look at his schedule. "It says Sarah James."

"I might have had Lyra make up a name to surprise you."

"Consider me surprised." He makes his way toward me, then wraps his arms around me in a hug. When he pulls back, he drops a quick kiss to my lips. "So, you're going to let me ink you?" he asks, wearing a huge grin.

"I am."

"Do you know what you want? I might need some time. I want this to be perfect for you."

"I think this one will be easy enough. I actually have two that I want to start with."

"Two? To start with?"

"Yeah, today I have two, and then maybe in a month or so, I want another one. But you might not be able to do them both today, but at least you'll know what I want and can be more prepared next time."

"My girl's got the ink bug." He grins.

"Only for things that are important to me."

"Okay. Well, let's hear it."

"Well, I want something like this." I pull the image of the knitting needles and yarn from my purse. "For Grandma Doris. Maybe on my shoulder or something?"

"Love this, Mags." He nods, staring at the picture I handed him. I can already see his wheels spinning with ideas. "What else?"

"This." I hand him Sean's footprint from the hospital. "Can this be done? Maybe with his name and date of birth on there somewhere."

"Damn, I want this one too." He picks up his phone and dials someone. "Hey, I need on your schedule." He's quiet. "Yeah, that works. Thanks." He hangs up the phone. "This can be done," he tells me. "I love this idea."

"Who did you call?"

"Rome. He's the only other one here tonight, and I want this too. We'll get matching tattoos for our boy."

My heart fills with love for this man. "I love that idea."

"Okay, well, which one do you want to do first?"

"I don't have a preference."

"Wait, you said you want another one too? What's that?"

"I don't know exactly where I want it, but I'd like to have 'Mrs. Noble' somewhere. However, it's probably a good idea for that to be my name before I do it. That would be weird having your mother-in-law's name on your body." I laugh nervously.

He grips my hips, lifts me onto his desk, and kisses me. His tongue slides against mine, and before Lachlan, I never would have thought it was possible to feel love through a kiss. It's more than just through his kisses, though. I feel it with every touch.

When he pulls back, he rests his forehead against mine. "I love you, Mrs. Noble."

"Future Mrs. Noble, and I love you too."

"You really want our name on you?"

"Yeah, I really do."

A throat clearing has him lifting his head and turning toward the door. "What's up?" he asks.

"Just thought I'd stop by and say hi to Maggie."

"She's busy," Lachlan says with no heat in his tone. He leans back against the desk, between my legs, and I wrap my arms around his neck.

"Hi, Rome."

"You getting some work done?" he asks.

"I am. I thought I'd find out what this tattoo thing was all about."

Roman laughs, and I can feel Lachlan's body shaking with his laughter.

"Take care of her," Roman tells Lachlan.

"Get out of here." Lachlan laughs. "You know I got this."

"Maggie, I'm just down the hall if you want some real talent," Roman calls out. He barely gets the words out over his laughter.

Lachlan turns and kisses the tip of my nose. "Give me a few to get these drawn up, and we'll get started."

"Thank you."

"Anything, Mags." Another quick kiss, and my man gets to work doing what he loves.

I'm excited that there will be a piece of him, a piece of his heart on my skin for the rest of my life. I want our love to be so entwined, we don't know where the other ends or begins. I never thought I'd find this kind of love, and now that I have it, I never want to let go.

LACHLAN
EPILOGUE

One Month Later

"TODAY'S THE DAY, BUDDY," I whisper to my three-month-old son who's in my arms, smiling up at me. "Mommy's gonna have our last name," I tell him.

We wanted a small, intimate wedding. We chose to stand up on our own, but I needed my boy with me, while we waited for his momma to walk to me down the aisle. When the music starts to play, I turn to look for her, waiting for the doors of the small venue we rented here in Ashby to open.

And there she is.

My bride.

"Momma's stunning, Sean," I tell my son. He coos up at me, looking adorable as hell in his tiny little suit Maggie found for him. He has no idea what's going on, but he'll have the pictures and the stories we tell him when he gets older.

My eyes move back to my bride, who is walking in on the arm of my dad. My chest expands with love for both of them. For the man who stepped up and showed me how to be a man. He showed me it's okay to wear your heart on your sleeve, and that being there for those that you love is important.

And Maggie, she swooped in and stole my heart when I wasn't looking. One night with her changed my life. Changed *our* lives. And I'm a better man because of her. She's wearing a long, white form-fitting silk gown. Her curves from having Sean make my mouth water. Her hair is pulled back, allowing me to see her long slender neck, and I can't wait to kiss her there.

To kiss her everywhere.

My parents are keeping Sean overnight while we go back home to our place to have some alone time. Maggie isn't ready to leave Sean just yet for a long period of time, and she's already back to work, so we're planning a honeymoon, just a long weekend, in a couple of months.

When they reach us, I swallow the lump in my throat. Dad kisses Maggie on the cheek before pulling me into a hug. He then holds his arms out for Sean, and I hand my son over as I take my wife's hands.

"You're beautiful," I tell her. I hear the ladies in attendance, hell, maybe even some of the men—it's just the Everlasting Ink family, and their families in attendance—making an *aww* sound. I didn't bother to lower my voice. My wife is a smoke show.

"You look handsome," she tells me, with tears in her eyes.

"You ready to do this, Mrs. Noble?"

She nods and blinks away her tears. Unable to handle her being sad, I lean in and kiss her softly. "Love you," I say. This time, my words are just for her.

"Hey, Lachlan, man, it's not time for that yet," Maddox calls out, and everyone laughs.

"Look at her. Do you blame me?" I call back as I watch the blush coat Maggie's cheeks.

I get lost in her eyes as the officiant leads us through our vows. I speak where I'm supposed to speak, all words and promises we've made to one another prior to today. Because of that, we chose to say traditional vows.

When it's my turn to place her wedding band on her finger, I swallow hard past the lump of emotions welling in my throat. My dad steps forward, holding a now-sleeping Sean, and passes me the ring. My hands tremble as I slide the diamond band onto her finger before lifting it to my lips and placing a kiss as my silent promise to never stop loving her.

My mom steps up and passes Maggie my ring, and her hands, too, are unsteady as she slides the ring onto my finger. "I love you, Lachlan. With all that I am," she says, her voice cracking.

We've already signed the marriage license, so this is a formality, and I need to kiss my bride. I don't wait for anyone's permission. I slide my palm behind her back, and one around the nape of her neck, tilting her lips to mine, and I kiss her. I kiss my Maggie Noble for the first time, and damn, does it feel good.

My heart pounds like a bass drum inside my chest, and the crowd cheers.

"Mr. Noble, you got a little ahead of yourself." The officiant laughs.

"I'm not sorry," I tell him, pulling my wife into my arms and giving her a fierce hug.

Our guests cheer again, and we raise our joined hands, united as one. The photographer that we hired rushes us off to take some photos before we join everyone in the adjacent room for the small reception.

The entire day feels like a dream.

She is my dream.

We eat an amazing meal. Everyone stops by the table we're sitting at in the front of the room to wish us well. Everyone we love is here. It's perfect, and what's better is my wife hasn't stopped smiling. Hell, I haven't stopped smiling.

"Can we get the bride and the groom out on the floor for their first dance?" the DJ announces.

I grin at Maggie, standing from our seats and offering her my hand to lead her out to the makeshift dance floor. Pulling her into my arms, I want her as close as I can get her.

"Today was perfect," she says, smiling up at me.

"It was," I agree. I slide my hand to the small of her back and pull her closer.

"Lachlan, I don't think you can get me any closer." She giggles.

"Can we try?" I ask her.

Her eyes light up, and she nods, before standing on her tiptoes, pressing her body into mine. She offers me her lips. Our kiss is slow and sweet, and exactly what the moment calls for.

"This is the first day of our forever, Mrs. Noble," I whisper against her lips.

THANK YOU

for taking the time to read **Can We Try?**
Want more of Lachlan and Maggie?
Scan the QR code below to read, **Can We Try?**

Never miss a new release:
Newsletter Sign-up

Be the first to hear about free content, new releases, cover reveals, sales, and more.
You can also find free reads and bonus content on my website.

CONTACT KAYLEE RYAN

Website:
kayleeryan.com/

Facebook:
bit.ly/2C5DgdF

Instagram:
instagram.com/kaylee_ryan_author/

Reader Group:
bit.ly/2o0yWDx

Goodreads:
bit.ly/2HodJvx

BookBub:
bit.ly/2KulVvH

TikTok:
tiktok.com/@kayleeryanauthor

With You Series:
Anywhere with You | More with You | Everything with You

Soul Serenade Series:
Emphatic | Assured | Definite | Insistent

Southern Heart Series:
Southern Pleasure | Southern Desire
Southern Attraction | Southern Devotion

Unexpected Arrivals Series
Unexpected Reality |Unexpected Fight | Unexpected Fall
Unexpected Bond | Unexpected Odds

Riggins Brothers Series:
Play by Play | Layer by Layer | Piece by Piece
Kiss by Kiss | Touch by Touch | Beat by Beat

Entangled Hearts Duet:
Agony | Bliss

Cocky Hero Club:
Lucky Bastard

MORE FROM KAYLEE RYAN

Mason Creek Series:
Perfect Embrace

Standalone Titles:
Tempting Tatum | Unwrapping Tatum
Levitate | Just Say When
I Just Want You | Reminding Avery

Hey, Whiskey | Pull You Through | Remedy
The Difference | Trust the Push | Forever After All
Misconception | Never with Me | Merry with Me

Out of Reach Series:
Beyond the Bases | Beyond the Game
Beyond the Play | Beyond the Team

Kincaid Brothers Series:
Stay Always | Stay Over | Stay Forever | Stay Tonight
Stay Together | Stay Wild | Stay Present
Stay Anyway | Stay Real

Everlasting Ink Series:
Does He Know? | Is This Love? | Are You Ready?
What About Now? | Can We Try?

Co-written with Lacey Black:

Fair Lakes Series:
It's Not Over | Just Getting Started | Can't Fight It

Standalone Titles:
Boy Trouble | Home to You
Beneath the Fallen Stars | Beneath the Desert Sun
Tell Me A Story

Co-writing as Rebel Shaw with Lacey Black:
Royal | Crying Shame | Watch and Learn

There are so many people who are involved in the publishing process. I write the words, but I rely on my team of editors, proofreaders, and beta readers to help me make each book the best that it can be.

Those mentioned above are not the only members of my team. I have photographers, models, cover designers, formatters, bloggers, graphic designers, author friends, my PA, and so many more. I could not do this without these people.

And then there are my readers. If you're reading this, thank you. Your support means everything. Thank you for spending your hard-earned money on my words, and taking the time to read them. I appreciate you more than you know.

SPECIAL THANKS:

Becky Johnson, Hot Tree Editing.
Julie Deaton, Jo Thompson, and Jess Hodge, Proofreading
Lori Jackson Design – Model Cover
Emily Wittig Designs – Special Edition Cover
Wander Aguiar – Photographer (Model Cover)
Chasidy Renee – Personal Assistant
Jamie, Stacy, Lauren, Franci, and Erica
Bloggers, Bookstagrammers, and TikTokers
Lacey Black and Kelly Elliott
Designs by Stacy and Ms. Betty – Graphics
The entire Give Me Books Team
The entire Grey's Promotion Team
My fellow authors
My amazing Readers

Made in the USA
Columbia, SC
04 May 2025

57530600R00135